DARKROOM

Darkroom

KATE WILLOUGHBY

HeartEyes
Press

In memory of Lisa B. Kamps

Forget about resting in peace.
I hope you're up there enjoying a giant margarita!

I miss you, my friend.

CONTENTS

The best mirror is a friend's eye.

--Scottish proverb

INDI

Even though the first day of fall semester here at Burlington University wasn't until tomorrow, I was in serious study mode. I wanted to become a doctor and planned to take the Medical College Admissions Test, or MCAT, in January. The MCAT is one of the hardest standardized tests known to man and I was supposed to spend between three and four hundred hours preparing for it, in addition to all my regular college coursework.

Unfortunately, I'd been so engrossed in my studies tonight I hadn't realized the time. It was almost eight o'clock, my stomach was painfully empty and I had nothing in my Carter Hall apartment but a pack of sugarless gum.

There was one campus cafeteria still open—The Marketplace —but I'd already taken off all of my makeup.

For most people, this would not be a big deal, but I was born with a large, irregular reddish-purple birthmark, called a port-wine stain. It covered the upper left quadrant of my face and made it look like I lost a no-holds-barred game of paintball. My white parents adopted me from the Chinese orphanage where I'd been abandoned, presumably *because* of this birthmark. My mom assures me there was a time when I didn't care what people thought about my face, but I don't remember it. I only remember being teased and stared at and eventually deemed too different to include in the group.

Until I started wearing makeup.

These days, my normal beauty routine took a half hour. Tonight, I didn't have that kind of time. The Marketplace was going to close soon.

I put on an oversized Mickey Mouse hoodie and wrapped a scarf over my nose and mouth. When I added sunglasses, virtually none of my face was visible. Hopefully, I'd be able to go in, grab something—anything—check out and leave without anyone noticing me.

I was good to go all the way to the dining hall, keeping to the shadows like a thief. But once I got to the brightly lit building, it was a different story. I checked my reflection in the glass double doors before entering and almost didn't recognize myself. Dressed as I was with my arms wrapped around myself and a slightly hunched posture, I looked timid and afraid, like I was the victim of a bad home situation. This wasn't me. Not anymore. I hadn't looked like this since I was thirteen, about to face another day of teasing and bullying.

Appalled, I immediately straightened my posture, lifted my chin and entered the building with my normal amount of confidence.

In an effort to make a healthy choice, I perused the array of salads. There was one chicken Caesar and one Greek. They both looked a little wilted, so I headed over to the pizza by the slice area. My family owned a successful pizzeria, Slice of Heaven, back home, so I was a bit of a pizza snob, but given the choice between wilted salad and pizza made with substandard dough in a less than ideal oven, I'll pick pizza every time.

The pepperoni looked like a safe bet. Even though they were generous slices, I got two—one for tonight and one to save in the fridge for tomorrow. Thinking I was home free, I was turning toward the cashier when I collided with someone.

A tall, very solid male someone.

The bowl on his tray upended as it hit the floor, detonating with a spectacular splash of hot chili. A large helping of cornbread bit the dust, too, as his spoon and my pizza slices skittered several feet away. Worst of all, he had a large drink that slid into his chest with quite a bit of force, enough to cause the contents of the cup to geyser up into his face.

People turned and gasped. I stood there, horrified, speechless.

As our eyes met briefly, my heart rate tripled and my mouth went dry.

Shit. I knew this guy.

He was Hudson Forte, darling of the hockey team. Tall, with blue-eyes and sun-kissed blond hair, he looked like he'd been plucked off the beach at Malibu. Freshman year, I caught him and my ex-roommate, Blair, just finishing a nooner in the dorm room she and I shared at the time.

He was just as ripped now as he was then.

His root-beer-drenched shirt clung to every muscle on his rock-hard torso. A pool of soda swirled around on the tray he was still holding. People were gaping at the spectacle. His friend had his phone out and took a picture of him as he set the tray of root beer aside.

"I'm so sorry," I exclaimed, my voice muffled by my scarf. "I didn't see you."

"Hey, accidents happen," he said, giving me a concerned smile. "No harm done. You're all right, aren't you?"

"Me? I'm fine. Just embarrassed."

As he peered more closely at my face. I realized my scarf had slid down a little and I jerked it back into place, hoping he hadn't noticed my birthmark.

Unfortunately, what he said next confirmed he had.

"You're absolutely sure you're okay?" he asked in a low voice. "Because if you need, um, support or protection or anything, there's a confidential victim's advocacy program on campus. I could get the number for you, if you need it."

This used to happen all the time. People would see my purple, moon-surface birthmark and think I was being abused by one or both of my parents. Even people in the medical field were sometimes unaware that port-wine stains existed. My dad always tried to joke around and say, "You should see the other guy," and my mother would usually try to explain that it was a vascular birthmark, but I used to get angry and defensive. Thanks to them, I'd grown up in a loving home with parents who barely even raised their voices to me, let alone their hands, and I wasn't about to tolerate anyone suggesting otherwise.

And yet, I had to forgive this guy. Now that I was an adult, I was more able to see things from a stranger's point of view. He was coming from a place of concern, not accusation.

I gave him a reassuring smile. "I'm not being abused."

"I didn't say you were." But he didn't look convinced. I couldn't blame him. On TV and in the movies, the victims always denied it, saying they fell down the stairs or ran into a door.

"But you're thinking it. I can tell," I said. "I swear to you I'm not being abused. I know the number for Campus Advocacy. It's on a poster in my dorm and I promise, if I ever need it, I will call. Honest."

One of the cafeteria workers came with a mop and started cleaning up the mess.

"If you're sure…" he said, still frowning.

"I'm one hundred percent sure. Do you want me to pay for your clothes to be cleaned? Or buy you a new shirt? Because I'd be happy to…"

He shook his head. "No. This is probably the oldest T-shirt I own. Don't worry about it."

"Okay, cool. See you around," I said and left.

But I felt his eyes on me all the way to the exit.

HUDSON

"So, that was interesting. Do you believe her?" my roommate AJ asked.

AJ and I both played hockey for Burlington University and at the start of each year, every athlete, male and female, had to listen to a serious lecture about what constituted sexual harassment and how to get help on campus. Apparently, it had been a problem sometime in the past, so now they made sure every athlete was well informed.

"I don't know," I said, watching the girl walk away.

She sure was dressed weird. From the shoulders down, she'd looked like any other co-ed, but her face had been covered up like she didn't want anyone to recognize her. At first, I'd wondered if she was a celebrity wanting to get her degree after she was already famous, like Emma Watson or Natalie Portman, which would have been cool. But then, I noticed the purplish mark on the side of her nose and my thoughts took a more sinister turn.

"Well, if she doesn't want to be helped, there's not much you can do about it," AJ said. "You did what you could, buddy."

"I guess," I said. He was right, but I was still troubled. I really hoped she was telling the truth. I resolved to keep my eye out for her in the next few weeks, even though I didn't really know what she looked like.

"So, I don't know if you noticed," AJ said, "but while you were trying to be her knight in shining armor, they closed the place."

"What? Really?" I looked around and every one of the food counters was dark. "Damn it."

"I didn't want to eat here anyway," AJ said. "Want to go to the Biscuit in the Basket?"

The Biscuit in the Basket was the unofficial, on-campus hangout of the hockey team. We went there after every home game to either celebrate a win or drown our sorrows if we'd lost.

"No. There's no way I'm showing up there like this." I reeked of root beer and the right leg of my jeans was a chili-infused abstract painting. "Let's just go home. I'll change clothes and we'll grab something in town."

We'd gone to The Marketplace because I was starving and it was close to the ice rink, but the neighborhood where we lived had a lot more dining choices there than here on campus. AJ and I shared a two-bedroom place on Lake Street in a historic building that was originally a railroad warehouse from the 1870s but had been converted a few years ago into apartments. Downtown Burlington was only a ten-minute walk away.

As we drove up to our place, AJ said, "Hey, your dad's here."

Sure enough, there was my father, just getting out of his cherry red '67 Camaro convertible. He was a big man who, at four inches over six feet, stood like a mountain. When he was playing for the NHL, he weighed two-twenty. Now, he had to be close to two-fifty. He still had most of his hair but was missing one tooth—a point of pride with him. The hole in his smile was a badge of honor.

"Dad, what's going on? Is Mom okay?" I asked as I got out of my car.

"You're mom's fine. AJ, Good to see you."

"Mr. Forte."

My dad and AJ shook hands.

"I told you none of that Mr. Forte shit," my dad said. "Call me Dom."

AJ had met my dad several times, but he still went starry-eyed around him. To me, he was just Dad, but to everyone else—especially hockey fans—he was D-Day Forte, the man who won the Calder Memorial trophy as the rookie of the year, the Hart Memorial trophy as most valuable player, and earned almost 1300 points during his colorful nineteen-year NHL career.

"Why are you covered in food?" my dad asked.

"I had a little run-in with someone in the cafeteria."

"Then you haven't eaten yet! Perfect. Let's grab some dinner. Is there a good steak house around?" my dad asked. "It'll be my treat. I'm in the mood for a porterhouse with all the fixings."

"Yeah," AJ said enthusiastically. "The Blue Spruce has steaks."

"Great," my dad said. "Why don't you ask some of your teammates if they want to join us? The more the merrier."

"The whole team?" I asked. "I don't think the Blue Spruce has a table big enough."

While this was true, the main reason I said this was because my dad was a bit of a braggadocio with a wealth of anecdotes drawn from his career, and if my teammates came with us to dinner, it was sure to turn into the Dominic Forte Hour, starring Dominic Forte.

"I'm sure the restaurant will accommodate us. Money might not buy happiness, but it can usually get me a table."

Resigned, I sent out a group text...

Hudson: *Who's up for dinner at the Blue Spruce? My dad's paying. You have five minutes to reply or you're out of luck.*

It didn't take long for the replies to start rolling in. No one likes a free steak dinner better than a college hockey player. We're always hungry and usually broke. When the five minutes were up, I'd changed clothes and we had eight RSVPs.

"...this place fairly clean," my dad was saying to AJ. "That must score you a lot of points with the ladies. You boys getting plenty of action?"

AJ coughed.

"Cut it out, Dad," I said.

With a head tilt, Dom just held his hands up in mock surrender. "Hey, I'm just sayin', hockey is king in this town and I know women appreciate little things like neatness, no matter how hot and bothered they are to nail a hockey player."

"*Dad.*"

"Okay, okay, I get the message."

Squeak squeak squeak.

My dad cocked his head. "What's that noise?" he asked.

"That's Deke, working out."

"You got another roommate?" he asked, looking around.

"In a manner of speaking," I said, gesturing toward Deke's elaborate two-story wood veneer abode. The top floor was for food, drink and exercise. The bottom floor, accessible by a plastic cylinder, was filled with soft bedding material and the occasional paper towel tube. Below that was a storage cabinet. The whole thing looked more like a piece of furniture than a pet habitat.

"What the fuck?" My dad drew closer, bending at the waist to see inside. "What is *that*?"

"It's a hamster."

Deke was a golden, or Syrian, hamster. Larger than most pet store hamsters, he had soft fur the color of honey that lightened to blond on his stubby legs. He was currently running on his exercise wheel, something he did for a long time every evening.

My dad turned to me with a comically horrified expression and I just smiled back at him. This was a familiar point of contention between us. Dad was an old-school manly man who believed everything he owned, wore or ate should have the appearance of masculinity. I, on the other hand, always had a soft spot for cute animals, even stuffed toy animals. This bugged my dad like nothing else. When we went to the zoo, as a kid I gravitated toward animals like the koalas, red pandas and the baby version of anything. My dad, of course, encouraged me to look at the lions, the gorillas, the crocs—anything that could potentially maim you.

"Jesus H. Christ. I hope this is yours, AJ."

AJ laughed. "Nope. Deke belongs to your son."

My dad dragged a hand over his face with a muffled sound of pain.

"Hey, this is your fault, Dad. You wouldn't let me get one when I was little, so here we are."

"Surely your landlord has rules against pets."

"Not hamsters. I checked."

"What an idiot," Dom muttered. Then louder, he said, "Well, just don't...don't post pictures of him on social media. Okay? Will you do that much? I don't want it getting around that my son..." He shook his head dejectedly.

"No promises, Dad. I am who I am. No apologies."

He gave a long-suffering sigh, which was more for show than it was from any true pain. As long as I was still on the pathway toward NHL greatness, that was all that mattered.

"We'd better get going," AJ said. "Dom called the restaurant while you were changing and they're going to have a table ready."

"Great."

"I'll drive," Dom said. "Unless you want to, AJ."

AJ's eyes went wide. "Are you fucking kidding me?"

"You have a license?" Dom asked.

"Sure, I have a license."

Dom handed him the keys to the Camaro and AJ looked happier than he had when we accidentally bumped into Billy Crystal in town last autumn. And he'd been pretty damned ecstatic because Billy Crystal was in AJ's favorite movie of all time —*The Princess Bride*. He was such a fan, he bet me once he could recite the entire movie, word for word. I stupidly took that bet. I say stupidly because not only did he win, I had to watch the entire movie with him talking over it the entire time.

3

INDI

By the time I got back to Carter Hall, my embarrassment had faded away, replaced by hunger. In my haste to escape Hudson, the sexy good Samaritan, I'd left my pizza behind and now here I was, still without dinner. But as I approached the suite style apartment I shared with my roommate, Ruby Chang, I smelled something delicious wafting out into the hallway.

Ruby and I had only met yesterday and so far, we'd gotten along pretty well. We both had big collections of makeup. We were both very serious about school and we both despised love stories with tragic endings, like *Me Before You* and *La La Land*. But last night had been a marathon of getting to know you questions and I wasn't ready yet for a repeat.

Holding my scarf up, I made a beeline for my room. "Hi."

"Hey," she said. "Are you hungry? I made authentic Hawaiian fried rice and by that I mean it's made with yummy SPAM."

Only steps away from the safety of my room, I stopped. Lord, I was hungry. Unfortunately, I hadn't shown Ruby my birthmark yet. The reason I'd avoided it so far was because she was breathtakingly beautiful. Hawaiian on her father's side and Chinese on her mother's side, she was an Asian Heidi Klum. She had gorgeous black hair with a natural wave in it that I envied. Her features were elegant and delicate, and even though her lips were on the thin side, her smile was arresting. Don't even get me started on her smooth golden skin or her long legs.

"Come on. You'd be doing me a favor. I made way too much," she said.

When I heard the scrape of Ruby's chair, I made a snap decision.

"Okay, but first I have to tell you something," I said, removing my sunglasses.

"That sounds a little ominous. Should I be worried?"

"No. It's not really a big deal," I said in what I hoped was a casual tone. "I just wanted you to know that I have what's known as a port-wine stain birthmark on my face."

Even though my heart was pounding, I tugged my hood down, unwound the scarf and turned around. If she was grossed out, it was going to make things awkward between us for the rest of the year.

"Wow. You weren't kidding," she said, putting down the bowl of rice. "That's...pretty sizable. Were you bullied a lot in school because of it?"

"I got teased every day when I was younger, especially in middle school."

She growled. "I hate bullies. Nothing good ever comes from bullying."

"I agree. It's horrible and I don't wish it on anyone, but I like to think it made me a stronger person."

"That's the spirit. I knew I liked you," she said, smiling. "Now come sit down and try my fried rice."

She grabbed an extra fork and we sat down at the table. Even though I was born in China, Chinese food was not my go-to ethnic cuisine, but I was so hungry, I didn't really care at the moment. I took a bite and was rewarded with a mouthful of deliciousness I couldn't deny. The SPAM was like a chewy, salty umami bomb in my mouth. Minced ginger gave it a sharp bite, the green peas added a sweetness and when I squirted Sriracha sauce all over it, it was game over.

"Ruby, this is really good."

She beamed at me. "Thanks. We eat fried rice a lot at home. It's easy because you can just use whatever you have on hand in the fridge. It's great for using up leftovers."

"Funny, pizza is kind of like that too. Sometimes for staff meal, we'd come up with the weirdest combinations."

"I'm sorry. What's staff meal?" she asked.

"My parents own a pizzeria. Staff meal is what you feed the restaurant staff before the rush."

"Oh my gosh, that's so cool. Did you work there? Can you toss the pizza like they do in the movies?"

"Yes, I can, but it's not really that hard. People we hire usually get the hang of it after a couple days."

"What's the weirdest pizza you've come up with for staff meal?"

I took a swig of water from my water bottle. "Well, one of my personal favorites was the cheeseburger and dill pickle pizza."

"Whaaat?"

"First, you spread ketchup and mustard on the dough."

"Okay. You can stop right there." She made a face. "Ketchup and mustard?"

"Hear me out," I said. "Ketchup and mustard as the sauce. Top that with cheese and cooked ground beef and bake. After it comes out of the oven, you put lettuce, chopped pickle, and onion on top and drizzle it with a sauce made out of mayo and—don't freak out—pickle juice."

Instead of instantly recoiling like she had before, Ruby thought about that. "Okay, actually that might not be that bad. It's like an open-faced burger on crust."

"It's delicious. Honestly. Another fave with an unconventional sauce is something my dad ended up putting on the menu, the Brat Bacon Pizza. The sauce is apricot jam and honey mustard.

The toppings are bratwurst, dry-cured bacon, grilled onions and cheese."

"Now, that sounds like it's to die for. Indi, where did you say your parents live again? Because you seriously need to take me to your pizzeria."

"They live in Brattleboro, about two hours south of here. We'll have to visit one weekend. You can have all the pizza you can eat."

"That sounds amazing."

After we'd finished and were cleaning up, Ruby said, "Hey, Indi, can I ask you a delicate question? It's about your birthmark."

"Sure."

"I saw how you were dressed before..." She made a circular motion with her hand around her face. "And I was wondering if your birthmark is supposed to be a secret, because if it is, I'll keep it until I die..."

"No, it's not really a secret. It's just...private. The only people who know about it are my very close friends and family."

"Okay. I get it. Thanks for clarifying. And for the record, I want to say that I'm really grateful you shared this with me. I think we're going to be great friends."

Touched by her sincerity, I had to blink back some tears. I'd been afraid that being so beautiful might have caused her to place a higher than normal value on looks, which would mean that once she saw my PWS, I'd become an object of disdain. I'd had it happen. One of my aunts was obsessed with her appearance, and she loved to dole out criticism about people's clothing or hair or whatever. She was a mean girl who never grew out of it and although she'd never said anything to my face, I knew she talked about me with pity when I wasn't around.

But Ruby was the opposite of a mean girl. People claimed you made some of the best friends in your life while at college, and so far, it seemed like that might be true.

HUDSON

When we got to the Blue Spruce, our teammates were already there, milling around the lobby. While my dad went to the hostess stand to tell them the whole party had arrived, Jason Nightingale pulled me aside. He was one of the incoming freshmen and from what I could tell, a nice guy. We called him Birdy for obvious reasons.

"Dude. Your dad is really D-Day Forte?"

"Yeah."

"I thought I was being pranked. I mean, I knew your last name was Forte, but I never put two and two together—that you were one of *the* Fortes."

"Yeah, well, it's not like I go around announcing it."

My family has had a player in the NHL since the day the league came into being. Over a hundred years of hockey playing men came before me, so the minute my parents looked at the ultrasound photo of my tiny dick and balls, my fate was sealed. I was going to play for the NHL or die trying—not an exaggeration.

After we were seated, the guys all spoke in hushed tones for a few minutes, like they were in the presence of the Pope or something, but by the time appetizers were served, my dad had them all eating out of the palm of his hand. He had long ago learned how to make people feel as if they were part of his inner circle.

"So, anyone want to play a game?" he asked.

Shit. I knew what was coming, but before I could think of a way to derail it, AJ said, "Sure!"

My dad grinned. "The name of the game is You're Full of Shit: Hockey Edition. I'm going to tell you ten facts about hockey and you tell me if I'm full of shit or not. If I win, you each chip in ten extra bucks for the tip, in addition to the twenty percent I'll be giving. If *you* win, I'll put a hundred into your team kitty. Deal?"

The team kitty was a stash of money that built all season. The captain and alternate captain decided which infractions required a contribution and, in the spring, the money was donated to a local charity.

Everyone was down for that. One of the freshmen mustered up the guts to ask for a selfie too, and my dad assured them they'd go outside after dinner and they could have all the selfies they wanted.

My dad pointed at me. "Hudson, you don't get to play."

"No, I know." I'd seen him do this many a time at parties and charity fundraisers. At one high end event, he raised ten thousand dollars with this game.

"And no fair giving them hints. No sign language, no eye rolls, nothing."

I held up my right hand. "I swear by all that's holy I won't help them."

My dad rubbed his hands together in anticipatory glee. "Let's start with an easy one. You all know what a Gordie Howe hat trick is, right?"

Rolling his eyes, Spencer Briggs said, "It's when you score a goal, get in a fight, and get an assist, all in one game."

"Correct. What would you say if I told you Gordie Howe only did that twice in his whole career? Oh, and no fair Googling. All phones on the table."

There were groans of protest, but they all complied.

Briggs said, "That doesn't seem possible. They named it after him. He must have done it more than twice."

AJ looked at me, but I gave him my poker face. A minute or so more of debate went on before my dad called for a "final answer" from me. I'd been designated as the team representative since I wasn't playing.

"The consensus is you're full of shit," I said with a laugh. Saying that to my dad never got old.

With a grin, my dad shook his head slowly. "Oddly enough, it's true. The record for Gordie Howe hat tricks is actually held by my brother Rick, with eighteen in his career."

"Good old Uncle Rick," I said. Not surprisingly, Uncle Rick also held the family record for the most missing teeth. Go figure.

"Brammy, did *your* dad score any Gordie Howes?" Birdy asked.

All eyes turned to Pete Bramley, admittedly not my favorite guy on the team. He was moody and not receptive to the couple of times I'd tried to be friendly. I was actually a little surprised he agreed to come to this dinner. Oddly enough, his dad had also played for the NHL. But Bramley hadn't been drafted. He told everyone it wasn't his life's goal to play professional hockey, that he wanted to be a screenwriter, but Burlington U wasn't exactly known for its TV and Film department. It was, however, known for its excellent men's hockey program and plenty of their players have gone on to the NHL without being drafted.

"No," Pete replied, "but he's a Stanley Cup champion."

"Who's your dad, son?" my dad asked. His tone was casual, but I could tell his dander was up. The fact that he'd never won the Cup really stuck in his craw. Everyone in the family knew not to bring that up in his presence.

"Craig Bramley. He won the Cup with Colorado but he also played for LA and Arizona."

According to his Wikipedia page, Craig Bramley was one of those solid—and I mean solid—physical players who got a decent amount of ice time, a good portion of it spent delivering hard hits. His career reminded me of Uncle Rick's.

"I remember your dad," my dad said, nodding. "We didn't play too often since he was in the Western Conference, but he's a good guy. How's he doing?"

Pete shrugged. "He's okay."

"Give him my best, will you?"

"Sure."

"All right, going back to the game," my dad said. "You all know the logo for Montreal, right? It's a big C with a little H in the middle. I'm here to tell you that contrary to popular belief, the H stands for hockey. Am I full of shit?"

Some of guys thought it stood for Habitants, but others said it stood for hockey. After a lot of arguing, they went with hockey and got a point.

The score was tied by the time the bill came and we had to finish the game before we left because the tip amount had to be resolved.

"All right, boys, it all comes down to this," my dad said. "Wayne Gretzky was captain of all four of the NHL teams he played for. Am I full of shit?"

"I know for a fact he was captain of the Oilers," Briggs said.

"Give me a break, Briggerton, everyone knows that," AJ said.

"What about LA?" Birdy asked. "Did your dad play with him, Bramley?"

"No, that was before my dad."

"But still," Birdy said. "You don't have any idea? Maybe your dad mentioned it in passing?"

"I don't know about you, but I don't remember every word my dad ever said."

"Okay, guys, come on," Seb Hunter said. "We can get this one. Dom said he was on four teams. Who are the other two teams?"

"The Rangers and the Blues, I think," Birdy said.

"Oh, yeah. He went to New York to play with Messier again before he retired," Hunter said.

"But was he captain there?" Pete asked.

Hunter groaned in frustration. "I don't know. I'm trying to picture him in the Ranger jersey and damned if I can remember if there was a C on it."

They argued about it a little longer, but even though there had been no consensus, they told my dad he was full of shit, only because he'd fooled them so many other times during the course of the evening.

My dad laid both hands on the table and leaned forward, a slight smile on his face. "Well, boys…"

My teammates all seemed to be holding their breath.

"You won! Congratulations," my dad said with a laugh. He closed the folio on his credit card and handed it to the waiter, who had hung around to hear if he was making an extra hundred. He looked disappointed, but I knew my dad would make good on that too.

"Which team didn't make him captain?" Briggs asked.

"It was the Rangers who didn't give him the C."

"That makes the Rangers dumber than shit, doesn't it?" Birdy said. "I mean, he's the greatest hockey player who ever lived."

"The C doesn't automatically go to the best player, son," my dad said. "Not to toot my own horn, but even though I was usually the top scorer on my team, I was never captain. No. You need a leader to be captain. Someone who will put the team ahead of everything. The guy who demands more of himself than anyone else, who knows how to motivate the team. That was never me," he said, laughing. "I'm way too selfish."

By the time we left the Blue Spruce, my dad had gained a couple dozen new fans. When he gave you his attention, it was like stepping into the sun after a month of cloudy skies. He posed for selfies with my teammates, the restaurant staff and several other patrons. It should have been a fun evening, and for the most part, it was, but as was often the case with my dad, he had an agenda tonight and I needed to confront him about it.

Back at the apartment, I asked AJ if he wouldn't mind going up without me, that I needed a word with my dad.

"Sure thing, Forts," AJ said handing my dad the keys to the Camaro. "Thanks again for dinner, Dom, and letting me drive your car. It was great."

"Hey, my pleasure. Thanks for feeding my kid. See that he eats a vegetable once in a while."

"Will do," AJ said with a two-finger wave goodbye.

I turned to my dad. "I know what you were trying to do back there at the restaurant."

"What? You mean like eat dinner?"

"Come on, Dad. You were really sly about it, but you were trying to convince the guys I'd make a good captain."

"I was? Because I'm pretty sure I never said, 'Hudson should be captain.' I didn't even talk about you."

"That's because you're too smart for that."

"Aw, he thinks I'm smart. And I didn't even go to college."

I gave him a hard stare.

"All right, fine. Is it a crime for me to want you to be captain? Christ. You know as well as I do you're the best man for the job. You came out of your mother a leader. I could see you were captain material when you were five years old, playing with your friends. You would organize everyone into teams of approximately equal strength and make sure the other boys played fair, especially against the littler kids. Everyone listened to you because you had their respect and you stepped up and got the job done."

I shook my head. "Look, Dad, I appreciate the dinner. All the guys did, but I don't want you trying to buy me the captaincy—no, don't even deny it. And besides, I'm only a junior and they usually pick a senior to wear the C."

"Ah, but the Graham boys have gone to Vegas and Seattle, and

I talked to your coach and he says even though that Bramley boy and some other kid..."

"Kurlander."

"Yeah, that was the name. Your coach said even though those boys are seniors, you're obviously the better candidate. He could be blowing smoke up my ass, but I don't think so. Your work ethic has always stood out. I saw to that."

"You're missing the point. The point is, if I get the captaincy, I want it to be because they think I'm the best choice, not because D-Day Forte schmoozed the fuck out of them."

"Actually, son, *you're* the one missing the point. The real point —the only point that matters—is that you've been drafted, yes, but you're not in the NHL yet. I know guys who were drafted higher than you and then floundered around in the AHL for most of their career, only getting called up once or twice. That will not be you, not if I can help it.

"The Dragons are looking at and weighing everything you do against who they already have on the farm team. This year, you're going to leave everything on the ice, every game because that's what Fortes do. If you're a leader in the room, all the better. Character guys are vital. The more ways you can make yourself indispensable the better."

I'd heard all this countless times before and not just from my dad. Uncle Rick, Uncle Matt, my late grandfather, and a couple of great uncles had all counseled me my whole life. I could probably write a book filled with their hockey advice.

"I know all that, Dad, and I appreciate how much you care, but there comes a time in a man's life when he wants to be trusted to live his life, to stand on his own two feet. I don't want you or anyone else in the family interfering."

"How am I interfering?"

"Come on, Dad! You talked to Coach Keller about me. You know how that looks? Like my daddy is watching over me like I'm fucking five years old."

Finally, he looked contrite. "Okay, you're right. I'm sorry about that. I just wanted to know what your chances were. I should have just asked AJ."

"No, you should have just waited to hear who was captain *like everybody else's father*." I unfastened my seat belt.

"But I'm not anyone else's father and you're not just anyone's son. You're a Forte, damn it and Fortes don't settle for second best."

While it was on the tip of my tongue to mention he had never won the Stanley Cup, I knew better than to throw that in his face. It would only make things worse. Anyway, what was done was done and nothing I said now was going to erase tonight's campaign dinner.

"So from now until the election," my dad said as I got out of the car, "you're going to bust your ass even harder and be the first in and the last to leave. Give a few extra pats on the back during practice. Do everything you can to show your team you can lead them to a championship in the spring. Then it won't matter that I took those guys to dinner. You'll have earned it."

When I finally left my dad and went up to the apartment, AJ was stirring some Ovaltine into a glass of milk.

"How do you even have room for that?" I asked.

"Hollow leg?" He shrugged. "Your dad's a fun guy. My dad would never just drop by and take the team out to dinner, even if he could afford it."

"My dad didn't just drop by. He was here trying to get them to vote me in as captain."

AJ put his glass down and licked the chocolate milk moustache off his upper lip. "No shit?" I could see him run through the events of the night in his head. "That was a pretty slick move. He even arranged for you to be sort of de facto 'captain' of the team in that trivia game."

"Exactly. He likes to pretend he's just your average schmo, the guy with a C average in high school, yadda yadda yadda, but his brain is always working the angles. He's a calculating SOB."

"But he's a *fun*, calculating SOB." AJ glugged more of his chocolate milk. "Your dad didn't have to bother. You're a shoo-in for captain."

"I am not. The captaincy always goes to a senior."

"Not true. Under certain circumstances, it can go to a junior. And I don't think anyone thinks Pete's a good leader. He can be such a dick sometimes. So can Kurly. You, on the other hand… you're reliable and easygoing but you're not a pushover. Hell, everybody likes you."

"You sure it's not just because I'm a Forte?" I asked.

"Honestly?" AJ said, "maybe a little. But for the most part, you just show up. All the time. You care about the team more than yourself and you make us all better, on the ice and off."

I scoffed. "You keep talking like that, asshole, and I'm going to expect an engagement ring."

5

INDI

As a psychological science major with an eye toward medical school, I was taking a lot of math and science and one breather course so I could stay sane. An aspiring immigration lawyer, Ruby was in the same boat, except she was weighed down with Asian studies, political science and history. We both ended up taking Photography Appreciation, which was supposed to be both an analysis of the history of photography and practical instruction on taking good photographs. I mean, who doesn't want to learn how to take better pictures? It's a skill that would come in handy for the rest of our lives. What sold us on the class was that the course description said you could complete all the assignments with a smart phone. As far as I was concerned, this would be an easy A.

Our photography instructor, Larissa Larkmont, didn't show up for the first two class sessions due to illness, but she didn't let us off the hook. We'd been given detailed instructions on how to create our required photography blogs where all the assignments for the semester will be posted.

Just after Ruby and I took seats in the second row, Professor Larkmont strode in. She was tall and had a commanding presence. Her gray hair came just down to her chin in a severe bob and she wore a belted knit dress with heavy-duty combat boots.

"Hello, everyone," she said. "Sorry about last week. Couldn't be helped. At least, through the miracle of technology, we could proceed anyway. One of these days they won't need human professors at all, but hopefully I'll be retired by then."

She spent a little time reviewing the syllabus and the assignments. To be honest, a lot of them sounded like fun. Some of the work was written. We were to read articles, study the work of professional photographers, and explain the meaning behind some of our photographs. Best of all, she had extra credit assignments. To me, extra credit was insurance. If you tanked a test, extra credit could save you. Even though I was adopted by white parents, I still ended up being the stereotypical high achieving Asian in school.

"Am I correct in assuming I have another contingent from the hockey team this semester?" Larkmont asked with an air of amused resignation.

Several whoops cut through the air. I turned to see a small group of guys all sitting together in a cluster near the back corner.

Hudson Forte was one of them.

Shit.

My heart rate elevated, I whipped around to face forward again.

"Oh my God," Ruby said in a low voice. "We've got to start going to the hockey games."

I didn't reply. He probably wouldn't recognize me from The Marketplace. Too much of my face had been covered up. I'm not sure my own mother would have recognized me. But he might remember me as Blair's roommate. I had my full face on today, as I had when I met him two years ago. I gave myself a fifty-fifty chance.

Larkmont said, "I hope everyone has prepared their introductory slide show. Any volunteers?"

For class today, we were to choose and present ten to fifteen photographs that inspired or represented us in some way. The photos could be amateur or professional.

Larkmont was answered by silence and chair scraping.

I raised my hand. When it came to presentations in class, waiting to get called on was ten times worse to me than actually standing in front of the class and doing my thing. Plus, as an added bonus, teachers universally appreciated someone getting the ball rolling. Did I mention the high-achieving Asian thing?

"And you are?" Larkmont asked.

"Indi Briscoe." I carefully kept my gaze away from the jock-populated part of the room.

"All right, Indi, let's see what you've chosen."

After I synced my tablet with the big screen TV at the front of the classroom, my first photo appeared.

"This is a picture of me and my parents on the day they adopted me from the orphanage in Chengdu, China."

I included this photo because you couldn't really see my PWS. My parents looked so joyful and young.

"How old were you there, Indi?" Larkmont asked.

"I was eight months old."

"Are you the only child they adopted? I know people often adopt several children."

"Like Brad Pitt and Angelina Jolie," someone called out.

"No," I said. "I'm an only child."

I showed a picture of my parents' pizzeria, our dearly departed family cat, Bonkers, and me on the day I got my driver's license. I was wearing makeup by then, so it was safe to show.

"Next is another baby picture," I said, advancing to a photo of a sleeping newborn in an elaborate butterfly costume.

Larkmont immediately recognized the work of Anne Geddes. "The queen of baby photography," she said. "What drew you to her?"

"Everything I saw of hers was magical and innocent and full of hope, in direct contrast to this…"

When my next photograph, one of a toddler with a severe cleft palate, showed up on the screen, there were gasps and even a few F-bombs.

I'd done that on purpose—shown them a beautiful, perfect infant and then contrasted it with one with a facial deformity.

"That is one ugly baby," someone said.

A couple of people laughed and, damn it, that was enough to set me off.

"Who said that?" I demanded, outraged.

No one responded.

"Well, whoever you are, shame on you. Because of people like you, life sucks for kids like this little girl. Not only are they ostracized, they often have difficulty breathing, eating, hearing and talking. When their mothers try to breastfeed them—what are we, twelve?" I asked when someone from the back row snickered. The guy wore an amused smirk as he balanced his chair on its back legs.

"Please ignore them," Larkmont said. "Unfortunately, from time to time we admit students who have yet to achieve full adulthood. Please go on."

Score: Larkmont, 1, Jocks, 0.

"As I was saying, when their mothers try to breastfeed their babies, the milk goes through the holes in the roofs of their mouths into their sinuses, causing them to choke. Some mothers don't know any other way to feed their babies and many infants are malnourished as a result. Fortunately, clefts like this one can be repaired and it's my goal in life to become a surgeon so I can help kids like this." I clicked to the next photo. "In comparison, this is the same little girl after surgery."

Except for two tiny scars beneath her nostrils, she looked adorable. This time, the class reaction was more appropriate. I saw people smiling in gladness and relief.

"I always thought the problem with clefts like this one was with the appearance," Larkmont remarked.

"I know," I said. "That's what most people think."

Later, I realized I should have closed the presentation with the cleft photos because the rest of my photos didn't garner near the interest, but I still thought I got an A.

As the presentations continued, I was impressed by how often Larkmont identified the professional photographers in the second part of people's presentations without being told. Someone remarked on it and she said, "I've been teaching this class for quite a while and believe it or not, out of the billions of photographs you can find on the internet, students gravitate toward the same images. And that's not coincidence. Good photography is something we can all recognize. The best images are the ones that retain their strength and impact as time goes by, regardless of how many times they're viewed."

Hudson was the last one to present. He walked with the self-assured grace of a natural athlete and his physique rivaled that of any movie superhero, especially his thighs and butt. Thick with muscle, his legs looked powerful enough to tow a midsized sedan. Now that I knew his sport was hockey, I wondered if he was a fast skater or if that much muscle ended up slowing him down instead.

"My name is Hudson Forte. I play hockey, and…"

His teammates whooped it up for him.

"…I can hear the word 'breast' without giggling."

He got some laughter, some of it from me, but it was reluctant.

Ruby typed something on her laptop and a moment later her text appeared on my tablet screen.

Ruby: Is it just me or is it suddenly HOT in here???? He's gorgeous and funny.

Indi: I actually know him.

When Ruby gasped, Larkmont gave us a glance and I had to ignore Ruby and turn my attention back to Hudson's presentation.

"Speaking of breasts," Hudson said, "my first photo is from

one of my favorite shows, *Game of Thrones*. For those of you who haven't seen it, the show is famous for its nudity. In fact, one fan site actually tallied up a grand total of eighty-two nude scenes across the seventy-three episodes."

A heightened sense of anticipation gripped the room and I realized he made that little statement about not giggling to trick us into thinking he was above the adolescent behavior of his teammates, only to follow it with a picture of boobs anyway. I expected him to justify his objectification by claiming it was art and / or a celebration the naked female form.

I was wrong.

The photo was not of boobs, butt or bush. It was a landscape I recognized, having watched *Game of Thrones*. In the foreground was a colossal statue of a helmeted warrior with a sword and shield. He straddled a waterway on which tiny boats could be seen. Behind him was a vast city bisected by more water. It was pretty awe-inspiring and reminded me of how much I admired the rich and intricate world that George RR Martin had created.

Hudson's other photos included that famous one of the construction guys eating lunch on the beam of a New York skyscraper and a personal one of himself as a kid in full hockey regalia, including a helmet with a full metal cage to protect his face. He was surrounded by professional hockey players, all wearing different uniforms, which didn't make sense to me, because even a non-hockey fan like me knew only two teams played at a time. Once again, the hockey contingent made a ruckus.

"D-Day! D-Day! D-Day!" they chanted.

Larkmont settled them down with a raised hand before she asked, "I'll assume you're not talking about the invasion of Normandy."

"No. The man with his hands on my shoulders there is my dad and his nickname is D-Day," Hudson replied. "He played in the NHL."

"His whole family played in the NHL and he was drafted last year by San Francisco, Coach," someone said.

Larkmont raised one gray eyebrow.

"Not Coach. Sorry. Professor."

Looking uncomfortable, Hudson presented the last few photos, ending with a funny black-and-white portrait of a tiny bow-legged Chihuahua, taken at his eye-level. Beside him you could see the owner's shoes and the massive paws of another dog, possibly a Great Dane. The tiny dog was wearing a knitted sweater, a knitted, brimless Gatsby cap and a comical, long-suffering expression that seemed to say, "Yup, this is my life."

The hockey players applauded and even though they were pretty insufferable, I had to admit Hudson's presentation was surprisingly entertaining, thought-provoking and intimate. Who knew a jock could have a creative side?

After class, Ruby and I grabbed some lunch at The Marketplace. She was munching on a chicken Caesar and I had gotten my favorite combo—the French dip and fries. The place was crowded and noisy, but the staff here had things down to a science. Even when there were lines, like today, they moved quickly. And I appreciated their commitment to offering healthy choices and changing things up so we never got bored.

"I am so glad we're taking that photography class," Ruby said. "Who knew it was going to be chock full of cute guys?"

"Yeah, who knew?"

"Ah, you did," she said with an arch look. "You said you know the cute hockey player who presented last. Who is he? Because he's gorgeous. He's what would happen if Thor and Captain America had a baby."

"Ruby, two dudes can't have a baby. Well, not unless they adopt. Or find a surrogate." I rearranged the meat on my sandwich so it was spread evenly across the entire roll, not bunched up in the middle.

"Where do you know him from?" Ruby asked.

I dipped my sandwich in the jus to let the rich broth soak into the bread then took a bite. "He hooked up with my ex-roomie once."

"Which one?"

"My first one. Blair."

"The one who had a thing for jock cocks?"

We'd both given each other the run down on our former room-mates in the first "let's get to know each other" session.

"Yes. That's the one. Anyway, one day, I got out of class early and when I opened the door to our room, there she was, wrapping up a nooner. She was still in bed, but Hudson was standing there buck naked, with his back to me and oh my God, was he gorgeous. I'd never been in the presence of thighs like that. And his glutes? There are no words. He was just reaching for his pants and I must have made a noise—okay, I might have moaned a little —and he must have heard me because he stopped moving and turned."

Ruby gasped. "Wait a second." She leaned forward. "Are you telling me you saw his ding-dong?"

"I saw his *penis*, yes."

She giggled. "Was it impressive?"

"Not particularly."

"That's because it was resting," said a voice, startling us.

6

INDI

Ruby gave a little yelp.

Somehow Hudson had come to crouch next to our table without being noticed. His handsome face was literally less than a foot away. I would have asked how much he had heard, but his remark made it clear he'd heard enough.

My face burned as he straightened to his full height of a little over six feet. I wanted nothing more than to magically disappear in a puff of smoke.

"As an aspiring doctor," Hudson said, "I'm sure you know that the male sex organ is flaccid the majority of the time and nothing in a flaccid state is ever impressive. Asparagus, for example."

"Are you saying that your penis in a non-flaccid state *is* impressive?" I asked.

He gave me a decidedly wicked smile. "No comment."

I tried very hard not to picture him with a hard-on, but it was impossible. Ever since that fateful afternoon, I sometimes fanta-sized about what it might have been like if he'd hooked up with me and not Blair.

Usually, I imagined we were in my dorm room and he couldn't

get my clothes off fast enough. He'd take me on top of the bed, or against the wall, or on my desk. I'd actually come up with quite a few scenarios and they all ended with us sated and sleepy.

His smile got even more wicked, as if he could read my thoughts.

"Would you like to join us?" Ruby asked, gesturing to an empty chair.

"Emerald, right?" He looked at her questioningly.

"Ruby."

He snapped his fingers. "I knew it was a gemstone. I'm Hudson."

"I remember."

"Okay, let me get some food. Be right back."

After he left, I whacked Ruby on the arm. "What are you doing?" I hissed.

"Giving you a chance to make your fantasies a reality."

I quickly checked to make sure he wasn't sneaking up on us again. "I don't fantasize about him," I hissed.

"Like hell you don't."

I bit my lip. "Okay, maybe once or twice."

"Then you need to go for it," she said. "Ask him out."

"Are you kidding? First of all, he's way out of my league. I also just insulted his penis. I have a better chance of curing cancer than I do getting a date with him."

"Don't sell yourself short, my friend. He did agree to sit down and have lunch with you," she said, slinging her backpack on her shoulder and picking up her tray.

"Wait a second. What do you mean, 'with *you*'? What are you doing? Are you leaving?"

"Three's a crowd," she said with an overly-bright smile.

"But then I'll be alone with him and I'll have to carry the conversation all by myself. I can't do that. I suck at small talk. Lunch will be one giant uncomfortable silence and he'll walk away thinking my tongue went on vacation."

She put a hand on my shoulder. "Indi, I have faith in you. You can do this. Ask him about hockey. Or his car, if he has one."

"Oh, good idea. Guys love talking about themselves."

"And if all else fails, talk about his penis some more." Then, hooting with laughter, she deserted me.

I didn't know if I wanted to hug her or strangle her.

When Hudson returned a few minutes later, he had the same French dip combo that I had gotten—times two—an apple, a banana, a spinach salad, potato salad and a jumbo glass of iced coffee.

"Did you just come off a fast?" I asked.

He chuckled. "I have practice later. I need energy for that. Where'd Ruby go?"

"She had class."

As he dug in, I tried to regulate my breathing. I was sitting at a table alone with Hudson Forte. He was close enough for me to see that his blue lagoon eyes were rimmed with green. He had thick lashes, a full lower lip and a tiny scar on a jawline that wouldn't have looked out of place on Clark Kent.

"You know, it's not every day I find two women talking about my penis and in such disparaging terms. I think maybe you owe me an apology." He raised an eyebrow, but there was a smile playing about his lips.

This was so unlike any conversation I'd ever had with a guy, especially a jock. It was so disarming. And funny. It felt like we were friends now that we had this private joke. Maybe that was the key. I had to think of him as a friend. That would take all the pressure off. Despite what Ruby said, I was under no obligation to ask him out or even think of him as actual date material. He was pretty much in the same category as a celebrity I had no hope of ever talking with again.

Taking a mental deep breath, I said, "I *would* apologize if you were actually hurt by what I said."

"I *was* hurt. I have an incredibly fragile ego. Inside, I'm weeping."

"Stop it. You are not. Inside, you're digesting."

He laughed. "Can't argue with you there. I love their French Dips here. The bread is killer because they grill it with butter and the *jus* is really beefy. I dip my French fries in it too."

"So do I," I said.

"You do not."

"Yes—" I picked up a fry "—I do," I said and dipped it.

His eyes narrowed and we sat there dipping and eating fries in silence, maintaining eye contact like we were in some kind of French fry eating throwdown. After a moment or two, he took three fries as if in challenge, dipped and ate them, all in one go. In response, I grabbed the rest of the ones on my plate—about five in each hand—dunked them into the *jus* and pushed them into my mouth, heedless of the liquid dripping down my chin and onto the table.

He laughed. "I give up," he said, hands in the air in a gesture of surrender. "You win."

I wiped my mouth and chin with my napkin, pretty relaxed now. The friend zone trick was working.

"They said in class you were drafted by San Francisco. I'm not really a sports fan so explain to me why you're here and not with the team that drafted you."

"Because it's not like being drafted into the military. You don't immediately report to the team for duty. What being drafted in the NHL means is that San Francisco has, I guess, reserved me, so that when I go pro, I play for them. That way, I get my college degree and they wait for me to finish."

"So you're going to live in San Francisco then?"

"Most likely."

"You'll be a Forty-Niner. Congrats!"

He got a pained look on his face.

"Gotcha!" I said, laughing. "I know that's a baseball team."

When the pained look didn't go away, I laughed harder.

"Ha! Gotcha again. The Forty-Niners play football. My dad loves the Patriots."

He chuckled. "Yeah? I'm a Giants man myself."

"So what *is* your hockey team? It's the San Francisco…?"

"Dragons. The San Francisco Dragons. And get this—they're not the medieval kind of dragons. This Chinese billionaire, Lillian Pei, owns the team, so dragon is like a snake with four legs. Being Chinese yourself, I thought you might appreciate that."

"Actually, I don't really consider myself Chinese," I said.

"Oh, shit. I'm sorry. I swear you said you were originally from China yesterday."

"I did say that. That's where I was born, but I grew up here in America, in Brattleboro, a couple hours south of here."

"So, you don't speak the language."

"No. I don't know much about China at all."

"Huh." He removed one leaf from his spinach salad and set it aside. "Don't let me forget that."

"What's it for?"

"My hamster."

"Shut up. You have a hamster?"

"Yup. His name is Deke and he lives like a king."

"I wouldn't in a million years have pegged you as a hamster guy."

"I love cute animals. Always have, always will. Now tell me why you don't know much about China. No judging. I'm just curious."

"I don't know," I said. "My parents weren't really into it and now, neither am I. In fact, most of the time I didn't want to be Asian, especially when I was little. It was embarrassing. It singled me out as different. When we went out as a family, we didn't look like other families."

"In a weird way, I kind of know what that feels like, to want to be like everybody else. My family was kind of a big deal in the NHL."

"Oh yeah, I remember. What did they say in class? That your whole family was in the NHL?"

"Someone in every generation has played for the league since it started a hundred years ago. There's no other family that can claim that. My dad's generation had *three* players—him and his brothers Rick and Matt. Is it something that I'm proud of? No doubt. But at the same time, people I don't even know walk around with my last name on their shirts."

"That must be weird."

"I'm used to it by now, but sometimes it *is* creepy." He shook his head. "I'm sure I sound entitled as shit right now. Poor me. My family's famous and it's such a pain."

"I sound just as entitled," I said. "My parents took me from a state-run orphanage and brought me to a country where I literally have all the opportunities I could ever ask for, but here I am complaining too. Big whoop. There are a lot worse problems to have than not looking like your mom and dad."

"Yeah, the grass is always greener." He ate the last bite of his second French dip and started digging into the potato salad. "Let me ask you something. If you could wave a magic wand and make yourself into the biological daughter of your mom and dad, would you do it?"

"No one's ever asked me that."

I thought about it a moment. Ever since I could remember, I'd wished I could be my parents' "real" daughter. I even used to make that wish when blowing out my birthday candles. But here was Hudson shining a light on that—let's face it—misguided, childish desire. With the benefit of hindsight and maturity, I could look at the situation with more knowledge about the world and about myself and see that I couldn't "fix that problem" and still be the person I was today.

If the wand could get rid of my birthmark, however, I would wave it like I was warding off a horde of Azkaban Dementors. That would have been a life-changing miracle I wouldn't think twice about.

"If I became the biological daughter of my adoptive parents," I said, "and my DNA would be a mixture of theirs, I would pretty much be a completely different person. I would have been born with different skills, tendencies and talents than the ones I have now, and I like who I am. So, no, I would not wave that wand."

"Okay. I get it. It's just an image thing, then," Hudson remarked. "You just wish you could look white."

"Um…no," I said, feeling suddenly uncomfortable. And bristly. "It's not about being white at all. Are you…implying that being white is preferred?"

"No, no, not at all!" he said, straightening in his chair. "I'm just trying to—"

I didn't let him finish. "Because, for the record, what I wished for was to look like my parents. If they'd been black, I'd have wished to be black. If they were Indian, I'd have wished for that. I wanted to *match*, not just be white, you pretentious racist."

As he stared at me, shocked into silence, I grabbed my backpack and left.

HUDSON

I hate doing laundry and will put off doing it until I absolutely have to. I'd tried to get AJ to do my laundry as part of the reduced rent agreement but he'd refused.

"Dude," AJ had said, "I appreciate the discount but there's no way in hell I'm touching your laundry."

"Like your dirty clothes smell any better," I'd countered.

"Not the point," he said. "I wouldn't care if your stuff smelled like lilacs. I will not touch anything that touched your balls."

And really, I couldn't blame him.

So, here I was, faced with a giant pile of laundry. Fortunately, the building had four washers and four dryers in the communal laundry room, so if no one was using the machines, I could bang everything out in about an hour.

Before I started the dreaded sorting, I went to Deke's enclosure and was glad to see he was stirring. Hamsters don't appreciate being woken up.

I removed the roof of his habitat and carefully scooped him up in my hand.

"Hey, buddy. How's your day been?" I asked, stroking his silky head. "Probably pretty chill. Are you hungry? I brought you a spinach leaf from my disaster of a lunch. Don't say I never gave you anything."

I held the leaf close to his face and he snatched it from me and started nibbling.

"What's *your* stance on laundry?" I asked him.

Still munching, he looked at me as if to say, *Clothing is a construct designed to inhibit your natural freedom. I pity you.*

I grinned. Deke was a deep thinker.

When he'd finished his treat, I put him back in the enclosure and put the roof back on. Hamsters are skilled escape artists so I had to make sure the lid was secure.

Unable to procrastinate any longer, I tossed my dirty clothes into piles of lights and darks and told Deke about my encounter with Indi two years ago after a one-nighter with her roommate.

"The thing is, I barely even remember the roommate. We hooked up once and that was that. But I did remember the girl who walked in on us as I was getting dressed. There was something about her that caught my eye and she was really funny. I thought about trying to meet up with her again, but it seemed like a dick move after I'd had sex with the roommate. But now, here we are, a couple years later having lunch. What are the chances?"

Deke snuffled around his food dish, perhaps looking for more spinach.

"Anyway, against all odds we're both in my photography class and she's still pretty hilarious, so I'm doing my best to charm her and everything was going great. We talked about some real personal stuff. But then I had to ruin it all by saying something completely idiotic."

Deke's nose twitched as he continued to look at me unblinkingly. I imagined, if he could talk, he'd sound like Morgan Freeman. *Silence is a source of great strength. You should exercise it more often.*

"Yeah, you're probably right. I should talk less and listen more. I should also apologize. Hopefully, she'll have cooled off by Monday."

I ended up with three bags of clean, dry clothes by the time I had to head to the rink for practice. I had to put all thoughts of Indi out of my head and concentrate on hockey. Our first game of the season against UConn was in three short weeks. The freshmen had a lot to learn. The rest of us were still adjusting to the loss of the Graham twins and Josh Gruber.

Even though there was a part of me that wanted to defy my dad, I was still one of the first ones to show up at the rink and found myself being a little extra cheerful and encouraging to the freshies. I bit my tongue and smiled when some of them complimented me on how great a guy my dad was.

Then as I was taping my socks, I heard someone's voice raised. It was Tate Adler. He and Callan Thomas were looking at something on his phone.

"There, see?" Adler said. "I'm telling you, she died. Look at the way the camera is moving. It's flying, like she's a spirit."

"Yeah, but when they open the door for her, that floating stuff stops. Replay it."

Curious, I ripped the tape, secured it to my sock and went over. "What are you arguing about?"

"Whether or not Rose dies at the end of *Titanic*."

I suppressed my laughter as I watched the ending scene on Adler's phone.

"All the people that are greeting her died at the end, like Jack. You can tell they're all in heaven because of the white light at the very end."

Thomas crossed his arms. "So you've watched the movie and confirmed that every single person in that last scene was shown to die when the boat sank." He said it as a challenge.

"No," Adler said, "but I will if I have to. She was a hundred years old in the movie. Of course she died."

"She was dreaming, I tell you. Did you ever really listen to the song? The very first line is about her dreaming about him every night."

Adler turned to me. "What do you think, Forts?"

"What do I think? I think that Jack was a fucking pussy. He tried *one time* to get onto that door. *One time.* That, my friends, is the definition of a quitter. He didn't deserve Rose."

Both of them stared at me then Adler held out his fist for me to bump.

"You are absolutely fucking right on that score."

"We should take a vote," Thomas said. "Raise your hand if you think she was dead." He counted the hands. "How many think she was dreaming?"

"It's a tie," Thomas said. "Brammy, you didn't vote."

Bramley didn't even look up from lacing his skate. "I never saw *Titanic*."

Thomas gasped. "What the fuck?"

"You've never seen *Titanic?*"

They both gaped at him.

"Dude," Adler said, "you've got to see it. It's like mandatory."

"Not interested," Bramley replied.

"But Kate Winslett is beyond hot in that movie. There's this really great scene—"

"The scene where he sketches her!" AJ exclaimed.

"Yes!"

Other guys were chiming in now, fast and furious. It seemed that scene was A Moment in a lot of my teammates' lives.

"OMFG. So hot."

"So fucking hot."

"We saw it when it was rereleased in the theaters. My mom tried to cover my eyes!"

"Mine too."

"Guys, tell you what," I said. "We'll all watch it at the hockey house next week and Brammy can break the tie. The rookies can make dinner for us. How does hot dogs with all the trimmings sound?"

Everyone seemed to think that was a great idea, especially when AJ said he'd bring his famous "totchos," which were nachos made with tater tots instead of tortilla chips.

But Bramley said, "You guys go ahead, but I'm not watching that lame ass chick flick."

He was so adamant that no one said anything after that. Someone turned some music on to fill the awkward silence that followed.

Pulling my jersey on, I went over to Bramley.

"Come on, Brammy," I said in a low voice. "It really is a great movie, especially the last part when the ship is sinking. It's so realistic. Really makes you feel like you're there. Don't let the team down."

He sighed. "All right, I'll go on one condition…that you stop campaigning for the C."

"What? What are you talking about? I'm not campaigning."

"Can you deny you want to be captain?"

"Let me put it this way, if they offer it to me, I'll accept, but—"

He scoffed. "I knew it. I knew it that night your dad took us all out to dinner to butter us up. Talk about obvious."

"I didn't ask him to do that. I didn't even know he was coming that night."

"Sure you didn't." He let out a harsh breath. "Look, never mind. I have to finish getting dressed."

⸻

Back at the apartment, AJ baked a chicken and prepared some brown rice and frozen vegetables he cooked in the microwave. As we dug in, I said, "Guess who I had lunch with today?"

He put on a thoughtful look. "Sultan Kösen, the current tallest man in the world."

"I can't believe you know that."

He grinned. "I know many things, young Forte."

"Obviously, I did not have lunch with the current tallest man in the world. Guess again."

"The Jonas Brothers."

"Wrong again. One more chance."

"That cute girl from photography class, the one who wants to save the world from ugly kids, one surgery at a time."

I stopped in the middle of cutting my chicken and stared at him in shock. "How did you...?"

"I saw you guys at the Marketplace," he said with a chuckle. "But being the excellent friend I am, I left you alone and sat a few tables away. When I left, you two were still talking. I hope you can introduce me to her friend. She's a babe."

"Well, I would, except I fucked up royally and I'm not sure Indi will ever speak to me again."

"What the hell did you do?"

I sighed. "I...I kind of accidentally implied that she wished she was white."

AJ looked at me, horrified. "How in the living fuck did you do that?"

I explained what happened and how it was just a misunderstanding.

"I didn't mean it the way it sounded."

"Of course you didn't," he said reassuringly.

"I was just trying to confirm that she just wanted to look like her parents and it came out all wrong."

"Well, my friend, seems like your only course of action is to apologize and explain, otherwise, she'll go on thinking you're the BROC."

I gave him a questioning look.

"Big Racist on Campus."

"Fuck you." I said, unable to hold back a laugh. "Yeah, I'll definitely approach her, but I probably won't see her again until class, next Monday. Damn it."

"You could always haunt the Marketplace and hope to run into her again."

"And have her think I'm a stalker as well as a racist? No thanks."

AJ shrugged and ripped a big bite off his drumstick.

"I'll just wait until class and implement my dad's relationship reboot."

AJ blinked at me. "I'm sorry...what?"

"The relationship reboot. It's this thing my dad does when he fucks up with my mom. I swear, it's practically foolproof. Works, I'd say, eighty percent of the time."

"Your dad's a relationship expert as well as an ace hockey player?"

I shrugged. "He played the field when he was younger but once he married my mom, all that stopped. He's devoted to her and they're pretty happy."

AJ laid his chicken bone to the side of his plate and wiped his hands on his napkin. "Okay, tell me how this reboot works."

"There are three important aspects. First is the apology. It can't just be, 'I'm sorry.' You have to be specific. 'I'm sorry for—' then you fill in the blank. That's really important. The details make it more sincere."

"This is fascinating," AJ said.

I narrowed my eyes and he held his hands up in a gesture of innocence.

"No, really. I'm not being sarcastic."

Because he did seem sincere, I went on. "The second thing is related to the first one. You have to look her in the eye. That's how she knows you mean it."

"*Do* you have to mean it?" AJ asked. "I mean, can you just go through the motions?"

"My dad insists you don't, but like I said, it doesn't work every time and maybe that's because he doesn't always mean it."

"Makes sense. What's the last part?"

Grinning, I picked a piece of food out from between my teeth and sat back.

"Aw, come on. Don't be a dick. What's the last part of the formula?"

"What's it worth to you?"

"I'll do the dishes."

"Done."

Our normal deal was AJ cooked, I cleaned up, so just by sharing my dad's pearls of relationship wisdom, I was going to have a dishes-free night.

"So the last thing you have to do is ask her, 'What can I do to make this better?' Then, you have to do it, of course."

"Yeah, but what if she asks for something you don't want to do?"

"I'll tell you what my dad said when I asked that same question—that's the price of fucking up."

I'd told AJ the reboot worked about eighty percent of the time, but I was still worried. I really liked Indi. Beyond her rocking body, she made me laugh and I wanted to find out more about her. I admired the way she'd handled herself when my teammate made that rude comment about the kid in her presentation and how she seemed as passionate about medicine as I was about hockey.

INDI

Nodding at Hudson, I said to Ruby, "There's the creep."

He'd just entered the photography classroom and was standing near the door scanning the room. When his eyes lighted on me, he took a deep breath and started toward us. I'd hoped we could politely ignore each other for the rest of the semester, but he wasn't cooperating.

"Oh my God," Ruby said. "Want me to run defense? Tell him off for you?"

Before I could answer, Professor Larkmont blew into the room and started talking before she even got to the lectern. While Hudson went to sit in the back with his teammates, I faced front and tried to pay attention to her presentation about the history of photography.

I wasn't too successful. Just seeing Hudson again stirred up all the nasty feelings I'd bathed in for the past two days.

Even though he and I had spent less than an hour in each other's presence, I'd felt as if I'd been betrayed. He'd been so easy to talk to and he had this way of asking me questions that not only made me really think but that I wanted to answer. I'd found myself voicing feelings that I usually didn't share with other people or even examine for myself. And then, like a slap in the face, he'd said that shitty thing and it had felt like someone had said, "Indi, congratulations, you just won a new car!" and then a moment later told me it was a joke.

I'd tried to forget about it and him but when he walked into the classroom today, it stirred everything up again.

Despite my scattered thoughts, I managed to take some decent notes, but at the close of the class, Professor Larkmont dropped a bomb on us.

"We're about out of time," she said, "so quickly, written assignment 1A is to choose two of the pioneering photographers from the list provided and write a total of five hundred words about their contribution to photography. That is due on Friday. In the meantime, you should be getting a jump on the first portrait assignment which is due on the twenty-fifth. For those of you who have neglected to read the syllabus, you must pair up with someone from class, someone you don't already know. You hear me in the back?"

Some grumbling from the hockey contingent could be heard as she dismissed the class. They weren't the only ones thrown for a loop.

I had read the syllabus and seen the assignment required a partner, but I'd assumed Ruby and I would work together. Now, compelled to find someone else, I broke out into a cold sweat. When I was a little girl, when a teacher told us to pair up or form a group, I was often everyone's last choice or worse, I was shunned. The person or group would close ranks or turn their backs on me. When this happened, the teacher would either force someone to be my partner or step in and be my partner herself. It was an exercise in humiliation.

I usually managed to hold in the tears in until I got home where I would tell my mother what happened. As she enfolded me in her comforting arms, she would remind me how perfect I was, that I should never change to fit someone else's ideal and when people were mean to me, I should feel bad for *them* because what a person was like on the inside was more important than what they looked like. Easier said than done.

Once I learned to cover my birthmark with makeup, I didn't have any difficulty finding a partner when required, but that didn't stop the anxiety, or the memories, for that matter, from reappearing in a rush.

As I packed up my things, my stomach in knots, I was surprised by a tap on my shoulder.

It was, of course, Hudson.

"Hi," he said with a tentative smile.

I nodded once, my jaw tight.

"I wanted to apologize to you for what I said on Friday. It sounded like I thought you wanted to be white, as if being white was something all non-white people aspire to, and that's not what I meant, or believe, for that matter." Sighing, he shifted his weight, a heavy-looking backpack on his shoulder. "I was just trying to confirm what I thought you were saying—that you'd wanted to be like your parents. That's all. And it came out wrong. Really wrong and I apologize."

He looked me in the eye during his entire speech and as I took in the remorse on his face, the anger and hurt I'd felt all weekend seemed to evaporate. He seemed sincere and I was no saint myself. I'd said things before that I wished I hadn't or had come out differently from what I'd intended.

"Apology accepted," I said and a smile broke out on his face.

Lord, that smile needed to come with a disclaimer. *Side effects of this smile may include raised temperatures, heart palpitations and increased sexual desire.*

"I want to make it up to you somehow," he said.

"You don't have to do that."

Two voices said simultaneously, "Yes he does."

Arms crossed, Ruby looked at the guy who was standing next to Hudson. "Who are you?" she asked.

He grinned. "My name is Inigo Montoya. You killed my father. Prepare to die."

Without skipping a beat, Ruby said, "I think you must have me confused with someone else. I only have five fingers." She raised her hands and wiggled her fingers to prove she was not the Six-Fingered Man from the movie.

"Ah, a fellow *Princess Bride* fan," he said, holding out his own hand.

Ruby shook it. "Ruby Chang."

"AJ Scoville." He jerked a thumb at Hudson. "This guy's roommate. Want to be partners for that portrait project?"

"Sure," she said.

As they stepped away to discuss the details, I pressed my lips together. It was my childhood all over again. When faced with a choice, people never chose me. But I had to rise above and not let my insecurities get the better of me. I was a twenty-one-year-old woman, not a seven-year-old child.

I turned to Hudson. "Hey, you wanted to know how you can make it up to me? Be my partner for the portrait project." I hoped I sounded carefree and not as if a lifetime's worth of angst was in my throat.

"That wasn't exactly what I had in mind," he said.

My mind immediately jumped to the worst conclusion, but then he said, "See, you're supposed to pick something that's like a punishment or a chore. At least, that's how it usually goes when my dad messes up with my mom. Partnering with you is the opposite of a punishment. I *want* to be your partner."

9

HUDSON

I was getting dressed for practice, thinking about how perfectly the relationship reboot had worked that morning when a burst of laughter came from the doorway. Birdy and Briggs ambled into the locker room. They seemed to be taking their time, which wasn't smart because Coach Keller did not tolerate tardiness and we were expected on the ice for practice in a few minutes.

I was debating on a course of action when Bramley said, "You guys better get a move on or you're going to be late."

Birdy laughed as he plopped down on the bench and toed off his shoes. "Yeah, but you know that moment when you have one more chicken wing and no more beer to wash it down with?" Birdy pointed to himself. "That's what happened to me. Had to have one more beer."

"And I couldn't let him drink alone," Briggsy said. "Tha's against the bro code."

"You guys can't drink before practice," I said. "*Holy shit.*"

"You're freshmen. How did you even get served?" Bramley asked. "Were you at the Biscuit?"

Briggsy nodded again. "That new girl, Tina. She serves us if we tip her ahead of time."

"So you bribe her," I said.

Birdy lifted his chin. "I prefer to think of it as a pre-tip."

While Bramley again told them they were going to be in deep shit if they didn't start dressing, I turned to AJ.

"See if you can scrounge up some coffee," I said.

AJ finished tying his skate. "On it." He took off as I reached out, snatched up someone's Axe body spray and spritzed the beer-guzzling lunkheads.

"Hey! What the...?" Birdy exclaimed.

"You smell like a biergarten," I said. "Get dressed. Fast. If you're late, you're going to call attention to yourselves and believe me you do *not* want Keller to find out you were drinking before practice."

Some of the team had already left the room, but most stayed behind to watch the drama.

"If Coach finds out," I went on, "you'll be sitting out three, maybe four games." I turned to Bramley, who shrugged.

"Maybe more than that," he said. "Depending on your blood-alcohol level. He has a Breathalyzer, you know, and I saw him make a guy breathe into it once in front of the whole team. Worse, if you're under twenty-one, he calls your parents."

I was pretty sure Bramley was pulling all this out of his ass, but I didn't say anything, especially when it seemed to work. Gone was their "I don't give a shit" attitude. They were all business now.

AJ came back with two lukewarm cups of coffee just as they were pulling their jerseys on.

"Drink that while Brammy and I lace you up."

About ninety seconds later, I checked the clock on the wall. We had one minute. That wasn't enough to get to the ice. You can only walk so fast wearing skates.

As they sprinted toward the door, I said, "Hold on," and hustled over to the clock on the wall where I turned the hand back three minutes.

"What are you...?" AJ asked.

"Never mind. Just act as if nothing's wrong. Walk at normal

speed. Let me and Brammy do the talking." I turned to Brammy. "Follow my lead."

Coach Keller didn't look happy when we passed through the gate onto the ice.

"Nice of you to join us, gentlemen."

"What do you mean?" I asked, all innocent like.

"You're late. When the little hand is on the five and the big hand is on the twelve, that means your asses need to be on the ice."

"Sorry, Coach. We're right on time according to the clock in the locker room." I inclined my head in that direction.

Bramley backed me up. "Yeah, Coach. Go look. We're right on time."

I couldn't tell if Coach believed me or not, but I had never given him any reason not to trust me.

After what seemed like a lifetime, Coach Keller called out to one of the equipment guys to check the clock and adjust it if it needed adjusting, and I breathed a quiet sigh of relief. Crisis averted.

Ironically, after practice, we went to the Biscuit in the Basket—the scene of the crime. AJ didn't feel like cooking so he convinced Birdy and Briggsy—or the Brewski Brothers, as they'd been dubbed—to buy him, Bramley and me dinner. More sober now, they realized we'd saved their asses and wanted to show their appreciation, and I wanted to tell the manager, Kippy, his new hire was jeopardizing his liquor license. Win win.

The Biscuit was a homey place. In fact, table seventeen—a long high table with about twenty stools around it—was usually ours. The wood-paneled walls were covered with photographs of Burlington U's sports teams through the decades.

I got a double order of their whiskey maple chicken wings,

cole slaw, fries and a pitcher of beer that was obviously off limits to Birdy and Briggsy.

"That was a pretty slick move, Forts," AJ said. "That thing with the clock."

"I hate to say it, but I have to agree," Bramley said.

I lifted my mug of beer. "Thanks. But that's a one and done stunt. Keller won't fall for that again."

AJ turned to the Brewski Brothers. "No offense, but if Forts and Brammy hadn't done anything, I'd have probably sat back and watched the shit hit the fan when Coach smelled the beer on you."

Judging from the nods, most of the other guys would have stayed out of it too.

"He wouldn't have noticed," Birdy insisted, pouting a little.

"I don't know about that," AJ said. "You both looked a little wobbly out there. Especially you, Lord Briggerton."

"Regardless," I said, "you don't drink before practice or games. Period. End of story. If it happens again, we won't lift a finger to bail you out and no one else should either. I believe in second chances, but not thirds and fourths. We're a motherfucking Division 1 school. That means you step up and represent."

"Hear hear," AJ said, raising his stein.

Jonathan Kurlander, a mouthy senior defenseman, said something I didn't quite catch.

"Fuck you, Kurly," AJ blurted.

Whoa.

"Hey," I said, "I missed that."

Kurlander shrugged. "I said not all of us think of hockey as the end-all be-all. Some of us are actually here to get an education."

Ever my wingman, AJ was riled up now. "If Forts didn't want an education, he'd be in the fucking NHL right now."

Well, that wasn't quite accurate. Most likely, I'd have been playing for San Francisco's farm team, the Celestials, first, but now wasn't the best time to point that out.

"Hey, settle down. Kurly's entitled to his opinion, even if it's wrong." I lifted my chin at Kurlander. "Just for the record, I'm majoring in Community Entrepreneurship."

"Entrepreneurship," Kurlander said. "That's a big word."

"Yes, it is," I said. "You know what it means?"

"Don't be an idiot. Of course I know what it means. It means you want to go on *Shark Tank*."

There was some laughter. I let it roll off my back. I had no desire to go on *Shark Tank*. I wasn't planning to start a business. Not for a long time anyway, not until I retired from hockey.

"Just say the word," AJ said under his breath. "Just say the word and I will wipe that wiseass smile right off his face."

I gave him a small shake of the head and said to Kurlander, "Nah. If all goes well, I'll be on TV playing hockey, not begging for money."

"Yeah," AJ said. "Forts won't need money. He'll be making millions himself."

"Exactly my point," Kurlander said. "His degree will be irrelevant."

"*You're* irrelevant!" someone shouted and laughter erupted as Kurlander tried to find out who'd said that and I signaled the waitress for another pitcher of beer.

"So," AJ said to me later at the apartment, "I think you gained a few captain votes today with the clock stunt, but it's safe to say Kurlander won't be one of them."

"AJ, stop."

"I think he's jealous of you. Right, Deke?" he said as he passed the hamster cage where Deke was running on his wheel.

"Silly me. I thought because you're not taking a psychology class this semester, I'd be spared the psychobabble." I slipped Deke the sprig of parsley I'd brought back from the Biscuit. He immediately left the wheel and gobbled it up.

AJ laughed. "Tell me you don't agree with me."

"I don't have enough information to agree or disagree, but I do know I'm not his favorite person on the team. I'm glad we're not on the same line."

"See? Another reason he's jealous. You get more ice time. Chubby Hubby or Cherry Garcia?" he asked from the kitchen.

"Cherry Garcia."

AJ got a pint of ice cream out of the freezer and tossed it and a spoon at me, rapid fire. I caught both, but the spoon almost got away from me.

"Anyway, I heard he was badmouthing you the other day, saying how all you do is ride on your daddy's coattails, expecting everything to be handed to you on a silver platter."

"Fuck him. I don't care what he says."

"He was also trying to convince people that seniors deserve the captaincy because they've paid their dues, unlike some other entitled piece of shit. Those were his exact words. 'Entitled piece of shit.'"

I held my hand up. "Not listening. Seriously."

"Fine." Propping his feet on the coffee table, he worked his spoon into the pint of ice cream and took a huge bite. "Let me ask you a non-team related question."

"Shoot."

"Do you think I have any kind of chance with Ruby? Because I keep picturing her in a grass skirt and no top, but with her hair all loose over her luscious..." He gestured at his chest with his spoon. "It's making me fucking crazy."

"You know, I can put your Ben and Jerry's back in the freezer if you need to go tug the slug—hey!" I laughed as he kicked my feet off the coffee table.

"Shut up, jerk wad."

"Hey, you're the one who's over-sharing."

"I can't help it. She's so gorgeous, but she's way out of my league."

"Shut up. She is not. She liked your *Princess Bride* pickup line. Didn't she?"

"Yeah."

"Then don't wuss out. Go for it."

"What about you and Indi? You guys meet yet for the photography project?"

"Not yet." I dug up a big spoonful of ice cream and ate it. I loved those dark cherries and chocolate shards in the creamy cherry ice cream. "We're meeting at the Green Bean on campus next Monday."

"Nice. You going to make a move?"

I lifted a shoulder. "I don't know. She doesn't seem to be the type of girl you just hook up with and I'm not looking for long-term. On the other hand, I really like her. She's gorgeous and smart and funny...and we have stuff in common."

AJ worked to free a pretzel bite buried in his ice cream. "What kind of stuff?"

"We both sometimes feel like we don't have a right to complain about stuff. Me because of my family and the money and all that, and her having been adopted from China. I mean, who knows what kind of life she'd have had? She was at a government orphanage with no family, no one looking out for her welfare but the state. Here, she has a loving mom and dad, a solid childhood, a bright future..."

"Everyone has different challenges, Hudson," AJ said. "Just because you have a lot of advantages doesn't mean you can't ever be angry about something or wish things were different. Just be grateful for what you have and live your life. If you spend all your time feeling bad about it, then what's the point? If you have it, enjoy it, otherwise it's a waste."

"Shit, AJ. That's pretty fucking philosophical."

"Right?" He grinned. "Sometimes I amaze myself."

INDI

The campus coffee joint, called Green Bean, was hopping with students grabbing a caffeine hit so they could face their afternoons. I loved the smell of coffee and was looking forward to treating myself with something sweet. They had a fairly decent variety of hot, iced and blended drinks.

"Right on time," Hudson said as he came up to me near the entryway. "Let's order. I already staked out a table for us."

"Great."

I ended up getting this crazy milkshake that was kind of pricey, a creamy blend of coconut, peanut butter, chocolate, ice cream and cold brewed iced coffee.

Hudson ordered the same thing and tried to pay, but I wouldn't let him.

"This going directly to my hips," I said after we sat down. "I should actually just never come in here. I always end up getting that almond croissant. It's irresistible."

"No kidding," Hudson agreed.

I scoffed. "With all that muscle on you, I'm sure you burn more calories just breathing than I would during an hour-long spin class."

"Probably," he said, glancing down at the arm holding his drink and flexing.

Yowsa. The sleeve of his T-shirt stretched to accommodate his bicep which did all sorts of crazy things to my insides. I'll say one thing about jocks, they're nice to look at. Hudson was wearing some well-worn jeans and a dark gray T-shirt that emphasized his impressive physique. His blond hair shone even under the fluorescent lights and the stubble on his face was dangerously sexy.

I took a sip of my Peanut Butter Mocha Tempest in an attempt to cool down.

"So, let's get to it. I have to be at hockey practice soon."

We pulled out our laptops and somehow positioned them onto the small circular table without knocking over our shakes.

The first part of the project required us to interview each other using a provided list of questions and write a two-paragraph essay about our partner and what traits we hoped to convey in the portrait. For part two, we were to take the photographs and title them.

"Did you read the list of questions?" he asked. "For some reason, I expected them to be a lot more generic."

"Me too," I said. "We're supposed to choose any five questions, but to be honest, there are a lot more than five that I found to be interesting."

"I'm pretty easy, so you pick."

"Okay."

I perused the list and read the first one that jumped out at me. "What is something you were afraid of as a kid and are still afraid of now? I'll go first on this one. Did anyone ever tell you when you were a kid that if you stood in the bathroom, turned the lights off and said Bloody Mary three times, she would appear in the mirror behind you?"

He laughed. "Sure. I heard that story."

"Well, because of that I will never look directly in the mirror in a dark bathroom. Not now. Not ever. Yeah, go ahead and laugh. I know it's dumb, but there it is. What about you?" I asked.

"Me?" He looked a little sheepish. "I'm actually really afraid of doctors. When I was a toddler, I had to have my blood drawn for some reason and the lady trying to do it was horrible. She couldn't find the vein and they ended up having to hold me down to get the needle in. Ever since then, I've been really afraid to go to the doctor."

"I don't blame you. That sounds really traumatic."

"All right," he said, "one question down and four to go. What's next?" He sipped his shake then scooped out a finger full of whipped cream and ate it with gusto.

Trying not to imagine him licking whipped cream off *my* finger, I flipped the page. I kept finding questions I wanted to know the answer to from *him* but that I didn't want to answer myself, like "What is something you're self-conscious about?" "What's your greatest fear?" "What were some of the turning points in your life?"

In the end, I said, "I can't decide, so pick a number between one and two hundred."

"Eleven. That's my lucky number," he said with a grin.

I consulted the question list. "Number eleven. 'What's worth paying more for to get the best?' Oh, my answer is makeup," I said without thinking.

He cocked his head at me, his eyes widening in interest.

Good job, Indi. Now I'd called attention to my makeup. The urge to check my face was so strong, I had to sit on my hand so I wouldn't pick up my phone. I prayed nothing had smudged.

"You know, I've never bought makeup myself," he said. "But is there really that much difference between expensive makeup and stuff you can get at the drug store?"

This guy had no idea what he was asking. There's a lot of trial and error involved in finding makeup that will cover up a purple blotch on your face and not make you feel like you're wearing a layer of flesh-colored plaster. When I finally found products that I liked, they were all pretty pricey, but the cost didn't matter to me.

"There's some stuff I buy at the drug store—mascara, nail polish, lipstick," I said. "For those things, the difference in quality doesn't matter to me. Other stuff, like foundation, concealer and powder, I pay a lot more for."

"Huh."

The puzzled expression on his face was kind of adorable. It was as if I'd just talked to him in Swahili.

"If you want to see what I mean," I said, "I'd be happy to demonstrate on your face."

His bewildered expression turned instantly to one of horror. "Ah, no thanks. Makeup's not my thing. Like, in a big way. This is my face and I'm happy with it."

That's because you got dealt the royal flush of faces.

"Not that I'm against dudes who want to wear it," he went on still clearly flustered. "Whatever floats your boat, you know? It's a free country. I just don't play for that team."

Like I needed reminding. Every cell in my body, especially the ones in my erogenous zones, were on high alert. Maybe virgins were genetically programmed to respond to virile males. I'd learned in one of my classes that it had never been proven that humans produced sexual pheromones, but I was pretty sure this particular human was emitting pheromones like an essential oil diffuser set on turbo.

But then I reminded myself he was a friend and classmate. That was all. Because to assume anything more was to doom myself to disappointment.

"So what, to you, is worth paying more for?" I asked. "A nice pair of heels?"

"Ha! You're funny," he said, laughing. "I don't know that I actually believe in that whole idea. I'm not the kind of person who always demands the best. I'm more interested in value. Expensive things can be worth it, but most times, I think, you can be just as happy with something that doesn't cost as much."

This attitude surprised me. I assumed, as the son of a professional athlete, he'd grown up surrounded by largesse. Those guys made millions a year, didn't they?

"Okay, we have three more questions but I only have that one lucky number, so let's do eleven times eleven, which is one-twenty-one."

I referred to the list one more time. "'Is there anything you wish would come back into fashion?'"

He thought for a moment. "This is going to sound strange, but I wish hats were something guys wore every day, stylish hats like the fedora. I liked that bit of panache they added. I really like how they could be used to show respect."

"You mean like when cowboys tip their hats?"

"Yes, exactly."

"You could start a new trend yourself, you know. Just wear a fedora. See what happens."

He laughed. "Very funny. You don't know hockey players very well. I would get so much shit from the team if I did that. It wouldn't be worth it. Besides, you have to be an influencer to start a fashion."

"You're probably right." I leaned back and squinted at him. "But you'd look damn good in a fedora."

I was rewarded with another one of his supernova smiles.

"What about you?" He stirred his drink with his straw. "What fashion would you like to come back?"

"I like your hat idea, but I already know you want me to come up with my own answer." I sighed. "You know, I have to say, I kind of wish there was no such thing as fashion and that we could all wear whatever we wanted to."

This was because the only reason I had outfits that went together was because I saw them in the window or on a mannequin.

"Theoretically, we can," he said. "But it would never happen."

"Why not?"

"Humans need to bond with other humans, to form groups. There's safety in numbers and, back in the caveman days, you were more likely to survive in a group than alone. Dressing like everyone else is part of that. That's my theory, anyway. So you wish everything would come back into fashion. Is that your answer?"

I looked around the Green Bean and imagined what it would be like if everyone dressed in a fashion vacuum.

I frowned and shook my head. "You know what? No. That would actually probably be too chaotic. Like every day was a comic con. I think our eyes would get tired of all the visual noise. Plus, too much choice makes it harder to choose."

"Yeah, that's called choice overload. It's a phenomenon that we're covering in my Behavioral Economics class. Lots of options get people to browse, but sometimes fewer choices can get them to buy. Isn't that crazy? In fact, there's this big grocery store chain that's actively working on reducing the number of items they sell, based on studies about choice."

"That's really interesting," I said. "You almost make me want to take an economics class. And that's saying something."

His phone alarm went off. "Damn. I need to get going soon. I have practice. We're electing the team captain today."

Even though I knew the afternoon couldn't last forever, my heart sank.

"I had a really good time. I like the way you think, Indi Briscoe."

"Ditto," I said. My heart started beating faster as he tilted his head just slightly and leaned forward reaching out with one hand.

I froze.

Was he going to…?

And then he did.

He kissed me. It was brief, over before I even registered the fact that his lips were on mine. But the kiss lasted long enough for me to notice how warm his hand was as it curled around the back of my neck, that he smelled like autumn and coffee and a hint peppery sweat and that my body needed his like Vegas needed gamblers.

Before he pulled away, he touched his forehead to mine gently and let out a sigh that was part regret and part desire.

"I like the way you taste too," he said in a voice that got me even more riled up. I wanted to *feel* those words against my skin, with both of us naked or close to, somewhere where we could do all the things that kiss begged us to do.

HUDSON

As a hockey player, I'm usually highly aware of what's going on around me, but right now, everything faded into the background and all that registered was the softness of Indi's lips and how she tasted faintly of chocolate and peanut butter.

She didn't respond at all at first. It was like kissing a mannequin. For a moment, I thought, okay, there wasn't any chemistry after all. It happens. But then, she woke up and started to kiss me back and I immediately realized that there was enough chemistry to light a building on fire. She was eager and responsive and I wanted more—a lot more—but I couldn't go to practice with a hard-on so, with extreme difficulty, I pulled back.

"Can we, ah, finish later tonight after practice? We can go out and grab dinner, my treat. It's my fault I didn't allot enough time for this. For some reason, I thought we could bang this out in an hour…"

She touched her full lips with her fingertips and I noticed how elegant her hands were. She had slender fingers and bare nails, short enough to be practical but long enough to be feminine. It was satisfying to my ego that she seemed a little dazed.

"Indi? Dinner?"

"Dinner's fine," she said, snapping out of it. "What time?"

"Do you live on-campus?"

She nodded. "In Carter Hall."

"I'll pick you up at seven."

When I got to practice, I didn't have much time to dress. My locker room stall was next to AJ's.

"So, how'd the date go?" AJ asked me in a voice pitched so the other guys wouldn't hear.

"It wasn't a date." I started undressing.

"Potato potahto," AJ said. "How'd it go?"

"Good. We didn't finish. We still have two more questions, so I'm meeting her after practice."

I wasn't about to mention the kiss because then I would get the third degree about it. Plus, you never knew who was listening in the locker room. I didn't want it getting back to Indi that I was blabbing about the kiss not a half hour after it happened.

"Persistence, dude. Good for you." AJ held out his fist and I bumped it automatically. "As for me? I spent two hours with Ruby and I'm in love. I'm in love with a Hawaiian princess and I don't care who knows it."

"Oh, for Christ's sake," Seb Hunter said.

AJ ignored him. "She's my Buttercup and I'm going to do everything in my power to prove I'm her Westley. I will devote myself to making her happy in all the ways that can be accomplished." He nudged me with his elbow. "Anything you can do to help would be appreciated."

AJ was one of those guys who fell in love all the time. There was no easing into it with AJ. There was no "like" phase. He was all-in right from the get-go. I had to admire that. He was fearless that way. I'd asked him once why he wasn't afraid of getting his heart broken.

"Dude, love is the most amazing thing of all. It's the reason we're here. If there's even the slightest chance of finding it, I'm going for it, pedal to the metal. You can't win big if you don't bet big."

"Remind me never to take you to Vegas," I'd muttered.

A little over an hour later, Coach Keller blew the whistle and motioned for us to gather around. We were hot and sweaty from the drills we'd just run. I grabbed a water bottle off the railing and took a deep drink.

"All right, boys. Time to elect your captain," he said, handing out pens and small pieces of blank paper. "I want you to remember, this isn't high school. This isn't a popularity contest. I want you to think long and hard about who can lead this team to a championship.

"It should be someone who constantly pushes himself, because he knows if he ever slacks off, that just gives other people an excuse to do the same. It should be someone who isn't always in his own head, thinking about himself. A captain has his finger on the pulse of every one of his teammates. He's aware of stuff that's going on. He's not insulated. He's aware.

"He also listens. He listens to us and he listens to you. He's a decision maker, he's courageous, he's fair. Coach G? Anything to add?"

Coach Garfunkle glided forward. "Coach Keller told you what the captain should be. I'm going to tell you some things he should *not* be. A captain isn't selfish. He doesn't think he's right all the time. He doesn't think he knows it all."

"He's willing to learn," Coach Keller interjected.

"Exactly. He doesn't lie, or cheat or treat people disrespectfully."

"He's basically Jesus," AJ said under his breath and I had to press my lips together to keep from laughing.

"So, we've put together a list of three candidates for you to choose from—Pete Bramley, Jonathan Kurlander and Hudson Forte. We've talked individually to each of these men and all of them said they'd be honored to lead the team, so write the name of your choice on the paper, fold it and give it to Coach G. After that, you can hit the shower."

When I got my ballot, I didn't know who to vote for. I honestly thought I was the best man for the job. I certainly had the experience. I'd been captain of almost every hockey team I'd played for. But Bramley had been right. I could wear the C next year and give someone else a chance. When the Brewski Brothers had pulled their little stunt, Brammy had stepped up and the two of us had handled the situation. My dad told me there should always be more than one leader in the room and that leaders weren't always designated as such. Sometimes they just worked in the background and that I shouldn't ever shy away from being that unrecognized character guy.

Of course, he seemed to have conveniently forgotten about this selfless philosophy lately, but sometimes he got tunnel vision.

In the end, I scribbled Pete's name, handed in my ballot.

Everyone seemed subdued in the shower and later in the locker room where we waited for the announcement. AJ couldn't keep still. I was pretty anxious too. I wanted time to go home and change clothes for my date with Indi.

Finally, the coaching staff came in and stood at the front of the room where the white boards were still covered with notes about the plays we were working on.

"Gentlemen, it is my pleasure to announce your captain, the man who will lead us all to the Frozen Four in April, is...Hudson Forte. At his side, as alternate captain, will be Pete Bramley."

AJ whooped it up like he'd just scored the game-winning goal.

Pete had a solemn look on his face as he shook my hand. "Congratulations, Forte."

"Thanks, Pete. Congrats to you for getting the A."

"Yeah."

"Aw, look at Kurly," AJ said, a little loudly. "He looks like he's gonna cry. Gonna go cry now because you didn't make captain? Because an *entitled piece of shit junior* got captain instead of you?" AJ made an exaggerated sad face and pretended to rub his eyes.

Kurlander's face went red. "Fuck you, Scovie!"

He looked like he was going to launch himself at AJ, so I quickly shoved myself between them.

"Knock it off, both of you," I said.

I couldn't believe I'd been captain all of five minutes and I already had to play referee to two knuckleheads, one of them being my best friend. This sucked.

"AJ, apologize."

AJ looked at me with shock. "What?"

"You need to apologize to Kurly."

"The fuck I do."

"You don't rub a win in someone's face," I said. "Especially a teammate's. It's not cool, bro. Now, apologize."

"It was a fucking joke."

I didn't say anything. We both knew it hadn't been.

"Fine." AJ cast me a dirty look then muttered an apology to Jonathan before stalking off in a huff.

Kurlander was standing there, dumbfounded. The rest of the team were taken aback too. Everyone knew AJ and I were tight and no one seemed to be able to figure out what this meant.

With a sigh, I went after AJ.

"AJ, wait up."

He ignored me and shoved his way out the double doors that led outside.

I went after him, but unfortunately, several of our teammates came too.

"Hey, the parking lot's the other way," I said, jogging to catch up. AJ didn't have a car, so I usually drove us home.

He stopped. His posture was rigid.

"Come on," I said. "It's a twenty-minute walk home and it's cold."

As if on cue, a gust of wind whipped past us, making me zip up my jacket.

He turned around and said, "Not as cold as what you just did to me back there."

"What I did to you? What about what you did to me?"

"I didn't do fuck to you!" he shouted.

"Yes, you did. You put me right between a rock and hard place."

"And you stabbed me in the back! In front of the whole team. Jesus Christ. I want to throw up right now thinking about having to apologize to that pencil-dicked show-off."

"Hey, look at it from my point of view. I'm the captain now. I can't play favorites and I can't let shit like that go. It undermines the team."

I was vaguely aware of some of the guys standing in the periphery, listening, but this had to be done right now and it wasn't necessarily a bad thing if they heard this too.

"You made me feel like I was five fucking years old."

"I'm sorry, Scovie. I didn't have a choice. The coaches were watching. Everyone was watching. I couldn't let my captaincy start out like that."

He didn't reply, just walked off in the direction of home. This wasn't how I'd wanted the evening to go. I'd wanted to be in a celebratory mood when I met Indi. I'd wanted to look forward to the coming season and leading my team to the championship. Now, my best friend and roommate was royally pissed with me and for good reason. Looking back, I wished I'd come up with some other way to diffuse the situation other than a forced apology.

But in all honesty, I was a little pissed too. AJ should never have tried to pull that shit in front of everyone. He could have just said that to Kurlander in private. Then it would have been between them. But the moment he chose to slam Kurly in public, I *had* to get involved. If I'd let that go, I'd have been immediately tagged as a weak leader who played favorites and nothing good came of that, team-wise.

INDI

"Oh my God," Ruby exclaimed, "he *kissed you?*"

Still wondering if it had been a dream, I nonetheless nodded.

"With tongue?"

"Ruby!"

"Answer the question."

"Unfortunately, no."

"Damn. But still, he kissed you. I told you he likes you."

"We're having dinner tonight too."

"Indi's got a boyfriend," she said in a singsong voice. "Indi's got a boyfriend."

"Stop it," I said. "It's not—"

"—a date. You said that last time, but I think it's common knowledge that a kiss—was it on the lips?"

"Yes."

"Was it platonic? Like a kiss between friends?"

I thought about his hand on my neck and how his voice got growly afterward when he told me he liked how I tasted.

"No, definitely not."

"Then I think we can safely say tonight is a date. What are you going to wear?" Ruby asked. "Not that, I hope."

I looked down at my loafers, jeans and gray sweater set. "What's wrong with this?"

"Nothing, if you're going for that 'I'm here to get a degree but then I'm joining a nunnery' look."

"Thanks a lot."

She went into my room and after pawing through my closet, she turned to me. I was sitting on my bed feeling inadequate. Fashion wasn't my strong point.

"I swear, Indi, judging from your wardrobe, I'd guess you were color blind."

"Why do you say that?"

"Because your closet is a sea of black and gray. Nothing but neutrals."

"But that way I know everything goes together and I don't have to do what we're doing now, which is spend a lot of time making a decision on what to wear."

"Okay, wait here. I'll be right back. In the meantime, put this on." She flipped a couple of hangers, pulled out my black turtle-neck. "Do you have black skinny jeans?"

"Yes."

"Put those on too."

A moment later, she was back with a red beret and a pair of red flats.

"A hat?"

"Don't argue with me. Put it on. The shoes too. Thank God we have the same shoe size."

After I'd slipped the shoes on, I noticed Ruby was turning in a circle, clearly looking for something. "I can't believe you don't have a full-length mirror. Doesn't matter." She nodded matter-of-factly. "We can keep mine in the living room. Put the hat on and meet me in there."

I did as I was told. Ruby had propped the mirror up against the wall next to the door leading to the dorm hallway. I approached it and as my entire body came into view, I had to admit, two tiny additions really made a huge difference.

"Now, I think heels would actually look sexier, but considering this is kind of a fishing expedition, I think low key is wiser. Red lipstick is a must. If you don't have any, you can borrow mine."

After I applied the lipstick, Ruby looked me up and down. "You look good, Indi."

"I do, don't I?" I turned and looked at myself over my shoulder. The hat and shoes added panache that my lived-in loafers couldn't compete with.

My phone signaled a text, startling me.

Hudson: I'm out front, if you're ready.

My heart started pounding.
"He's here."

"Nice ride," I said as I got into his late-model Jeep Wrangler and buckled up.

"Thanks. It's got some really nifty features like this big touch-screen. There are heaters for the seats and the steering wheel but the coolest part is the doors come off."

"You're joking."

"I am not. It's too cold right now, but you can take the doors off and enjoy more of the fresh air while you drive than you ever thought you could. I like your hat, by the way."

"And I like yours."

Along with khaki pants and a white shirt, he was sporting a leather fedora that made him look pretty damned sexy.

"Yeah?" He ran his fingers along the brim. "This hat was my Indiana Jones costume from a couple of years ago, minus the whip. After we talked this afternoon, I decided I can damn well wear a hat every day if I want to. Apparently, you did too."

He grinned at me.

"Well, if I'm honest, my roommate made me wear it. She made

me change my whole outfit because apparently I looked like a nun."

He glanced at me. "Wait. You were going to wear a Halloween costume too?"

I laughed. "No, never mind."

As he drove along University Place, I looked over at him and wondered how I'd gotten so lucky. I was going out with Mr. Hockey McHottie. Maybe it was that manifestation thing in action. I'd read an article once about how to make miracles happen in your life by thinking about what you want down to the last detail and opening yourself up to the universe giving you what you want. The trick was not to just sit back and wait. You had to be aware of opportunities and grab them. Obviously, since I'd actively fantasized about him, I had that first part down pat. As far as grabbing the opportunities? I'd asked him to be my project partner, so damn. I was turning out to be the master of my own fate.

Now all I had to do was manifest him all the way into my bed. Because I was pretty sure sex with him wouldn't suck, even if it was my first time.

We exited the campus and headed toward Burlington. He had a five o'clock shadow that was super sexy. I'd always been a sucker for a five o'clock shadow.

"So who's the new team captain?" I asked.

"Well...I am."

"You don't look very happy about it."

He frowned. "Is it that obvious? I'm sorry. It's just...something happened right after the election. I was put into a lose-lose situation and now AJ hates me."

"I'm sure he doesn't hate you. What happened?"

He told me how AJ had teased someone who was also up for captain and how he'd stepped in and made AJ apologize.

"Yikes. If it means anything, I think you did the right thing."

"Really? Because I've been second-guessing myself ever since. I could have taken AJ and Jonathan aside and resolved it privately. I could have just made a brief statement and not gone down the 'apologize *now*' route…"

"Hindsight is 20/20. What's done is done. Hopefully AJ will come around. It sucks when your roommate is pissed at you."

When he parked in front of Tito's Wood Fired Pizza, I gave him a look.

"What?" he asked. "You don't like pizza?"

"No, I love pizza. It's just…my parents own a pizzeria in Brattleboro. It's called Slice of Heaven."

"Oh shit. I had no idea. We can go somewhere else, if you want."

"No, it's totally okay. We can eat here," I said. "I could really go for a deep-dish pie anyway. We don't serve deep-dish at Slice. Do they have deep-dish here?"

"I've never ordered it, but I know they do."

The restaurant's interior was warm and toasty and I immediately took my jacket off. They had wooden tables with iron accents and multicolored chairs that looked institutional yet cool at the same time.

I inhaled the familiar but tantalizing aromas of tomato sauce, basil and oregano, garlic, sizzling cheese and beer. We got a table right away. I sat with my back to the wall and Hudson faced me. The walls were large brown tiles and two huge chalkboards on opposite walls displayed the menu.

"Pick out whatever you want. I'm easy," he said. "Are you twenty-one?"

When I nodded, he pulled two beers out of his coat pockets.

"Hudson, ah, what are you doing?" I glanced around to see if any of the wait staff was watching him produce beverages from his clothing.

He grinned, a lock of his blond hair dipping down over his forehead. "Don't worry. This place is BYOB, one of the main reasons I like coming here. But their pizza is good too."

He popped the tops and handed me one. It said Saucer Pass IPA on it. The label reminded me of an old-time sci-fi movie poster in that there was a UFO in the night sky, but on closer inspection, I saw it was a hockey puck.

He took a pull from his beer and I couldn't help but watch his Adam's apple bob as he swallowed. Call me crazy, but the sight was so sexy, I had to cross my legs.

We went with the Detroit Triple Threat—bacon, sausage, pepperoni—and were told that because it was a deep-dish, it would take a little longer. Someone brought us a small bucket of ice to chill the two more IPAs Hudson had brought.

"If the pizza has a thick, fluffy crust and a lot of cheese bark, it'll be worth the wait," I said.

"Cheese bark?" Hudson asked.

"Yeah, it's that cheese that adheres to the side of the pan and gets all crispy in the oven. It's the best part of deep-dish." I patted his hand. "Stick with me, kid, and you'll know all the pizza lingo in no time."

"So, why do your parents not serve deep-dish? Are they anti-cheese bark?"

"Kind of. My dad is, anyway. He just loves the traditional Neapolitan crust. He claims it's easier to tell the difference between a superior pizza and a substandard one when it has a traditional hand-tossed crust. I do have to agree with him, but man, once in a while I just crave that crunchy, cheesy edge."

"I always thought deep-dish pizza came from Chicago."

"It does, but the Detroit kind has the sauce drizzled on top and is baked in pans that aren't quite as deep as Chicago's. They say that the original Detroit deep-dishes were baked in pans sourced from the automotive industry."

"So we're actually having not-quite-as-deep deep-dish pizza."

"Shut up," I said, laughing. "It's good. You'll see."

The pizza was excellent. Hudson was surprised to see a rectangular pan arrive and I was happy to see a nice crunchy edge with the highly anticipated cheese bark. It crunched when I took a bite and a rich tangy umami mixture of the crust, toppings and sauce exploded in my mouth.

"Oh my God, this is so good," I said, panting a little because it was still piping hot.

"I don't even have words," Hudson said, after taking a bite. "This is the best damn pizza I've ever had."

For a couple of minutes, we didn't speak. We reveled in pizza nirvana. The beer was the perfect complement and we clinked bottles when we started on our second.

After he polished off his first piece, Hudson said, "We have two more questions to get done, right? So choose a number."

"Let's go with our table number, 16."

He scrolled down the list. "Okay, I'll go first with this one. 'What do you strongly suspect but have no proof of?' I strongly suspect you like me, but I don't have any solid proof. I'll have to kiss you some more to be sure."

My face turned red but I gave him my flirtiest smile.

"I plead the fith," I said. *Damn it.* "Fifth. I plead the fifth."

"I also strongly suspect someone is a lightweight, and I think I do have proof."

I scoffed, even though he was right. It didn't take much to have me stumbling over my words.

"Whatever. I'm not sure why being able to drink a lot of liquor is such a laudable thing. The way I see it, I can get the same buzz as everyone else but for a lot less money."

"Touché," he said, tapping my bottle with his. "Your turn. What do you strongly suspect but have no proof of?"

Unfortunately, this question hit a little close to home.

"Hey," Hudson said, sitting up in his chair. "What's wrong? All of a sudden you look like you got bad news."

He reached across the table and took my hand. His was cool and damp from the condensation off his beer bottle, but I didn't mind. I was heating up from the way he was looking at me, his eyes full of concern.

"It's nothing," I said. "The question reminds me of something that happened when I was a kid that I really should be over by now."

"You want to talk about it?" he asked, his thumb stroking across the back of my hand. "I'm a good listener."

"No, it's ancient history. I don't think about it that often." I shook my head to clear out the bad memories. "To answer the question," I said, "I strongly suspect money *can* buy happiness. No, there's no real proof of that, but I'd be happy to test the theory any time."

"Has your family had to struggle?" he asked, concern still shadowing his brow.

"Oh, no," I assured him. "No, we've always had food, a roof over our heads, all the necessities. I just meant I fantasize about how much easier life would be if I didn't have to worry about money."

"Honestly, my family has money."

Ha. They *were* wealthy.

"But if you don't have money worries, you end up worrying about other things. And it doesn't guarantee happiness. That's for damn sure. Not the real kind anyway, not the lasting, deep-in-your-heart kind of happiness." He frowned and scratched at something stuck to the table. "I think real happiness comes from things like loving and being loved, doing good things, fulfilling some kind of purpose. The work you're going to do, for example. Helping those kids live normal lives."

My heart did a little somersault when his eyes met mine. Tonight, they were the color of the hydrangeas that bloomed in my parents' garden—deep blue with a hint of lavender and that intriguing green ring around the irises. I couldn't look away.

"That's the kind of thing that will make you happy."

"What about you?" I asked. "Does hockey make you happy?"

"Sure it does. It's what I'm meant to do."

"That's what your family thinks. I want to know what you think. Does hockey make you happy?"

This time *he* was the one who looked thoughtful.

"It does," he said after a long moment. "I love being part of a team, because there's nothing better than being in sync with your teammates and executing a perfect play. There's a lot of trust that has to occur on the ice and when you give your trust to a teammate and they come through, or vice versa, it's the best."

"And there's the satisfaction of putting everything you know into practice too," I said. "Using skills you've honed with hours and hours of work."

"Exactly. I love that too. Hockey is never easy, but that's what I like about it. All the highs you experience—scoring a goal or killing a penalty or winning the game—they're sweet *because* of the challenge."

"So meeting challenges can bring real happiness, too," I said.

"Yes, absolutely. We should write a book," he said with a laugh.

After tackling one last question—an easy one since we both just wanted to be done with it—he paid the bill and we headed back to the campus.

I was pretty drowsy—a result of the delicious pizza and the two beers. I must have fallen asleep on the five-minute drive back because I woke to find we were parked in front of Carter Hall.

"Oh my gosh. I can't believe I fell asleep."

"Don't worry about it."

"How long was I out?"

"Not long. About five minutes. You were so peaceful, I didn't want to wake you."

The air was cold, but I was warm with anticipation. He was going to kiss me again and oh, did I want him to. This time I wasn't going to settle for a one and done. No, I wanted to feel his mouth on mine for a long while. I wanted to feel his tongue parting my lips, his strong arms around me.

We looked at each other and every one of my nerve endings tingled with awareness. My heart was beating so hard, I could feel my pulse in my fingertips. I swallowed and let my lips part and I saw his eyes drop to my mouth.

This was it.

I leaned forward and he brought his head closer to mine, reaching toward me to cup my neck as he had just a few hours ago at the Green Bean. Giving in and preparing for the kiss of my life, I closed my eyes.

Our lips met gently, again and again. With each soft kiss, he explored a different part of my mouth, pressing, nibbling, tasting. Then he drew back and gazed into my eyes as if gauging my reaction. I smiled and he came back for more and I was happy to give it to him. Kissing Hudson was more intoxicating than any cocktail I'd ever drunk. In a matter of moments, I was breathing hard, moaning softly and there was a restless ache between my legs.

We started fogging up the windows as he deepened the kiss, demanding more from me and getting it. Outside it had to be in the fifties, but inside the Jeep it was hotter than the tropics. I was contemplating taking his hand and putting it on my breast, but he placed it on my face instead and I was so lost in the kiss that I let him do it. I loved the feel of his big hand on my face and how his thumb stroked my cheek.

Shit. That's when I realized.

He was stroking my cheek—the cheek with the birthmark on it.

HUDSON

I'll never understand the opposite sex. I know I'm not the first guy to ever say that, but I'd never been so baffled by a girl as I was by Indi that night. I mean, we were making out and it was great. Fantastic. Those little sexy moans of hers...fuck. I'd wished I'd worn pants with a lot more room in the crotch.

Then, all of a sudden, she freaked out. She gasped and pulled away like she'd been burned. And I hadn't even been trying for a feel.

Before I knew it, she was out of the car, babbling an apology before she dashed up the concrete walk.

I sat there, alone and horny as hell, going over what had happened bit by bit but for the life of me, I couldn't figure out why she'd bolted.

I picked up my phone and texted her.

Hudson: Are you okay?

The three dots appeared, indicating she was composing a return message. I sat and waited for her reply and for my erection to go away.

The dots disappeared.

Then they reappeared.

This happened twice more while I considered going up to her room. I didn't actually know which place was hers, but I might be able to find someone in the halls who would tell me.

Indi: I'm sorry I left in such a hurry.

Hudson: It's not a problem. I just want to know if you're okay.

Indi: I'm fine. I just…I have this…

Three dots, more waiting.

Indi: I have this thing about people touching my face. I know it's weird. I probably should have told you.

Hudson: No, it's not weird. Everyone has their Kissy crakes.

Damn it.

Hudson: Stupid autocorrect. I meant idiosyncrasies. My dad won't let anyone touch his feet. TMI?

Indi: Ha ha. No. Not TMI.

Hudson: So are you free sometime next week to shoot the portraits?

My phone rang. It was Indi.

"Yes. I only have two classes on Tuesdays and Thursdays."

"Hey, me too, but I have practice every afternoon."

"Do you have a problem waking up early? Because I was looking at the sign-up for the studio and everyone wants the later times. For the darkroom too."

"Wait. What? I thought the darkroom was extra credit."

"It is. I always do extra credit. Are you telling me you want to wimp out and just do the minimum? Because it'll be easy, especially with two of us figuring it out. The instruction video is only fifteen minutes long and I already signed out one of the SLR cameras. There's something cool about real prints. It'll be like cooking something on an open fire versus your stove, you know?"

"I hadn't thought about it like that."

"And maybe they'll come out good enough that I can frame one for my parents for Christmas."

"Great idea. Don't let anyone tell you you're just a pretty face," I said.

She didn't reply for a second.

"Indi, did I lose you?"

"No, sorry. I'm here. I have to go. I'll see you on Wednesday in class."

I got a weird vibe from her goodbye, but I felt I'd fixed everything for the most part. All I really cared about was spending more time with her, especially in a conveniently private darkroom. I couldn't stop thinking about her. Our conversation at Tito's had been as satisfying and fun as the one at the Green Bean, and I felt like we'd really made a connection.

When I got home, AJ was playing a video game. He didn't look up when I sat next to him on the sofa. I watched him battle it out against aliens in a military installation on a distant planet. This was a level we'd both tried time and time again to get past. There were just too many aliens for the arsenal we were able to amass, but he had to be getting close. I saw him edging toward a pillar and on the other side, there was a disintegration grenade. Shit. That could shift the balance.

When there was a tiny break in the assault, AJ scooped up the grenade and launched it toward the enemy. When it exploded, it took out only four aliens.

"Damn it," he swore. "Should have held it until...now."

The creatures gathered in a tight group near a box that was labelled with alien markings. If that box held something explosive, he could take out all of them. AJ kept playing until he ran out of ammo and weapons and got torn apart limb from limb.

"How did you find that grenade?"

"While you were gone, I spent about seventeen lives just searching the room for something, anything we hadn't found before."

"Go ahead. Finish it."

He picked the controller back up and restarted the level. I leaned back on the couch and watched him move through the rooms, systematically taking down the aliens with moves we'd perfected from repetition. When he got to the big warehouse with the pillars, I leaned forward, resting my elbows on my knees. This was it. He could do it.

Once again, he edged toward the pillar and picked up the grenade, but this time, he waited until the aliens formed a cluster near the mystery box.

"Now!" I urged just as he threw it.

The explosion was three times as big as before. Smoke billowed and the music hit a crescendo as bodies and shrapnel flew through the air. AJ had his shields up, so he was unharmed.

I gave him a high five and he grinned as he set the controller down. "That was epic."

"Yup." He turned the TV and the console off. "I'm going to bed."

"Hey, hold up a second. We need to talk."

"Ya think?"

I looked him in the eye. "I'm sorry for that shit with Kurly earlier. I shouldn't have called you out on it in front of the team."

"Damn straight you shouldn't have. I mean, what the fuck? I've supported you the whole fucking time, telling everyone who'd listen you'd be a better captain than those two seniors. I defended you when Kurly called you an entitled piece of shit."

"I know. You're a good friend. You're my best friend and I'm really sorry. Tell me how I can make it up to you."

It took him a moment to realize I was using the relationship reboot on him but when he did, he laughed. There was a hint of evil in that laugh.

"What can you do to make it up to me? Let's see. You can clean my fucking bathroom.

"Oh, fuck you, man."

"Okay. I guess you're not as interested in redemption as I thought you were."

I sighed. AJ wasn't a slob and our bathrooms had handheld shower heads, so it would be relatively easy to sponge down the walls, door and floor with cleaner and hose it clean. I just needed to block out the fact that those walls probably had dried jizz on them. And the toilet…Fuck. I didn't even want to think about it.

"Oh, all right. I'll clean your bathroom," I said. "Will that square us up then?"

He met my eyes. "Yeah." We shook hands and he said, "For the record, you were right. I *did* put you on the spot, and I'm sorry about that."

"Sorry enough to let me out of cleaning your bathroom?"

"Hell no."

A week later, I met Indi at the photography studio at seven a.m., which was hella early for me, especially considering the fact that I stopped at the Green Bean on the way to school and picked up lattes and croissants for us.

"You got me an almond croissant?" she said, delighted when she opened her pastry bag.

"I remember you said that was your go-to."

"It is. I love the filling and the toasted nuts on the top."

After breakfast, we got down to the business of shooting the photos. There was a stool, a background and lights already set up for us. We were supposed to be capturing an aspect of the person that we'd discovered during the interview. I wasn't quite sure how to do that, so I just made a game of it, pretending that she was a high fashion model. There was one of those wire things that allowed you to click the shutter by pressing a button in your hand, so I didn't have to glue my eye to the viewfinder.

"Show me happy. Sexy. Pouty. You're a goddess. You're a vamp. Now you're contemplative…now, calculating…"

And she did the same when it was my turn to pose. We laughed a lot and by the time our allotted studio time was up, we'd used up two rolls of film.

The darkroom was not the little closet-sized space I'd expected. It was almost the size of the photography classroom. There were six machines called enlargers along one wall and the same number of developing stations. It smelled weird and I wondered briefly about the effects of inhaling the fumes of the chemicals we would be using.

To our surprise, there was a darkroom assistant named Randi there to develop the film on a giant machine and guide us through the rest of the process—using the enlarger, the three-step process for developing, adjusting contrast and making the final print. While this made our work a hell of a lot easier, I wasn't getting the alone time with Indi that I'd hoped for. So with the third wheel in the darkroom, I had to get creative.

As Randi demonstrated how to adjust the enlarger to ensure the proper print size, I stood very close to Indi and placed my hand on her ass. She turned toward me, one questioning eyebrow raised, but I maintained a look of innocence as I slowly squeezed. Her eyes widened as Randi droned on about refocusing or something. I wasn't paying that much attention. I was too busy enjoying the luscious handful I had in my hand.

Indi tried to listen to Randi, but, bad boy that I am, I persisted. I slid my hand down and between our bodies. She was wearing jeans, but I could tell she liked what I was doing by the way she subtly arched her back to give me a little more access.

Then, I felt her hand on *me*, which wasn't something I had anticipated when I'd started this. Shit. My jaw clenched as her fingernails scratched their way from the bottom of my fly up to the button at my waist and then back down again.

That was some sweet fucking torture right there. In a matter of moments, I was hard and ready with shit-all I could do about it and no one to blame but myself.

"Now, shift the card every five seconds to expose one more inch or so of the paper each time," Randi said. "Like this…one, two, three, four, five, shift. See? One, two, three, four, five, shift. We do this to determine the correct exposure time…"

Indi, that evil woman, timed her ministrations to Randi's count, *stroke, stroke, stroke, stroke stroke*, but on "shift" she squeezed the head of my cock.

Jesus H Christ. I was going to lose my mind.

Eventually, I couldn't take it anymore. Beaten at my own game, I removed my hand from her behind and she let go of my package. I really hoped Randi hadn't caught onto our darkroom hanky-panky. I'd tried like hell to keep my breathing even. But even if she *had* noticed, I'm sure it wasn't the first time.

"Okay, any questions?" Randi asked.

"I think we can handle it," I said. Frankly, I didn't care that much if we messed up. We'd taken some photos with our cell phones as back-up, so if we screwed up the prints, no big deal.

"Okay. Good luck," Randi said and left.

"Alone at last," I said.

I grinned as I flipped the switch so the room was bathed in that lurid red light. Handily, this also turned on the "No-Entry - Darkroom In Use" sign outside in the hallway. That handy bit of information, I'd paid attention to.

"Hudson, what are you doing?"

"Making sure we aren't disturbed," I said before taking her in my arms and sealing my mouth over hers.

Unlike the other night, this kiss was incendiary right off the bat. Hot and wet and eager. I put both hands on her butt now so I could grind up against her. She moaned in my mouth. I wanted to kiss my way to her ear, but remembered that her face was off limits, so I went for her neck instead. Breathing a little faster, she shuddered in my arms, and it was such a turn on that she loved what I was doing. I covered her neck and throat with kisses and she started moaning louder.

Normally, I wouldn't care who heard us, but if there's anything a hockey team loves more than hockey, it's pranks. All it would have taken was a teammate taking note of my name on the sign-up, hearing the moaning, and recording it on his phone for broadcasting later in the locker room. Now, it would be a pretty big coincidence that they happened by the darkroom at just the right time especially since it was pretty early in the morning, and I could easily laugh it off and claim the prankster just recorded sound off a porno and was saying it was me. But better safe than sorry, I figured.

I got my phone, chose some music and maxed out the volume. When I turned my attention back to her, her lips were parted and a little swollen. Her hair was mussed, her eyes a little glazed. I advanced on her and took her mouth again in a hot, wet, deep kiss and she kissed me back, tangling her fingers in my hair and holding on like she wasn't ever going to let go. I loved it. I'd wondered if the other night had been a fluke, but here was proof positive it hadn't been. My body felt like it was on fire.

Pulling back, I brushed my thumbs across her nipples, right over her shirt. Gasping, her eyes rolled back into her head and I toyed with her breasts. A tad more than a handful, they were soft and yielding. Her nipples hardened against my palms and my cock pulsed in my pants.

Even as a wave of need rolled through my body, I wondered how far we were going to go. Right now, I was at about seventy-five percent go-for-the-gold and damn the consequences, but something inside me didn't like the idea of quick and dirty for our first time together.

Because I wanted more than a quick bang with Indi. I'd had enough one-night stands and awkward morning-afters to realize the two of us connected on a deeper level. We looked at a lot of life in the same way. She was low maintenance and she freaking dipped her French fries. How could I not fall for a girl who dipped her French fries? And yet she had a deep side too. There was a lot more to her than met the eye and I'd seen glimpses of parts of her, vulnerable parts, that I wanted to explore and understand.

INDI

Hudson Forte was driving me insane. I knew this was a fact because I was ready to blow off the extra credit and drag him back to Carter Hall so he could bang my brains out. My body was flushed and ready, and his was hard and hot. I hadn't made my bed and there were dishes in the sink, but he wouldn't care.

The only thing preventing me from suggesting we go to my place was a promise I'd made to myself not to repeat the mistake I'd made with my ex-boyfriend, Austin. Unable to deal with my birthmark on the night we planned to have sex for the first time, Austin had torn apart my self-esteem. I'd learned the hard way, if I couldn't trust a guy enough to see my real face, I shouldn't trust him with the most intimate areas of my body, not to mention my heart.

But if there was ever a time I wanted to break that promise, it was now. Hudson was compassionate and interested in my hopes and dreams in a way Austin had never been. And his kisses, his touch, the feel of his hot breath on my skin flooded me with a need I'd never felt before.

He pulled away and stood there staring at me intensely, breathing hard. His hair looked a little wild and so did his eyes.

"You're a good kisser," I said, gratified to see him as hot and bothered as I was.

He blinked then grinned. "You too. I didn't want to stop."

"Me either."

"But this isn't the right time or the right place."

"Agreed."

Someone knocked on the door. "Hey, are you at a good stopping point yet?" a voice called.

"Sure, just a second," Hudson replied.

After we smoothed our clothes and I finger-combed my hair, Hudson pulled me close for one last kiss.

"I'm not finished with you, Indi Briscoe," he said with a banked fire in his eyes.

I certainly hoped not.

After an hour of trial and error and a few more stolen kisses, Hudson and I emerged from the photo lab with some decent prints, which surprised me, considering how divided my attention had been when Randi was giving us the instructions. Of course, the real test would be if, a few days from now when we turned them in, they hadn't turned some weird color because we didn't dip them in the right chemical for the right amount of time.

"So, what do you think?" I asked Hudson.

He examined the three prints. "I actually really love these. This paper has some real weight to it. I also like the way the image has a frame of white around it, like it's matted. It makes it look like real art."

He got out a spiral notebook and carefully sandwiched the prints between the pages. "Got a question for you," he said.

"Shoot."

"Our home opener is on Friday—"

"You're having a housewarming?"

He laughed. "No, no. This Friday is our first hockey game at home and I want you to come."

Burlington U had an excellent hockey team, but sports didn't interest me. I'd only ever been to one game in the past two years because I always had more studying to do and I went home to Brattleboro for the weekend as often as I could, and all the games were on the weekends.

But that was before I'd made out with Hudson Forte. After the way he'd talked about how much he loved the game, I really wanted to see him play.

"Of course I'll come. It sounds like fun."

His face lit up like I'd told him it was Christmas tomorrow and that made me feel good.

Later, however, I couldn't concentrate. It took me almost four hours to read two chapters of Organic Chemistry. I found myself getting to the end of a page, realizing I didn't remember anything of what I'd just read and having to start over. This happened multiple times because I kept thinking about Hudson and what we'd done in the darkroom.

I still couldn't quite believe how on fire I'd been. He turned me on so much, it felt like I would die if I didn't get naked with him as soon as possible. I'd read about this kind of erotic insanity in books and saw it in the movies, but until today, I kind of thought it only existed in people's imaginations. Now that I'd experienced it myself, I understood completely why sex was such a powerful motivator. All he had to do was look at me with that hungry expression on his handsome face and I wanted him to touch and kiss and lick me everywhere. I wanted to touch him too—especially those thighs—to see if his body was as hard as it looked.

And now I was all worked up again. Damn it.

Frustrated, I jammed the cap back on my highlighter, stalked across the room to turn the lights off and lay down on the bed.

Time to get you out of my head, Hudson Forte.

Closing my eyes, I slid my hand into my panties. Maybe if I gave my body what it wanted, I could get some real studying done.

I brought my mind back to the moment when I felt his hard cock and how that red-lit room had seemed provocative and exciting when just moments before it had been cold and sterile. And when he looked at me with that hunger in his eyes how my body had responded with a rush of heat that centered between my legs.

As before, I'd felt the effects of his kisses everywhere. Every one of my nerve endings seemed to be on high alert and when he brushed his thumbs against my nipples, even over my shirt, I felt it right in my hoohah. Were there nerves connecting the two, I wondered?

That's when that guy had knocked on the door, but now, in my fantasy, it was still just me and Hudson in that room.

He undid his jeans with practiced movements as I did the same. I only managed to get one leg out of my pants, but that was enough.

"Put your arms around my neck," he growled.

As I did so, he hoisted me up, my back against a bare wall that hadn't been there in real life. Amazingly, he held me there, suspended, as he reached between us, took his hard cock in his hand and pushed it inside me.

In my fantasy, I was irresistible and experienced, so when he entered me, I felt no pain, only pleasure. Intense and immediate, raw and urgent.

Imagining what it would feel like when he thrust himself in and out of my body was all I needed to launch me into orgasm. I pressed my lips together tightly as the waves of pleasure coursed through me. I continued rubbing my clit to milk every bit of feeling out of it that I could.

I lay there, still tingly all over, staring at the ceiling, and wondering if that was what it would really be like with him. Or was I shooting myself in the foot by creating this perfect dream that the real experience would never match?

Well, there was only one way to find out.

15

HUDSON

Today was our home opener and the arena was going to be filled to capacity with avid fans dressed in green and white. Hockey was to Burlington U what football was to Notre Dame. Our fans were devoted, numerous and we sold out every home game. Even at away games, we could always count on a sizable contingent of people rooting for us. Inside the arena, the energy was unbelievable.

Burlington was one of the twelve NCAA Division I hockey schools and our championship tournament, known as the Frozen Four, took place in the spring. We won it last year so the entire town was hungry for a back-to-back. I usually didn't go a day without someone mentioning it to me.

Many of my family members had gathered at my parents' house in Brooklyn to watch on TV. The good luck texts had been coming in all day.

And I was fucking freaking out.

I tried to tell myself that my brain and body knew what to do. But all the practice and training in the world didn't guarantee good performance. I saw it all the time—professional players going into a weird tailspin that lasted for months. I couldn't afford that kind of slump. I had to be improving every single game because, even though I knew there wasn't a Dragons representative attending the games or even religiously watching video of my play, it *felt* like they were. Every mistake I made, I wondered if they were going to see it and to mark it down on a tally somewhere of Hudson Forte's fuckups. I had a dream once where the league commissioner was dressed like Santa but instead of his list saying "Naughty" or "Nice," it said "In" or "Out" and my name was on the top of the Out list in big bold letters.

AJ made pregame meals for us of turkey burgers with pepper jack and this mustardy mayo he whipped up himself, oven roasted sweet potato wedges and spinach salad with honest to God warm bacon vinaigrette. It tasted great at the time, but as we headed to the rink, my stomach started feeling weird.

"Hey, that turkey was okay, right?" I asked AJ. "It wasn't expiring or anything…"

"No. It was fine. Why?"

"I just…" I shook my head. "I feel a little…unsettled."

"It's because Indi's going to be there tonight," he said. "You don't want to look like an asshat in front of her."

"Probably."

And it was also my first game as captain. The coaching staff and my teammates would be looking at me, wondering if, as a junior, I'd been the right choice. So there was one more thing I had to prove.

Eventually, drenched in sweat, even though the most strenuous thing I'd done was put on my gear, I realized I was going to vomit. I made it to the men's room just in time to hurl my dinner, which was a sickening combination of brown, orange and green.

As I flushed the toilet, my phone signaled a text. I quailed when I saw it was from, Adam Kee, the President and CEO of the San Francisco Dragons.

Kee: On behalf of the entire Dragons organization, good luck, tonight, Forte. Knock 'em dead. We'd all love to see Burlington go all the way in April.

I wanted to reply, *I'll put it on my list of things to do*, but I didn't.

Hudson: I'll do my best, sir.

Kee: And that's why we drafted you. You always come through.

After I read that, I threw up some more.

When I got back to the locker room, I guzzled some Gatorade.

"Are you okay?" AJ asked.

"I'm good." I didn't want him to know how fucked-up my stomach was. If I did, he'd think it was his fault. Plus, I promised myself when we made this cooking for rent money deal, I would never complain about the food.

"Bullshit. You're still thinking about Indi."

"Maybe a little," I admitted. "Aren't you thinking about Ruby watching you?"

It was a given that Indi would bring Ruby with her.

"Hell yeah, but honestly, you win some, you lose some." He checked the tape on his stick and smoothed down a spot that was lifting. "I don't plan on playing like shit, but if by chance I do and she doesn't want to see me anymore, so be it. Don't get me wrong, if she rejects me I'll cry in my pillow for a month, but life's too short to be with someone who only values you for your hockey playing."

He wasn't saying anything I didn't already know, but I wasn't really afraid Indi would drop me if I stunk up the ice. I hadn't known her long, but I knew her well enough to be sure she wasn't that shallow. Her life's goal was to help repair the messed-up faces of little kids, for Christ's sake. No. My anxiety centered more around a yearning for her approval and respect. I wanted her to look at what I did and be impressed. More than that, I wanted her to be proud to be seen with me, to be dating me.

Too late, I realized that meant I had added one more name to the catalog of people monitoring my performance.

Shit piss fuck damn.

UConn got two in a row in the first five minutes of the game and the entire first period and five minutes of the second went by without an answering goal from us. We weren't even getting any good chances. Everyone seemed like they were skating through tar.

"Come on, boys. Turn the juice on," I yelled, reaching for a water bottle as I sat on the bench catching my breath.

I watched as my teammates followed the UConn players down the ice. Their guy swooped around behind the net with the puck and passed it to a teammate on the blue line who fired it and missed.

The puck bounced off the boards right to Lex Vonne, who scooped it up and whizzed past one of their guys. He passed center ice, passed the blue line and sent it across to Callan Thomas. Thomas shot. It went wide. Two players were fighting for the puck which was wedged against the boards with some-one's skate. I couldn't tell much from the angle but—

"Forts!" AJ batted me on the arm. "I was talking to you."

Shaken from my reverie, I looked at him. "Sorry. I didn't hear you."

"I said, we look like dicks out there. You especially."

I was definitely off my game. The C on my jersey felt like a big fat lie. Captains didn't play like this. Certainly, draft picks didn't play like this.

"No kidding."

"Number forty-five is beating you on the boards every single time," AJ said.

"Fuck. I know. I'll fix it."

Out on the ice, the whistle blew. Kurlander had drawn a penalty so for the next two minutes, we would have one more player on the ice than the opposing team. As a member of the power play offensive unit, I hopped the boards and headed out to take the faceoff dot.

As Kurlander passed by me, he said, "There you go, Forts. Time to shine."

Gritting my teeth, I kept my eyes on the ice and the players, resolutely refusing to look up in the stands.

Focus. Focus. Focus.

As I skated to my spot, my opponent sneered at me. "So you're the famous Forte, huh?"

I said nothing. I just met his stare.

"Let's see what you've got then," he said.

I hunkered down to lower my center of gravity and tried to concentrate on the task at hand. A lot of people think winning a faceoff is a simple matter of being faster than your opponent, but in reality, there are some pretty sweet moves you can pull, moves my Uncle Matt taught me. Because this guy gave me some attitude, when the linesman dropped the puck, I blocked his stick, pivoted and shouldered him away while I kicked the puck aside with my foot.

Put that in your pipe and smoke it, asshole.

AJ picked it up and we formed up in their zone, looking for an opening. The pressure was on because we were two goals down. We moved the puck back and forth across the ice, circling, crossing, searching for a chance to score. They cleared a couple of times but in the last few seconds of the power play, AJ deked and sent me the puck.

I had a wide open net.

Come on, baby.

With a quick wrist shot, I fired the puck toward the net...and hit the pipe.

FUCK.

Time ran out on the power play, their fifth man came back out on the ice and the moment was gone.

I continued to play like shit and as the minutes ticked past, I felt more and more guilty. We were able to tie the score at the end of the third period, and just when we all thought we were going into overtime, Kurly, of all people, scored a game-winning buzzer beater. Those of us on the bench leapt up and over the boards to congratulate him. Even though he was often a dick, he deserved some accolades.

In the locker room, I presented Kurlander with the Burlington U game MVP poncho, a busy pattern of crazy yellow, orange, tan and brown crocheted zigzags. No one really knew who made it, maybe some long ago coach's great-grandmother. Kurlander stuck his head through the hole and as it settled it over his shoulders, he flapped his arms to make the fringe move, as tradition demanded.

The mood was jubilant and I plastered a smile on my face for the sake of the team. We'd won our first home game of the season. But inside, I was angry and frustrated with myself for my overall craptastic performance, especially that missed shot on the power play. I mean, the net was wide fucking open.

Maybe I needed an eye exam.

After showering and changing back into my suit, I grabbed AJ and we headed out to meet Indi and Ruby.

"Congratulations! Great game!" Indi gushed. She had a huge smile on her face and just the sight of her lightened my mood considerably.

"Did you see my assist?" AJ asked.

When the girls looked at each other, AJ laughed. "You're not hockey fans, are you?"

"No," they admitted.

"Did you even understand what was going on?" I asked. Nothing like three hours of watching something that didn't make a lick of sense to you.

"I think so," Indi said. "The puck is supposed to go in the net, right?"

I almost fell for that, but I saw the twinkle in her eye.

"Very funny," AJ said. "Yeah, the puck's supposed to go in the net."

Elbowing each other gleefully, the girls laughed. I didn't join in.

"So the team goes to the Biscuit in the Basket after the games," AJ said to the women. "We have a reserved table there on game nights. How does that sound?

"Sounds fun," Ruby said. "Indi?"

Indi nodded her agreement. "Sure. Why not?"

A blast of raucous cheers greeted us when we got there. A win really pumped everyone up and the place was crowded. When Briggs, our new goalie, spotted us, he yelled our names and waved us over. We threaded our way through the people and obtained stools for the ladies. Our usual table, table seventeen, had plenty of seats left but it would be full before long.

AJ made introductions while I flagged down a server and ordered us a big basket of assorted wings, fries and a pitcher of beer. The girls asked us questions about the game and AJ and I did our best to answer without mansplaining.

After about fifteen minutes, Indi said, "Well, I still don't really understand icing, but I think I have the gist of the game."

"You were really impressive out there," Ruby said to AJ. "I want you to score a goal for me tomorrow."

Someone said something at the other end of the table I couldn't quite make out, but it must have been amusing because there was some chuckling. AJ didn't seem to hear it either. He just gazed at Ruby and said, "As you wish."

"I'm going to the restroom," Indi said. "Ruby?"

"Sure. I'll go with you," Ruby replied.

When they were out of hearing distance, Kurlander asked, "Hey, Forts! Think you're gonna score tonight?"

When I didn't honor that dickhead comment with a reply, he said, "I hope so, since you sure didn't score on the ice tonight."

The whole table oohed.

"First of all," I said, "don't talk about her like that. Do it again and you'll regret it."

That got another round of oohs.

"Second, fuck you. At least I was taking shots. You scored the game winning goal but most of the shots on goal tonight were mine. Let's take a tally at the end of the season and see who's on top."

I realized too late that my tone had gotten sharp and defensive.

"Shit, Forts. Can't you take a joke?" Adler asked.

"Yeah, we won tonight, so let's celebrate," Thomas said, lifting his beer stein.

I didn't answer as our food arrived and the ladies returned.

Still feeling touchy, I grabbed a chicken wing and even though I knew they were way too hot to eat yet, I took a bite anyway and burned myself.

"Damn it."

"What?" Indi asked.

"It's too hot," I complained, waving a hand at the wing.

"Want me to blow on it?" Indi asked with a teasing smile.

Ruby giggled and after a glance at Indi, AJ hooted a laugh.

I knew she was just flirting, but my brain supplied me with an image of Indi, gazing up at me, her gorgeous lips wrapped around my cock, which was a huge mistake, considering that I was in the middle of the bar with my teammates all around. If one of them noticed, no doubt he'd attribute my aroused state to the wings and dub me Chicken Bone for the rest of the season.

But at least it pulled me out of my sour mood.

The rest of the evening was fun and thankfully, no one else teased me about the missed goal. Honestly, I didn't blame them. A five-year-old could have made that shot, and looking back, I should have taken Kurly's chirp in stride. I *could* take a joke. I really could. I was usually the first one to make a self-deprecating remark. I chalked it up to having thrown up my pregame meal and needing some body fuel.

As AJ, the girls and I got up to go, I swallowed my pride and offered Kurlander my hand. "Great goal tonight, man."

Kurlander nodded. "Thanks."

"See all you bastards tomorrow," I said.

It was chilly outside, cold enough to see our breath. The campus was quiet except for the muted music and voices coming from the Biscuit.

"Oh, it's such a beautiful night," Indi said, looking up. "Look at all the stars."

I obediently gazed up. Thousands of points of light decorated a black velvet sky. One lacy cloud drifted across the view like a slow-motion spray of snow from a skidding skate blade.

"I feel like walking," she said. "Will you walk me home?"

Carter Hall was only a five-minute walk from the Biscuit.

I glanced at AJ who shrugged. "Wanna walk?" he asked Ruby.

"Not really. It's too cold."

"Okay," I said. I tossed AJ the keys to the Wrangler. "You drive Ruby back and I'll meet you at home."

"Cool."

My arm around Indi's shoulders, we ambled down the walkway toward their dorm as AJ and Ruby headed toward the rink lot where I was parked.

"Did you have fun?" I asked.

"Yes, but I don't think you did."

"What makes you say that?" I asked as my phone rang. "I had fun."

"Really? Because I got the feeling like something was bothering you." She gave me a sidelong glance. "Aren't you going to answer that?"

I pulled my phone out of my pocket, afraid it was Adam Kee calling me out on that missed goal. It wasn't.

"It's just my dad."

"That's so sweet. He probably wants to congratulate you."

"Not exactly. Now that he's retired, whenever he can, he tries to stream the games live. That way he can give me pointers as soon as possible, after the fact."

She stopped. "Wait, really? He really calls after every game just to critique you?"

"He believes there's a prime window of opportunity between execution and critique and that the sooner he talks to me, the better it will sink in. Personally, I don't think it works that way, but he's my dad, so I just grin and bear it. It really is helpful though. He's an amazing hockey player. People say he'll probably make it into the Hall of Fame."

"Wow. That's impressive."

"It really is. But even so, I'm not going to interrupt our date just so he can tell me everything I did wrong."

"Good choice," she said, taking my hand and starting toward her dorm again. "So, was that why you looked tense back there at dinner? You were expecting your dad's call?"

"I looked tense?"

She nodded and rubbed the spot between her eyebrows. "You had a tiny little line here most of the time."

"Dad's call doesn't bother me that much. I'm used to that. I didn't like how I played."

"Really? I thought you looked really great out there."

"That's because you know almost nothing about hockey," I said, squeezing her hand. "Take my word for it. My performance tonight was a ridiculous string of mistakes and miscalculations. I'd list them all for you, but I don't want to bore you."

"I wouldn't be bored, honestly, but I also don't want to encourage you to beat yourself up any more than you already have, especially when your dad is already waiting in line to do that." She snuggled closer.

"He's not the only one."

"What do you mean?"

"I'm under a lot of pressure. A lot of people are expecting great things from me." I laughed humorlessly. "It's been like that almost my whole life."

I told her how, when I was a kid, the expectations from my family didn't really register on my radar. Hockey was something I did for fun. And because I was good at it, I didn't really have to practice that hard. My innate skill allowed me to skate circles around almost everyone.

But as I grew older, things got more serious. I still had fun in middle school, but practice wasn't just playing around with my friends anymore. It was work. My parents, especially my dad, expected constant excellence. I had to be the star, the lead goal scorer, the MVP, the one with the most ice time. No one ever came out and said it, but if I hadn't gotten drafted, I'd have been a disgrace.

"I remember thinking once I got drafted, I'd have it made. I'd get some breathing room. Everyone would relax. I'd have a contract and a team who believed in my potential. I couldn't have been more wrong. If anything, the pressure is ten times worse. I vomited before tonight's game."

She winced. "This is exactly why you can't put pressure on yourself. You already have too much external pressure."

"Easier said than done," I said as we finally arrived at Carter Hall.

"Do you want to come to the game tomorrow?" I asked, trying to sound nonchalant. I really wanted her to see me play a decent game.

"Yes. I really liked seeing you out there. It was exciting and now that I know the rules, I'll be able to enjoy it even more."

I lifted my hands and almost cupped her cheeks but remembered at the last minute and detoured them to her shoulders. She snickered, so I guess I wasn't as smooth at the detour as I thought. She wrapped her arms around my waist and stepped close as I bent my head to kiss her.

She felt so good in my arms. I threaded my hands in her hair, marveling how silky it was. Her mouth opened under mine and I took full advantage. The kiss got deep and hot. I knew Carter Hall had suite style rooms which would mean we could take this upstairs.

I laid a trail of kisses along her jaw down her neck and she panted softly, which excited me even more. When I sucked her earlobe into my mouth, she gave a low moan. Fuck. That was only her earlobe. I wondered what kind of sounds she would make if I went down on her.

But then she pulled back and said something in a voice too soft for me to catch.

"I'm sorry. I didn't hear you."

"I just said I need to go. It's pretty late."

"Sure. That's fine. It's all good." I gave her what I hoped was a I-have-no-problem-with-that smile, even though I was sporting a steel rod in my pants.

"I'll see you tomorrow," she said, her cheeks flushed, her lips wet from my kisses.

"Tomorrow," I agreed.

As I turned to go, I surreptitiously adjusted my cock to a more comfortable position, but there really was no such thing as comfortable for me at the moment. I was so hard and so hot, it was a wonder steam wasn't forming around my crotch.

INDI
—

I woke up the day after the home opener when Ruby knocked on my bedroom door.

"Indi, are you awake?" she asked softly.

"I am now," I said with a groan. It was just after nine.

Ruby opened the door and leaned against the door jamb. "AJ wants to know if I want to go to dim sum with him in town and I haven't had dim sum in *ages*, but it's boring if you go with just two people and I told him to ask Hudson if he'll come too and now I'm asking you." She said all of this rapid-fire while my brain was still coming online.

"Hold on. Slow down." I sat up. "What's dim sum?"

"Sorry. I forgot. Dim sum is sort of like a Chinese buffet that comes to you. You go to the restaurant and sit at the table and they wheel these carts around. Each cart has different things to eat —small plates—and you just pick what you want. I had no idea you could get dim sum in Burlington. This could be *life-changing* if it's good."

"I don't understand how the number of people have to do with how good it is."

"If you have more people, you can order a bigger variety of things. That's what makes Chinese food amazing. Most other cuisines you order your one thing, but with Chinese food, it's family style and you get to share everything." She came to the bed and got on her knees. "Please say yes, Indi. I know you're not... crazy about Chinese stuff, but I want to go so bad. Having dim sum would be the next best thing to being home and I also kind of don't want to go on a solo date with AJ."

"What? Why not?"

She wrinkled her nose. "He's really nice, but you know how people say, 'He's just not that into you?' Well, I've got the opposite problem. He's really intense and last night I got the feeling he was on a mission to find things we have in common. He wanted to know everything about me. I mean everything. But I want to give it another chance before I make a decision, so I really need you to come to dim sum."

"All right, but you owe me," I said.

She scoffed as she sent a text to AJ. "Like you don't want to see Hudson again as soon as possible."

"I can't deny it," I said, grinning like an idiot. "I really really like him. In fact, I think I might want to sleep with him."

"*Might* want to?"

"Okay, I definitely want to sleep with him, but I..." I bit my lip. "I'm a virgin."

"You are?" She looked up from her phone. "Sorry. It's fine. I'm just surprised. I just sort of assumed."

"Exactly. Hudson's going to just assume too and that's the problem. I feel like I should tell him, but it's so embarrassing."

"I'm sure he'll be fine with it. He seems like the kind of guy who'd think it was sweet."

"So you think I should tell him first?"

"Absolutely. You should also—and tell me to butt out because it's really not my business—but you should also share your birthmark with him. Unless you're planning on a one and done."

"No, I made a promise to myself a while ago that anyone I slept with needed to be fine with my birthmark."

"Good plan. Because if they aren't okay with your birthmark, they don't *deserve* the glory of your goddess body. Now," she said, getting to her feet and pulling me out of bed, "unless you want him to see that birthmark this morning, we'd better get ready. They're coming to pick us up in forty minutes."

"You're looking sharp this morning," I said to Hudson after Ruby and I got in the back seat.

He was wearing jeans, a sweater, and his Indiana Jones fedora.

He tipped his hat at me and grinned. "Why thank you. I wore this just for you."

"I thought you wore it because you thought it was Halloween," AJ said.

Hudson congenially flipped AJ the bird before starting the Jeep.

"Where are we going?" Ruby asked.

"It's a place on Church Street called Wang's," AJ said. "It hasn't been there very long, but the word has spread and it's gotten pretty popular."

There were people waiting outside when we got there, which wasn't surprising, since the place was small. But people waiting meant they were doing something right—food or service or both.

Five minutes later, we were weaving our way through the restaurant. I was surprised to see quite a number of Asian diners. Back home in Brattleboro, I could go a year without seeing another Asian. People wearing aprons were pushing aluminum carts full of stacked metal cylinders. As I passed one, the attendant lifted the lid off one of them to reveal white buns with a little daub of pink on them. Another held flat white noodles folded like blankets with tiny shrimp in the folds. It all looked very different from the food I was used to.

As soon as we sat down, a pot of tea appeared on the table while someone parked their cart next to our table. Ruby and, surprisingly, Hudson indicated what they wanted and the server picked up the small plates and containers with tongs and put them on the table, then stamped our check, one stamp per plate. Before we could even start eating, another cart came by and more goodies where chosen. We hadn't even been seated for five minutes and we already had a table full of food.

"Okay," Ruby said, "let me give you the rundown of what we got. That's *siu mai*, which is pork, shrimp and shitake mushroom wrapped in a noodle. That's my favorite. That's *ha gow*, rice noodle filled with shrimp. This thing that looks like a deep-fried football is *haam siu gok*."

"What's inside of that?"

"Pork and vegetables."

"I dip everything in the soy sauce mixed with the chili oil," Hudson said.

I noticed a little pot of orange-colored oil with what looked like flecks of hot peppers in the center of the table.

"It looks hot," he said, "but it's not that bad. The mustard is good too, but it'll clean out your sinuses if you're not careful."

"How is it you know so much about dim sum?" I asked him. I scanned the tabletop. Not a fork in sight. I sighed inwardly.

He shrugged. "My family lives in Brooklyn and we eat out a lot. Honestly, I think one out of every ten restaurants in New York is Chinese."

"Okay, I'm going to try one of those footballs first. It's deep fried and anything deep fried has to be good." I flagged down one of the staff. "Can I have a fork please?"

"I'm sorry," AJ said. "Did you just ask for a fork?"

I bristled. "Something wrong with that? Just because I look like I do doesn't mean I automatically know how to use chopsticks."

AJ gaped at me in surprise and frankly, I was pretty shocked by my outburst too. It was uncalled for and I was immediately swamped by remorse.

"Sorry, Indi," AJ sputtered. "I didn't mean anything by it. Honest."

"No, *I'm* the one who's sorry, AJ. You're fine. I overreacted. I don't know what came over me. I'm really sorry. It's just…I'm touchy about people making assumptions about me based on how I look. My mom and dad brought me home from China when I was a baby, so I'm as American as you guys. I just don't look it."

"It's cool. I understand," AJ said. "Won't happen again."

"You know, you wouldn't have a problem if you just learned how to use these," Ruby said, sliding an unopened pair of chopsticks toward me.

It bugged me that she was right, of course, but I tore the wrapper off them anyway.

You can do this, Indi, I told myself. *How can you expect to wield a scalpel if you can't even use chopsticks?*

"Okay, here goes," I said.

Concentrating on my grip, I reached for the football. It actually looked like the most difficult thing to get a hold of because of its shape, but I'm nothing if not stubborn. As my chopsticks slipped off the rounded surface over and over, I felt like everyone was watching and judging me. It was obvious I was a poser and didn't know a fortune cookie from a pagoda. Heat rose in my cheeks and I almost grabbed it with my fingers when Hudson bumped my arm.

"This is how I do it." He showed me how to spear the football with one of the chopsticks. "Now just pinch, like this. See? It's cheating a little bit, but it gets the job done."

It totally worked. I got the football to my plate feeling triumphant. After dipping it into the soy sauce, I bit into the crunchy dumpling and oh my gosh, it was really strange, but so good. The outside shell was delightfully crispy while just under that was a chewy, slightly sweet layer and in the middle of the mostly hollow football was a bit of seasoned ground pork. The soy sauce brought out all the perfectly balanced flavors and textures.

Ruby and Hudson were watching me intently and I nodded slowly. "Amazing," I said around the mouthful. Using Hudson's spear-and-pinch method, I took a *sui mai* and it was just as delicious.

Afterward, Hudson asked if Ruby and I wanted to hang out at their place until they had to go dress for their second game against UConn.

Ruby shook her head. "I have to study, but you should go if you want, Indi."

I didn't hesitate. "Okay. That sounds fun."

"Aw, come on, Rube," AJ said. "We can play video games or ping-pong or watch *The Princess Bride*."

"Sorry," Ruby said. "School comes first."

"Okay. Sure. I understand," he said, looking dejected.

Because they were low on groceries, AJ dropped Hudson and me at their place before taking Ruby home and then heading to the store.

I really should have hit the books too. I had a quiz tomorrow, but so far, my psychopharmacology class was pretty easy and a quick review of my notes before I went to bed would probably be enough.

Their second-floor apartment was almost right in the center of town, with gorgeous views of the lake and mountains. Hudson told me the building used to be a railroad warehouse until they converted it a few years ago into apartments.

The interior of their place was big and I was jealous of how much space they had. There was a TV show about downsizing to live in tiny houses and I wondered if any of the people on the show had ever lived in a dorm. My personal hope was that I would never in my life have to live in such crowded quarters again.

"I like your place," I said. "It's really nice, like something out of a Pottery Barn catalog."

The whole apartment was a collage of warm grays and cream and looked like it had been professionally decorated. The furniture looked new and there were accent rugs and plants and artsy knick-knacks that gave the whole place a cohesive style. Neither AJ nor Hudson seemed like people who would buy a floor vase filled with eucalyptus sprigs so I wondered if their apartment had come furnished. The only thing that defined this as the domain of two college guys was the green ping-pong table in the middle of the dining area and the tally of game wins taped to the wall.

"Funny you should say that because it *did* come from a Pottery Barn catalog," he said with a laugh. "Page fifty-six. The Hudson Collection. I'm not even kidding. When my mom saw that, it was a no-brainer."

I took a peek in his bedroom and saw a similar muted style. A queen-sized bed with a thick oversized-plaid comforter and actual matching throw pillows dominated the room. The furniture had black iron accents and a huge plush rug made everything cozy.

That's when I noticed Deke's house. I didn't see him on the top floor, so he must have been nestled in all the fluff on the bottom level. Hudson noticed my interest and came over.

"He's asleep right now and unfortunately, he doesn't like to be disturbed otherwise I'd let you hold him."

"That's okay. Some other time. I guess hamsters need their beauty sleep too."

"So, you want something to eat?" he asked. "I have some graham crackers or yogurt. Or I could make you a peanut butter and jelly sandwich."

"You're not serious, are you?" I asked, plopping down on their comfy sofa. "I'm stuffed from the dim sum."

"Yeah, I noticed you packing it in."

I scoffed. "Like you weren't eating a good ten minutes after I was finished." I sighed. "Do you think AJ's okay? I really didn't mean to snap at him like I did. It's just one of my hot buttons when people assume stuff because I look like I'm Chinese."

"I hate to break it to you, lady," he said with a chuckle, "but you *are* Chinese."

"No, I only *look* Chinese."

He shook his head as he sat down next to me. "I don't really understand, but that's fine."

"It's like this. If you go into Wang's and you don't know how to use chopsticks, no one judges you. But if I do the same thing… it's embarrassing."

"But you *used* the chopsticks today. Sure, you weren't great at it, but you did it. Problem solved. But let's say you didn't. Let's say you decided to use the fork. Who cares? I mean, I think Forte is an Italian name but I'm honestly not sure, and where my mom's side of the family comes from is a muddle too. So if I don't know anything about my heritage, why should you?"

I had honestly never looked at it like that. He was right. Just because my ethnicity was more obvious than his didn't mean I was more obligated to know about the culture of my ancestors. And yet, I couldn't pretend the feelings weren't there.

In the end, I decided this was a "me problem." I really felt bad about how I'd snapped at AJ so I decided, if this particular hot button was pushed in the future, I'd suck it up and deal instead of lash out. I didn't want to put it on other people to walk on eggshells around me because I had mixed-up feelings about my heritage. At the same time, I would try not to care as much what strangers thought of me.

Feeling like I'd turned some kind of corner, I turned to Hudson. "What you said makes a lot of sense, but if you don't mind, I don't want to talk about this anymore."

"Honestly, me neither. Mostly," he said with a mischievous grin, "because I haven't kissed you today yet."

"I hadn't really noticed," I said then yelped as he tickled me.

"Liar," he said. "You probably spent the night dreaming about my kisses."

I squirmed to escape because I was really ticklish.

"Admit it!" he said, mercilessly finding all my most ticklish areas.

"Okay, okay! I did dream about you last night. I dreamt we did it in the hockey arena."

He stilled. "No shit. Really?"

Flushing, I nodded.

I almost never had sexy dreams and this had been a doozy. We were making out in the penalty box of the empty hockey arena. Hudson was wearing street clothes and I was wearing nothing but his jersey—the one he'd worn during the game. Normally, I'd think this was gross because of all the sweat, but in the dream, it was a huge turn-on, for both of us.

He was kissing me hard and I was freezing but I didn't care. I was burning for him from the inside out and his warm hands were roaming all over my body. My back, my sides, my waist, my ass. Miraculously, his clothes disappeared and I was pressed up against the side of his Wrangler. He had hoisted one of my legs up and he fucked me hard.

"What happened?"

"In the dream?" I gasped. "I'm not telling you!"

"Come on." He pulled me close and nuzzled my neck. "I promise if I ever have a sexy dream about you, I'll tell you all about it."

Even though a whole-body shiver went through me and my heart was beating faster, I said, "No. No deal. Absolutely not."

"Can you at least tell me if I was good or not? I mean, I need to know if I have a lot to live up to."

He kissed me and his lips were warm and giving and as always, my body heated immediately. As I reveled in his closeness, part of my brain wondered if a person could get addicted to another person, like to through withdrawals and everything. I knew that cravings were one sign of addiction. Check. Another was indulging even when you knew it was detrimental and I was blowing off studying for my quiz for Hudson Time, so check again.

"You were actually horrible. You didn't make me come and then you went to get a hot dog. That's probably Freudian for something."

He chuckled. "Well, you're the one who dreamed it, so whatever the hot dog represents, that's all you."

"Jerk," I said, smiling as he pushed me onto my back.

As we made out with hot, long, deep kisses, I surrendered to the heady feeling of Hudson on top of me, his tongue in my mouth, his erection hot against my leg. Lord, the man knew what he was doing. I was awash with delicious sensations and when he slid his hand under my shirt and squeezed my breast, I arched. My nipples contracted and hardened and he groaned into my neck.

Desperate to feel more, I shifted so that one of my feet was on the ground and he was wedged between my legs. I was rewarded with direct grinding pressure on my clit. Yesss. It felt divine, especially when I wrapped my other leg around his hips to intensify the feelings.

We were both breathing hard now. My head was crowded against the couch cushions and I really wanted to shed some of my clothes. But Hudson was thrusting and rubbing himself against me and I didn't want him to stop. The only orgasms I'd ever had were the do-it-yourself kind, but that seemed like it was going to change. I could feel it building. As long as he kept doing what he was doing…

Beep-beeeep. Beep beep beep. Beep-beeeep. Beep beep beep.

At the sound of the car horn, Hudson stopped moving. "Shit damn piss fuck."

"What?"

"That was AJ warning me he's back."

He sat up and ran a hand through his hair. I followed suit, tugging my shirt back into place.

"You want to continue this in my room?" he asked with a hopeful smile.

Even though I was really turned on, I was reluctant to have sex for the first time while AJ was out here twiddling his thumbs, trying to ignore what was happening on the other side of the bedroom door.

"I don't think so. You have a game to play soon and you need all your energy."

"It wouldn't take that much energy," he whined.

"Good to know," I said with an arch smile.

A split second later when he got the dig, he scoffed and said, "Now you're going to get it!" And when AJ came in a minute later, I had to beg him to stop Hudson from tickling me to death.

17

HUDSON

Two weeks had passed since our home opener and we'd really begun to gel as a team. We had won both games the weekend before, which left us confident and ready to face the eight games scheduled for November. Seb Hunter, one of our top defensemen had returned after a minor injury took him out for a week and my own performance seemed to be back on track.

At least, I thought it was back on track. Unfortunately, that didn't turn out to be the case. Once again, life decided to pile a hat-trick-plus-one of shit on.

First, we were up against the Eagles. Tied for the record of the most Frozen Four appearances, Boston College was a tough opponent with a strong defense and even stronger forwards. On top of that they'd won the game last night, so we had our work cut out for us.

Then my dad called to tell me the "good news" that he would be there. While I was grateful he cared enough to make the trip from Brooklyn just to watch me play, Dad's game analysis was always more brutal if he attended live. Not only that, but Indi went home to visit her parents and because Brattleboro was only a couple of hours from Boston College, they were all coming to the game.

Despite that extra stress, I thought I had a handle on everything.

Then later that morning, we were on the bus headed for Chestnut Hill and I got a call that upped my anxiety level to seven point five out of ten. Doug Lyddane, one of the player development guys for the Dragons, said he, too, was coming to the game.

"I'd love to touch base with you afterwards," Lyddane said. "See if you need anything."

I wanted to tell him I needed a fucking Valium but managed to hold my tongue.

"Great," I told him. "Looking forward to it."

We held our own in the first period with neither team scoring, but in the second period, I caused a turnover by falling onto the ice, and my mistake resulted in a goal that went unanswered into the third period.

Now, ice is obviously slippery and sometimes a skater just loses his edge or hits a weird spot in the ice, but this was my third fall of the season and I was known for my skating. It was as if I'd traded bodies with a high school varsity player with big dreams and substandard skating skills.

I managed to disgrace myself one more time that night by completely missing a pass from Bramley.

"I gave you a heads-up," he accused when we were back on the bench after our shift.

"I didn't hear you."

"Then get your fucking hearing checked, for Christ's sake."

After the game, Doug Lyddane came to see me. My dad was on his heels, looking worried.

"I'm sorry you had to see that," I said to them both. We'd lost the game, 3-1.

Lyddane shook my hand and clapped me on the shoulder. "Don't apologize. I'm not sorry at all. You're a fine player, Forte. You just had a bad night." He turned to my dad. "He's a chip off the old block, Dom. You should be proud of him."

"I am very proud," my dad said with a fixed grin.

"And team captain, too," Lyddane said. "I forgot to congratulate you on that, Hudson."

"Thank you, sir."

After Lyddane left, my dad said, "How about we grab some dinner and then I drive you home to school? We can catch up on the way."

"Gee, Dad, that sounds great, but Indi is here with her parents and I'm having dinner with them and then Coach said it was okay if I drove back with her."

His brows rose. "You're meeting her parents?"

"I am."

"You're not getting serious about this girl, are you? Because judging from your performance today, you can't afford any distractions. Don't get me wrong. All work and no play makes Jack a dull boy and I would never try to tell you to deny yourself in the sex department, but in my experience, there's a tipping point with women and once you get past that they start demanding more of your time and attention." He touched my chest with his index finger. "You cannot afford that right now. Once you've made it into the NHL, fine. Get serious with whoever you want, but right now? You need to be focused one hundred percent on hockey."

I knew from experience arguing wouldn't do any good, so I just said, "Right, Dad. One hundred percent."

I wasn't sure if I could focus on hockey any more than I already was.

"All right. Good to see you, son. We'll get together soon," he said, giving me a backslapping hug.

I arranged for AJ to make sure my gear got home safely, told Bramley he was in charge and headed to Spinners, the restaurant where I was to meet Indi and her parents, Kevin and Bonnie.

After I kissed Indi hello, Bonnie gave me a hug. "So, you're Hudson. We've heard so much about you." She wore frosted pink lipstick and smelled like flowers.

"We're sorry for your loss," Kevin said giving me a hearty

handshake. "Your hockey loss, that is." He was a big man with a ruddy complexion and the sort of body you'd expect from someone who owned a restaurant.

"You win some, you lose some," I replied.

We sat down and opened the menus.

"How is it you're not sick of pizza?" I asked Kevin because Spinners was a pizzeria.

"We're always checking out the competition," he replied then leaned forward. "You never know when you're going to discover a new flavor combination you want to put on your menu."

"Isn't that…?"

"Pizza plagiarism? Not really." Lifting his chin, her dad leaned back in his chair. "You ever seen barbecue chicken pizza on a menu?"

"Sure. All the time."

"Well, listen to this. The barbecue chicken pizza was invented by a chef, name of Ed LaDou, for California Pizza Kitchen's first menu. This was back in the late Eighties, before you were born. Now it's everywhere. And just to prove my point…" He ran his finger down his menu and pointed. "There you go, barbecue Chicken."

"I had no idea," Hudson said.

"Happens all the time in the restaurant industry."

"You see anything interesting here?" Hudson asked.

Kevin glanced at Indi. "What do you think, sweetheart? Indi has a knack for recognizing good flavor combinations. I keep trying to convince her to join the family business, but she has her heart set on being a doctor."

"How about this one?" I suggested. "The Killer B. It's genoa salami, tomato sauce and mozzarella and a local hot honey. If it's good, I'm sure you'd have no problem finding artisanal honey in Vermont."

"That's a great idea," Indi said. She jerked a thumb at me. "Hudson is majoring in Community Entrepreneurship."

"I've never heard of that before," Kevin said.

"It's a business major with an emphasis on community development and the responsible use of natural resources," I explained.

"Really?" Bonnie said. "Maybe *you* should join the family. Business. The family business."

"Mom…" Indi said, blushing furiously.

"Freudian slip," Bonnie said with a carefree laugh.

The Killer B ended up being pretty damned good. I'd never in a million years have thought about honey on a pizza, but it was delicious. The salami and the honey were a perfect salty sweet combo. Kevin and Bonnie were great—funny and smart, just like their daughter and I had a great time.

We were just boxing the leftovers when a young woman stopped by the table.

"Well if it isn't Juicy Briscoe! And Mr. and Mrs. Briscoe! It's me, Jessica Burnuzzi."

Jessica was a sassy brunette with a big nose and tight sweater.

Kevin and Bonnie greeted her warmly but Indi remained seated with a smile on her face that didn't quite reach her eyes.

"What are you doing here?" Kevin asked.

"I go to school here," Jessica said. "At Boston College. I'm majoring in communications."

"Isn't that nice," Bonnie said.

"Where did you end up, Juicy?" Jessica asked Indi.

"Burlington U."

"Gotcha. And who's this?"

"Hudson Forte," I said with a big smile. "I'm Indi's boyfriend."

Under the table, I took her hand and squeezed it.

"Well now, isn't that nice," Jessica said. "Well, it was good seeing you," Jessica said.

"What a small world, Bonnie exclaimed after she'd sashayed away. "Jessica and Indi went to elementary school and I think middle school together. Right, Indi?"

Indi nodded.

"What was that she called you?" I asked. "Juicy?"

"It was just a stupid nickname from school."

"A nickname, huh? I sense a great story here," I said. No one loved nicknames more than hockey players. Most of us were just known by iterations of our last names, but some, like my dad, got something out of the ordinary. Often, when you were the new guy, you were gifted with something that cemented your low stature on the team. There was a kid I knew in middle school who was notorious for getting boners in gym class. A lot of the guys called him Woody, as a result. He threw it back in their faces saying at least he was always ready, which just earned him another nickname—Eveready.

Indi reached down to get her purse. "No story. I liked Juicy Fruit gum. That's all."

"Is that where that came from?" Bonnie asked. "You learn something new every day."

"Should we start calling you Juicy now?" Kevin asked jovially.

"No."

All of us started at her sharp tone.

"Sorry," she said, standing up. "I don't chew Juicy Fruit anymore. Please don't call me that."

Now I *really* sensed a story there, but not a great one. Indi's body radiated tension and she had a tighter-than-normal grip on her purse strap.

"I like Indi better anyway," Bonnie said as we all stood to go. "Hudson, did you know her full name is Indira? We named her that because it means 'beautiful.'"

"I did *not* know that, but I agree," I said, putting my arm around her shoulders and giving her an earnest smile. "She is very beautiful."

Coach Keller gave me special permission to drive back to Burlington with Indi, a much more pleasant experience than I would have had on the team bus or in my dad's Camaro. Even though all the hockey equipment was stowed in the storage area, the stench still contaminated the coach. Luckily, seniority counted for something and the freshmen usually got assigned the seats where the smell was the worst.

"Your parents are really nice," I told her as we whizzed north along I-93.

"Thanks. I think they're sort of goofy."

"We all think that about our parents."

"They were really impressed with your hockey playing."

I scoffed.

"No, really. No one in my family is athletic, so anyone who's even mildly good at sports is to be admired."

"Too bad they had to see me lose the game for us," I said sullenly.

"Are you talking about when you fell?"

"That and when Brammy sent me the puck and I just let it go by, yes."

"But that could happen to anyone, right?"

"Not to me." Not until lately, anyway.

"Oh, come on. Don't tell me you're one of those guys who pouts after losing."

"All right, I won't."

"But you are," she said.

"Are what?"

"Pouting."

I pointed to my forehead. "This isn't pouting. This is frowning. *This* is pouting," I said, pushing out my lower lip.

She laughed.

A few miles went by as I analyzed the game in my head. Even though I'd narrowly escaped my dad's critique, I ended up doing it myself here in Indi's car. I systematically identified each of my mistakes, misjudgments, and fuckups, along with ways I could have avoided them. I was mired in these thoughts when Indi's voice broke through.

"Is it normal for hockey players to mentally flagellate themselves when they make mistakes? Because I can tell that's what you're doing. It's like your dad conditioned you to go through this routine after games."

It was disturbing how spot-on she was, but I didn't let on.

"You don't understand. My dad wasn't the only one watching tonight. Someone from the Dragons was there too, one of the player development guys all the way from San Francisco. Of all nights for him to come see me. I probably would have been fine if he hadn't called ahead of time and let me know. I would have been blissfully ignorant. I mean, half of what we do is mental. It's not all just physical. So once something starts messing with your concentration and focus, you're screwed. It's all connected. If my mental game isn't there, I play like shit, which just makes me more stressed and it's a vicious circle."

"Maybe you should talk to someone. Maybe a doctor can help."

"You know I hate doctors."

"So what? Suck it up and deal."

I shook my head. "There's also the extra pressure of being captain. I've been team captain before, but college sports are a hell of a lot more intense than high school."

"What do you get out of being captain? Maybe you should resign," she said.

"I'm not a quitter," I snapped.

"Oh, please. Don't give me that macho baloney. You'd be making your health a priority, something I'm sure all pro athletes do."

"It's not macho baloney and I do prioritize my health. I just need to get used to this extra pressure. Believe me, if I have the career I want, I'll probably look back at these four years and think those were the good old days when I didn't know what real pressure was."

"Okay, change of subject," she said, "you said I was your girl-friend back there…"

"Yeah, sorry. I said that spur of the moment because we've

been seeing each other for a few weeks now and it didn't feel right to say I was your friend. You're okay with that, aren't you? I should have asked you if it was okay before I blurted it out."

"No, I'm glad you blurted it out. I loved the look on Jessica's face when you said that."

"Is there some bad blood between you?"

"You could say that," she said, but she didn't elaborate.

INDI

"So how did dinner with your parents go?" Ruby asked.

She and I were heading to the Green Bean for some coffee before our first classes of the week, and boy, did I need it. Not only had it had been a long drive back from Boston, but Hudson and I took a while to say good night.

"It was great," I said. "They really liked him, and he's officially my boyfriend."

"Oh my God! Congratulations. I'm so happy for you. He's such a great guy."

"He really is, but I'm worried about him."

I told her about how the stress was getting to him.

"I told him he should think about going to a doctor, but he thinks the stress here isn't anything compared to being in the NHL and that he needs to just acclimate."

"AJ told me he throws up before the games."

I gaped at her. "I thought it was just the once, at the home opener."

Ruby shook her head. "Nope. AJ says every game. Hudson's trying to keep it on the down low, but AJ sees him sneaking off to the bathroom just before they go out to warm up."

"That's not good."

"No, it isn't."

"Speaking of AJ, I think I'm going to tell him I just want to be friends. He's a lot of fun, but I just don't feel any spark when he kisses me. Like zero spark."

Which was the opposite of my experience with Hudson. I felt a bazillion sparks when Hudson kissed me.

"I'm sorry," I said. "He's really into you."

"I should have told him sooner, a lot sooner, but I felt bad. He's going to take it really hard."

We were just steps away from the Green Bean entrance when an Asian woman waved at us.

"Well, if it's isn't Ruby Chang," she said. In her mid-forties, she was short with pixie cut black hair and a leather briefcase that was stuffed to the gills.

"Ms. Tan!" Ruby exclaimed. "Indi, this is one of my favorite teachers."

"Call me Helen, both of you."

"Her Intro to Asian Studies class was what made me want to specialize in immigration law," Ruby said as they air-kissed. "Are you here to get coffee?"

"Can't live without it," Helen said.

We got in line and the two of them caught up with each other. I checked my phone for messages from Hudson. There weren't any, but I knew I'd see him later in Photography.

"So, I'm having some people over to make dumplings Wednesday evening. We'll drink some wine, whip up a big batch together and stuff ourselves. Would you like to come? You, too, Indi. I know it's not anywhere near the Lunar New Year, but sometimes I just get a hankering."

"Right? Boiled dumplings are the ultimate comfort food," Ruby said. "And I haven't made them since my grandma died three years ago."

"I've never had them," I admitted.

"Then you absolutely have to come, Indi," Helen said. "I probably still have your email address, Ruby. I'll send you the details."

"Sounds perfect."

When Wednesday rolled around, Ruby tried to convince me to go with her.

"Gee, I wish I could, but I have this paper due tomorrow…" I gestured at my laptop.

"Come on, Indi. This is your chance to embrace the food of your people, woman!"

Because I didn't want to seem like I had some sort of weird mania about my fake heritage, I said, "I had chicken and dumplings at a friend's house once and I am not a fan. Dumplings are tasteless blobs of bread dough that fell in some soup by accident."

She laughed. "Chinese dumplings aren't like that. Chinese dumplings are stuffed with meat and vegetables and you dip them in this amazing sauce. When you bite into it, an unctuous broth fills your mouth and oh my God, it's so good. You have to trust me. If you liked the dim sum, you'll like the dumplings."

"Thanks, but like I said, I have this paper…"

Ruby crossed her arms. "You know what? I call bullshit. You don't have a paper. If you had a paper due tomorrow, it would have been finished on Friday."

Damn it. She knew me too well.

"And you know what else?" she asked. "I think you're prejudiced against Chinese things."

I gaped at her in astonishment. "Me, prejudiced? That's ridiculous."

"Is it? Let's see. Do you like Italian food?"

"You know I do."

"How about Mexican? French? Barbecue?"

"Yes and yes and yes. Get to the point."

Ruby narrowed her eyes and I couldn't help but feel I was on the witness stand. "*Do you like Chinese food?*"

"No." But I frowned, suddenly uncertain about my answer.

"See...I don't think that's true."

"Are you calling me a liar?"

"No. I think you're just really confused. You liked my fried rice and you loved everything we had at dim sum."

"All right. Maybe I do like Chinese food more than I thought I did, but not liking a certain cuisine doesn't make you prejudiced."

"But it's not just the food, Indi." Her voice had softened. "I know you don't like to admit it, but you're a Chinese-American, my friend. There's no getting around that fact and honestly, it makes me a little sad that you're so against anything that has to do with the Chinese culture because I kind of hoped we'd be like sisters that way."

"We still can," I said, but even *I* heard the reluctance in my voice and she chuckled.

She didn't say anything for a moment and just as I was about to tell her I would go with her to make dumplings—because, you know...sisters—she said, "Does it bother you that your biological parents left you at that orphanage?"

I blinked at her in confusion. "Well, that came out of left field. I don't understand how this is relevant."

"Let the record show the witness is balking at the question."

"All right, fine. Even though I know I'm much better off here with my adoptive parents, it *does* bother me that my birth parents abandoned me and I don't think it's wrong of me to be upset about it."

"Of course, it's not wrong. That's not what I'm saying. It's perfectly natural to be upset. They rejected you, their own flesh and blood."

"Then what *are* you saying?" I asked.

Angry tears sprang to my eyes. Most of the time, it was easy to forget I'd been set aside by my own parents. All I had to do was remember how wonderful my adoptive mom and dad were and those feelings of being unwanted went away. But every once in a while, negative emotions rose to the surface anyway.

"I'm saying that maybe, just maybe, your feelings about Chinese things—the food, the culture and even me—are because it feels like China, not just your biological parents, rejected you, and now you're returning the favor."

"Oh my God." I inhaled sharply and it was as if someone had yanked the string on a window shade and sent it spinning. "Oh my God, Ruby, I...you're right. You're right! My whole life I've been operating under this...this creepy, brainwashy response to something I don't even remember."

Suddenly, so much of my weird behavior made sense—why I routinely checked off "decline to answer" when asked to identify my ethnicity, why I'd never been bothered by the overwhelming whiteness of my hometown, why I didn't like buying products made in China, and why I had an inexplicable aversion to using chopsticks.

"So, fight back then," she said. "Now that you know you have an unconscious bias against China, you can make a *conscious* choice about things when they come up. Like this opportunity to make dumplings, for example. What do you want to do? I think it's fine either way, I really do, but if it were me, I wouldn't want to close myself off to things I might enjoy out of some Freudian reflex."

"No, I don't want to either. I want to be in charge of my own life, so give me five minutes to change clothes," I said. "I'm going with you."

Helen lived a fifteen-minute walk away in a charming two-story house, dark green with brown trim. Birdfeeders abounded and a gentle breeze coaxed a calming melody from a set of pewter wind chimes. Her yard was a little overgrown but a tire swing hung from the branch of a large linden tree. I'd never played on a tire swing, but they looked like a lot of fun.

At our knock, Helen opened the door with a broad smile. She

wore an apron over a T-shirt and billowing palazzo pants. The apron said, "Exercise? I thought you said EXTRA RICE."

"Ruby, hello, hello. Indi, I'm so glad you made it!" Helen said, motioning us through the door enthusiastically.

Helen led us to the farm-style kitchen that continued the green theme with cabinetry painted the color of moss with rustic hinges and handles. From the look of things, we'd be working at the large butcher block kitchen island. Two bowls, both covered with plastic wrap, sat alongside a stack of parchment-lined baking trays, two thick wooden rods and a canister of flour.

An Asian couple were pouring themselves a glass of wine. The woman, her hair in an elegant chignon, wore a pretty, bright pink flowing blouse over slacks and heels. The man was dressed in a pale green sweater and jeans with an ironed crease.

"Harold and Elizabeth Wong, Indi and Ruby. Ruby is a former student."

Elizabeth said something in Chinese and I was flabbergasted when Ruby replied. I hadn't known she spoke Chinese.

This was exactly why I hadn't wanted to come. Talk about not fitting in.

Then I remembered what Ruby and I had talked about. This was the reflex in action.

You're not an android, Indi.

There was a lull in the conversation and I realized they were all looking at me.

"I'm sorry, I don't speak Chinese," I said, but Helen just smiled and waved her hand.

"Not a problem. Now that we know, we'll stick to English. I was just saying, I have aprons for everyone." She went to a drawer and pulled out several. "I have a thing for funny aprons. Here you go. One for Harold, one for Elizabeth…"

Harold's had just words, "WTF. Where's the food?" Elizabeth's had a drawing of chopsticks with the words, "Not chopsticks. Food pliers." Ruby's just had a cute little cartoon of a Chinese takeout box. Mine said, appropriately, "I'm just here for the Chinese food."

After we all put on our aprons and washed our hands, Helen said, "Correct me if I'm wrong, Ruby, but I thought you said you had experience making dumplings."

"I do, but it was a long time ago and I wasn't very good. I was only nine."

"It's like riding a bike," Helen said. "What about you, Indi?"

I shook my head. "I'm a complete beginner," I confessed.

"Don't look so worried," Helen said. "It's not that hard. By the time we're done, you'll be an expert."

"Indi's parents own a pizzeria," Ruby said. "She'll pick it up in no time. She's really good with her hands, which is a good thing since she's going to be a surgeon."

"My dad wanted me to be a surgeon even though I get queasy at the sight of blood," Harold said. "A lot of doctors in my family. He said if I wanted to avoid blood, I could be a psychiatrist and I'd say, 'Dad, I would *still* have to go through medical school and he would wave that away as if that was just a bothersome detail."

"So what did you end up doing?" Ruby asked.

"I'm an optometrist, which to my mind was a kind of compromise, but Dad doesn't consider me a real doctor."

"Why not?" I asked, a little outraged on his behalf.

"Because optometrists are doctorate doctors, not medical doctors. Big difference in his mind."

My parents had been nothing but supportive. That's not to say they didn't have any expectations. They did, but they didn't try to fit me into a box that didn't suit me and for that I was grateful.

"All right," Helen said, "I don't know about you, but I'm getting hungry, so let's get started. Indi, you're going to be prepping the dough for rolling. Elizabeth and I will be rolling it. Harold and Ruby, you're filling."

Helen removed the plastic lid off one of the bowls. "This is the dough. We keep a damp cloth on it to keep it moist."

She removed the ball of dough, cut a hunk off of it and

returned the rest to the bowl, making sure to cover it again with the damp cloth.

"Did you ever play with Play-Doh when you were little?" Helen asked.

"Yes," I answered.

"Then this part will be familiar."

Using her flattened hand, she rolled the hunk into a foot-long rope and cut the rope into pieces that looked like the peanut butter filled pretzel bites my dad liked to eat. She then demonstrated how to make sure each piece was flattened with flour on it, top and bottom, so it didn't stick to the board or the rolling pin. The result was a little disc about two inches in diameter.

"I think I can handle that," I said with confidence.

"Fantastic. After you make them into rounds, Elizabeth and I will take over."

Elizabeth and Helen each took one of the flattened discs, turning them around and around while moving the rolling pin back and forth. In a few seconds, they were a little thicker than kettle chips. By the time they had a few of them done, Harold was showing Ruby how to drop a spoonful of the filling into the center of the disc and crimp them shut.

"Make sure they're sealed tightly," Elizabeth said.

"I remember," Ruby said. "I got scolded if there were any leaks."

Still rolling the dough, Helen laughed. "So did I! My mother got so mad when I did that."

We all got into a rhythm and before long we had an entire sheet tray of dumplings, lined up in neat rows ready for cooking. They were cute and plump, like tiny calzones. But we didn't bake them and they weren't in the least tomatoey. After an extended dip in the boiling water, Helen scooped them out and put them in a shallow saucer.

"All right," she said, "dig in!"

And using their "food pliers," everyone picked up a dumpling, dipped it in one of the two sauces and started eating.

Except me.

This time it wasn't using the chopsticks that was holding me back, it was the appearance of the dumplings. They were slimy looking and white—again, the complete opposite of calzones. But I couldn't very well refuse to eat one.

"So good," Ruby said as she chewed, a dreamy expression on her face. Out of sight of everyone else, she nudged me with her foot.

I decided to eat *one*, no matter how slimy it was, and then say I wasn't feeling well and walk home. Someone else could take over dough prepping. Half the time, Helen and Elizabeth were rolling so quickly, Ruby and Harold fell behind. But I attributed that to the fact that sealing the dumplings was the most important job, so they had to be thorough.

I used Hudson's stab-and-pinch method to nab the dumpling, dip it in the sauce and lift it to my mouth. As I took a bite, some of the rich broth ran down my chin, but I didn't care because—oh my God—it was oh, so delicious. The dough wasn't slimy at all. It had a smooth but chewy texture and a burst of rich pork and shitake mushroom flavor bathed my tongue as I chewed. The sauce was a winning combination of soy, a little sugar, garlic, a little punch of vinegar and nutty sesame oil.

I moaned. "This is the best thing I've ever tasted. Even better than dim sum."

"Good thing you're wearing an apron," Ruby said with a smile as I grabbed a napkin to wipe my chin.

We polished off half the sheet pan before we started the assembly line back up. Amazingly, we ran out of dough and filling at about the same time, but by then we had about a hundred dumplings. Most of them had been frozen and bagged and Helen made us take a large Ziploc's worth home with us, plus a little container of the dipping sauce.

As we walked home, Ruby asked, "So was that so painful?"

"A little bit, at the beginning when you guys were all speaking Chinese. I didn't even know you were bilingual."

"I'm actually tri-lingual," she said. "I speak Hawaiian too."

I gave her a deadpan look. "Of course, you do. Any other languages? Latin? Dutch? Portuguese?"

"I know a few words of Tagalog a friend taught me."

I glowered at her.

"Okay, okay," she said with a laugh. "Sorry. Don't be mad. It's not like it's my fault. My mom taught me Mandarin and my dad insisted I go to Hawaiian school after regular school."

My jaw dropped. "Really?"

She nodded. "Every day, I went to another school to learn, not just the language, but everything about Hawaiian history and culture that you could want to know. For instance, I know how to roast a whole pig in a pit."

"A handy skill," I remarked.

"Right? You never know when you'll need to feed fifty people."

We stopped at an intersection and waited for the light to turn. The fall foliage was spectacular and there was a definite chill in the air that made me turn the collar of my jacket up.

"So, be honest. What did you think?"

"I had a good time. I thought it was going to be torture, but I had fun."

"You should be proud of yourself. At the end there, you even tackled filling and sealing, and that's the hardest part."

"I did, didn't I?" I said, shaking the bag of frozen dumplings.

"You, Miss Indi Briscoe, are a little more Chinese now than you were a few hours ago. How does it feel?"

I smiled at her. "It feels pretty good, actually."

19

HUDSON

I was just about done tidying up the apartment when AJ came home with a long face.

"I thought you were spending the afternoon with Ruby," I said.

"I thought so too, but she broke up with me, dude," he said, dropping his backpack on the floor.

I'd sort of seen this coming but hadn't said anything. After that double date for dim sum, AJ was even more gaga over Ruby than ever, but it seemed like the feelings weren't mutual. Like Indi and me, he would have gotten together with her every night if she'd let him, but more and more she gave him excuses. They were plausible excuses, but people make time for what's important to them and AJ didn't seem to be high on Ruby's priority list.

"What happened?"

He went to the fridge for a beer and held up two bottles. "You want one?"

The reason I was tidying up was that Indi and I were going to study together. Even though it didn't seem right to be drinking a beer before she got here, when a friend got dumped, the Bro Code demanded you have a drink with him in sympathy.

"Sure."

He popped the tops and we sat on the couch.

"You know what she said to me? She said I had no sex appeal."

"That's pretty fucking rude."

"To be fair, she didn't use those exact words. She said she didn't feel any spark, and that's pretty much the same thing. When I kissed her, she didn't feel diddly squat." He took a swig from his beer. "Maybe I should join a monastery."

I held back a laugh. "Dude. That's the way it goes sometimes. It's got to be mutual. You don't want to be with someone who's not into you, right?"

He heaved a sigh and took another pull on his beer. "She was my beautiful Hawaiian Buttercup. I would have loved her forever. I *will* love her forever."

I doubted that. I'd seen AJ fall in love three times since I'd known him. Had he truly been in love with those girls? Maybe. He certainly believed it. But I knew he'd probably be over this in a week.

"And now I have to see her in photography class for the rest of the semester," he moaned. "I don't know if I can stand it."

"I'm sorry," I said again. "That really sucks."

"How are things with you and Indi? There are sparks for you two, right?"

"Yeah, lots of sparks."

There was a fucking conflagration whenever we made out. My cock got so hot, my pants should have ignited.

AJ clinked his bottle against mine. "I'm happy for you, bro. I truly am."

There was a knock at the door. "Speak of the devil," I said.

AJ just sighed and drank more beer.

I opened the door to see Indi standing there bundled up in a sweater, scarf, coat and jeans, a backpack hung on her shoulder. She had a knit cap on her head that for some reason made me want to kiss her. Not that I needed any excuses to kiss her.

"It's so cold outside!" she exclaimed, stomping her feet. A bright pink blush stained her cheeks.

"I'll warm you up," I said, bending my head and pressing my mouth to hers. Her lips *were* pretty chilled.

She put a hand on the back of my head to extend the kiss a moment longer and when we broke apart, she whispered something I couldn't quite make out.

When I gave her a confused look, she pulled me out into the hallway. "I said, Ruby broke up with AJ."

"Yeah," I replied in a low voice, "he just told me. I was commiserating with him over a beer."

"I know you're talking about me," AJ called from inside.

Indi gave me a sad smile as she came through the door.

"Hey, AJ," she said. "I'm really sorry you and Ruby aren't together anymore."

"The woman broke my heart," he said bluntly. "I may never recover. But just because I'm single now doesn't mean I want to stand in the way of you guys' love, so I'll be in my room. Do me a favor, will you, Indi?"

"Sure. What?" She unwound the scarf from her neck and put her backpack on the kitchen table.

"Don't tell me if Ruby gets together with some other dude."

"Of course I won't, AJ."

He nodded. "Thanks." He got to his bedroom door before turning and saying, "And tell her...tell her I hope she has a life filled with happiness and success and everything she deserves."

"I will."

When the door shut behind him, Indi said, "He's taking it harder than I would have expected. I mean, they only went out twice."

I went to AJ's door and put my ear close to it. I could hear his TV.

"Yeah, I know. AJ has a tender heart, but he'll be okay. You want a beer?"

"Sure. Thanks." She opened her backpack and pulled out a

thick textbook and three highlighters. "So guess what I did yesterday."

"What?"

"I made authentic Chinese dumplings."

"Get out. You, the most stubborn non-Chinese person I know?"

"Shut up," she said, giving me a mock punch on the arm. "Ruby and I ran into one of her old professors and she invited us to make dumplings at her house. I wasn't going to go at first, because I…I've always made it a point to distance myself from China, and until yesterday, I never really understood why. But now I know."

"Well, don't keep me in suspense," I said, handing her the beer.

"I've been rejecting China because, basically it—meaning my birth parents—rejected *me* first."

I rolled that around in my brain. "That makes a hell of a lot of sense, actually."

"I know, right? It was like *boom*." She flicked the fingers of both her hands to mimic an explosion.

"Good for you, Indi. That's really great."

"From now on I'm going to be trying to combat my instant dislike of anything Chinese. If you play your cards right, I might even make authentic dumplings for you."

"I would love that," I said.

After taking a sip of the beer she said, "Hey, this is that same beer you gave me when we went to Tito's."

"I bought it on a lark once because it's made by three guys who used to play for the San Diego Barracudas. They retired from hockey and started a craft brewery there. Now I buy it because it's good."

"You know, this is a really interesting coincidence. I wanted to float something by you—a theory I came up with."

"This sounds interesting." I sat and leaned my forearms on the table.

"Promise me you won't get offended. Or mad."

A little wary now, I said, "I'll do my best."

"In my EDT class—"

"EDT?"

"Emotional Development and Temperament. Last week, in my EDT class the professor was talking about something called Imposter Syndrome and I think you have it. Listen to what my book says."

She got out one of her huge textbooks and opened it to a page she'd marked with a pink Post-it.

"'Imposter Syndrome, or imposterism,'" she read, "'is a psychological pattern in which individuals doubt their skills, talents or accomplishments and have a persistent, internalized fear of being exposed as a fraud. It can develop because someone grows up in an environment where self-worth is tied to accomplishments. Or perhaps praise was offered in the form of helpful criticism. People with imposterism often feel they do not live up to the expectations of their friends or loved ones.' Doesn't that sound exactly like you and your dad?"

I frowned. "Let me see that."

There wasn't much more about imposterism in the book. I even checked the index, but it was disturbingly on the nose.

"Huh. I'm not sure that really describes what's going on with me. My anxiety attacks happen *before* the games."

"And the self-doubt hits you afterward. Don't even try to deny it. I spent hours in the car the other night witnessing it."

I didn't say anything.

"Now here's where the coincidence comes in. Look at this." She showed me an article on imposterism on her phone.

"See there? It says it can be helpful to identify someone you admire and find out what their challenges are, what they struggle with. So have you heard of Booth MacDonald? He plays for the Barracudas in San Diego. You know, *where they make Hat Trick beer.*"

"Isn't *that* a weird coincidence. Yeah, I've heard of him. He's a goalie."

"Right. Well, I found this interview of him where he talked about how he had pregame panic attacks when he was a teen and I thought, maybe through your dad's connections, you might be able to talk to him about what you're going through."

"Interesting theory. I'll give it some thought," I said.

"Great. I'll text you a link to the interview. Why are you looking at me like that?" she asked.

"You're just really intuitive, is all. And thoughtful."

I liked that she cared enough about me to spend time trying to find a solution to my stress problem.

We turned to our books then and managed to study for quite a while before the sound of Deke at his water bottle broke the silence.

"Deke's awake!" she exclaimed, dashing over to pick him up.

Indi had long since made friends with him by bringing him bits of parsley or carrot and, as a fair-minded rodent, he'd allowed her to handle him without biting her. It was fun watching her stroke his head with her finger. For his part, Deke stared blankly into the distance as she cuddled him and cooed about how cute he was.

It is a testament to our bond that I endure this, his expression seemed to say.

"It's a pretty sad state of affairs when a guy is jealous of his hamster. I think Deke's gotten more loving from you than I have tonight."

"What can I say?" she said as she eased Deke back into his habitat. "I'm a sucker for bulging cheek pouches."

"Okay, now, you can't dismiss me until you've gotten a load of *my* cheeks." I puffed out my cheeks as I walked toward her.

"Those *are* pretty sexy," she said with a laugh as I took her into my arms.

Deke ignored us as we stood right in front of him and kissed. Indi melted against me as our mouths met over and over. So soft, so warm, her lips caressed mine as I slid a hand down her lower back to her gorgeous ass.

She arched her back and my cock stiffened. My bedroom was three feet away. I wanted to walk her in there and get her into my bed, but I didn't want to stop kissing her. Then she surprised me by taking my hand and placing it on her breast.

Fuuuuck.

I felt her nipple harden against my palm even through her sweater. Her breast filled my hand and I squeezed and massaged it so eagerly, I must have seemed like a teenager copping his first feel. When I couldn't stand it anymore, I slid my hands under her sweater and unhooked her bra.

Our eyes met as I thumbed her taut nipples. She closed her eyes and let her head fall back, so I took the opportunity to feast on her neck. She tasted like husky laughter and lazy afternoons in bed, and I reveled in every soft moan that came from her throat.

Heat and hunger pooled in my groin as I inserted my knee between her legs and pulled her closer so that she was riding my thigh. She took the hint and put her hands on my shoulders, rocking her hips back and forth, getting what she needed. I was content to just watch her pleasure herself. The heat from her pussy burned through my jeans and for a dangerous moment, I imagined what it would be like to be pressed against her, skin to skin, my cock head poised at her tight entrance.

Groaning, I put my mouth to her ear. "How about we take this to the bedroom?" I asked. "We'll have more privacy."

She stilled, her breathing a little ragged.

"I'm sorry. I can't," she said with a sigh. She reached behind to refasten her bra and gave me an apologetic smile. "In fact, I should really get going. Early day tomorrow."

"Are you sure?" I leaned forward and nuzzled her neck again.

She giggled but pushed me away. "I'm sure."

"One of these days, you're going to say yes," I said, as she gathered her things and put her coat and scarf on. "And when you do…watch out. It's going to be outstanding and you're going to wonder why we wasted so much time."

She gave me a kiss and a cheek caress as she passed me on the way to the front door. "I don't doubt it. See you in class."

"See you."

After I closed the door behind her, I heard the telltale squeak of Deke's wheel as he started his nightly marathon.

Squeak squeak squeak squeak…

I knelt in front of his enclosure so he was at eye-level. Even though his short little legs moved too quickly to track, watching him spin that wheel at top speed was hypnotizing.

"I struck out again, buddy."

Squeak squeak squeak squeak.

"What am I doing wrong? I know she wants it."

"Spoken like a true asshole," AJ said, having poked his head out of his bedroom. "I heard Indi leave."

"Unfortunately."

"She didn't break up with you?"

"No."

"Then, just a reminder, even blue-balled, you're better off than I am." He headed for the kitchen. "I'm going to make a grilled cheese. You want one?"

"Shit yeah." AJ's grilled cheeses were off the hook.

"Get that tube of slice-and-bake cookies out of the fridge. I want some of those too."

We both loved slice and bake chocolate chip cookies and sometimes we even just ate the raw dough with spoons. While the oven was preheating, AJ got out the ingredients he needed for the sandwiches: cheese, butter, bread, and his secret ingredients—garlic powder and grated Parmesan. I got out the cutting board and portioned out the cookie dough onto a baking sheet.

"Before she left, Indi and I talked about…my pregame nerves and she said she thought I had something called Imposter Syndrome. Have you heard of that?"

"No. What is it?"

As he slathered butter on the bread then sprinkled the garlic powder and Parmesan on top, I explained what imposterism was.

"Indi's pretty smart. That sounds exactly like you."

"It does. The article says that something I could try was to find a mentor who's gone through something similar and talk to them about it."

"Easier said than done," AJ remarked, pressing the bread, butter side down in the hot skillet. It sizzled and almost immediately the aroma of garlic, Parm and butter filled the air.

"Miss Smartypants already found me a potential mentor." I filled him in about Booth MacDonald as he laid slices of cheese on the bread and then topped each sandwich with the other piece of buttered bread.

"I just…I don't know if I want this getting around the league. There are like over a thousand players, but it's still a small community when it comes to things like that. Because if the Dragon organization hears about it…"

He nodded. "Yeah, there goes your spot on the roster."

"Exactly."

I put the cookie sheet into the oven and set the timer. AJ flipped the sandwiches to reveal the perfect crispy exterior. Just a few more minutes…

"I think you have to assume that if you asked him to keep it to himself that he would honor that. Only a dick would flap his lips to someone about it after you expressly asked him to keep it quiet. I think you should go for it."

AJ turned the heat off and delivered the sandwiches to the plates I'd gotten out. We sat down and I took that first glorious bite. The crunchy, cheesy exterior gave way to the melted cheese inside. I burned my mouth but it was worth it.

"AJ, you could quit school right now and get a job as a chef. Swear to God."

"Don't think I haven't thought about it," he joked. "Especially during finals."

We ate in silence, just enjoying the piping hot gooey deliciousness of our sandwiches. Talk about comfort food. I actually forgot about my problems for a few minutes, especially when the cookies came out of the oven. But eventually AJ returned to the conversation.

"Have you talked to Coach Keller about all this?"

"Hell no, for exactly the same reason. I don't want word getting back to the Dragons."

"Yeah, I get that." He took another bite. "So, go ahead and try that whole mentor thing. See if MacDonald has anything worthwhile to say. Who knows? Maybe whatever he does before games will work for you too. But if it doesn't..." He held up a hand. "I know I was the one pushing you to become captain and I stand by that. You're a great captain. But if wearing the C is putting too much stress on you, dude, maybe you should let it go."

20

HUDSON

I wasn't kidding when I said the NHL was a tight community and proof of that was how easily I tracked down Booth MacDonald. As it happens, I played hockey with a guy who got drafted by the Barracudas two years ago and was in the middle of his rookie year in San Diego. I just gave him a call and asked if he could let Booth know I'd like his advice on a personal matter. The next day, I got a call from the man himself.

"Mr. MacDonald, thank you for getting back to me."

"Call me Mac. My pal Booker said you needed to talk to me. What can I do you for?"

I briefly filled him in about my situation—my draft number, the captaincy, my persistent pregame nausea and shit show game performance.

"My girlfriend saw an interview you did that made her think you might have had a similar problem."

"I did, indeed. How old are you, Hudson?"

"I'm twenty-one."

"Okay. I was a little younger than you are, but I went through pretty much the same thing. I was on the cusp of my professional career and the pressure just…it got to me. I felt like a fake, like I'd been drafted by mistake. That the scouts just happened to see me on a good day and it was all just luck."

"It's the same with me except I feel like I am where I am because of my family, that all anyone sees is my last name."

"It sucks, doesn't it?"

"It sucks balls, Mac. My girlfriend said it's something called Imposter Syndrome."

"Your girlfriend's a smart cookie. That's exactly what it is."

"She also said that finding a mentor who's been through the same thing can be helpful."

"Wait a second. You're talking about me, right? I'm the mentor you're talking about."

"I hope so."

Mac gave a whoop. "I've never been anyone's mentor before. Wait until I tell the guys."

"I'm sorry, Mac. I meant to tell you before…I'd appreciate it if you could keep our conversation between us."

"Oh, okay. I get it," he said in a more serious tone. "You don't want your dad finding out?"

"Among other people, yes."

He paused.

"Well, I guess I'd better get out of the locker room and take you off speaker phone."

I let out a fervent f-bomb.

"Ah ha ha ha ha ha ha ha! You're not on speaker," Mac said, laughing. "I was just fucking with you. Someone should have warned you I'm the team prankster."

I exhaled in relief. "You almost gave me a heart attack."

"Kid, you're too young for a heart attack. I'm not really in the locker room. In fact, you said you play for Burlington University, right?"

"Yes."

"I happen to be on my way to Burlington right now with the little woman."

"Don't call me that," said a woman I assumed was his wife.

Mac laughed. "The team flew into Montreal last night and *my beautiful wife*, Janie, wanted to take a little day trip to Vermont to see the leaves and pick apples and shit. You want to meet up?"

"Yes, sir, I do."

We made a plan to meet in a few hours at Indi's dorm. Because it had all been her idea in the first place, we were going to surprise her and then go grab lunch in town. Maybe even dim sum. I thought she'd get a kick out of meeting the man she'd picked out as a mentor for me. I also thought she might offer some valuable input to the conversation.

I met the MacDonalds outside Carter Hall. I recognized Mac right away, having checked out his Wikipedia beforehand. The top-notch goalie was a bear of a man, well over six feet tall, most of him solid muscle. His wife was a pretty brunette with intelligent eyes and a rounded body.

After introductions were made, I knocked on the door. I was so amped, I could barely stand still.

I heard music coming from inside and the sound of footsteps. This was going to be so great.

The door opened and Indi stood there. She had something purple on the left side her face so I thought I must have caught her in the middle of a home facial. Moments like this, I was glad to be a guy. The only thing I had to do to my face was shave it and make sure my nose hairs didn't get out of control.

"Surprise!" I exclaimed. "This is—"

But before I could go any further, she slammed the door in my face.

"Ah, okay," Mac said with a nervous laugh. "That was interesting."

I knocked again. "Indi? What's going on?"

"Hudson, I'm sorry," she said through the door. It's just that I'm really...sick. I'm contagious, really contagious, and I don't want you to catch it."

"Is there anything I can do? Want me to bring you some chicken soup?"

"No, I'll be fine. I just need to get back in bed."

"Okay. Feel better," I said.

Even though I was worried about Indi, I had a good time at lunch. Mac and Jane were easygoing and easy to talk to. Mac regaled me with stories of his many pranks, like the time he'd convinced the Barracuda rookies he'd gotten hold of a package of "orgasm mushrooms."

"'It was discovered in the recent Hawaiian lava flows,' I told them, 'and it's been proven to cause instantaneous orgasms in women just from the odor it gives off.' Those boys were so eager to believe it, they didn't bat an eyelash. I told them that it was going to take a while to get them to San Diego because of governmental red tape but because I believed in sharing the wealth, they'd each get their own. I tell you, I had them on the string for weeks. When I finally gave them the mushrooms, we were on a road trip and they couldn't wait to hook up with some of the local puck bunnies so they could reap the benefits, if you know what I mean. The next morning, the disappointment on their faces was priceless."

Jane clucked her tongue. "Serves them right for thinking they could cheat like that."

"Oh, I don't know," Mac said. "I wouldn't mind not having to work so—ow!" Mac flinched as Jane thwacked him on the arm. "I'm kidding, honey. I love every second I spend taking care of you in bed."

Sighing, Jane shook her head. "All right. I've had enough. I'm going to go shop on Church Street for a while. Booth, we'll need to get back on the road by two thirty."

"Yes, dear," he said and laughed when she playfully boxed his ear.

"It was nice to meet you, Hudson. I'm sorry Indi couldn't make it. I hope she feels better."

"Yeah, me too."

After Jane left, Mac started in on his fourth piece of pizza. "Do me a favor. Don't tell the little woman I ate this," he said.

"Mum's the word," I said. "And you probably don't want to call her that."

"Ha! You're quick, Forte." He wiped his mouth with his napkin. "Why don't you run through a typical game day for me?"

"Okay, but first I want to say again how grateful I am to you for taking time out of your day to meet with me."

"Glad to do it, kid. You know, what goes around, comes around. Your dad and uncles were idols of mine when I was growing up."

I once again described what I was going through, from the moment I got up from a shitty night's rest to the mental agony I went through on the bench to the fuckups that felt like a guerrilla demon was sabotaging my game for kicks.

"So, let me say first, I feel for you, kid. I really do. Everything you just described brings me right back to when I was your age, but kudos to you for having the courage to speak up about it. A lot of guys I know would just grin and bear it, cross their fingers and hope it went away."

I didn't tell him that's exactly what I'd been doing before Indi and AJ pushed me to do something about it.

"But honestly, that's gotta change. I mean, I respect that you want to keep this quiet and all your reasons for that are solid. But as a league, we need to make it safer for guys to get the help they need and not feel like they have to suffer in silence." He looked at the half a piece of pizza left in his hand, made a face, then put it down. "My eyes were bigger than my stomach," he said.

"It's good pizza," I said, choosing not to comment on the other stuff he said about making the NHL a safe place.

I agreed but didn't think it would ever happen. Hockey players were bred to be tough, to suck it up, so much so that we'd gained a reputation for enduring. I had never played for the Stanley Cup, but from the way my family members talked, nothing short of death could stop an NHL player from a playoff game. I'd heard stories of guys playing through broken ankles, broken wrists, mild concussions, and slipped discs. Men who couldn't commit to the sport with that kind of dedication…well, let's just say word got around.

"All right, let me do some actual mentoring. Like your girlfriend, Janie is a very smart woman. She, too, recognized that I had a problem and was unlikely to do anything about it unless she intervened. So she came up with a routine that works for me every time."

He then described five things he did before every game, things that helped calm the chaotic feelings of self-doubt and fear of failure that never failed to surface.

"I know a lot of this sounds like New Age mumbo jumbo," Mac said, "and that's what I thought it was at first too, but I'm telling you, it works. And I've also come to realize on my own that it can help to flip your mindset. You probably go into the game thinking about what you're going to do, down to the last detail, as if it's all up to you. Now, I don't know your skill level, but despite your imposter feelings, they don't draft guys by mistake, man. They just don't. But even if you're Connor McDavid's clone, the games won't be won or lost by just you alone. You play on a team. So when you're on that fifth item—the pep talk—mix it up a little. Visualize what you're going to do as an individual, of course, but don't forget to include ways you and your teammates are going to dominate as a unit. That's just as important as your individual contribution. Oh, before I forget, I printed it all out for you."

By the time we said goodbye, I couldn't believe how good I felt. Mac gave me so much valuable information. I had a plan of action. I had a mentor, someone who had walked through the fire and gotten through, unscathed.

I had hope.

But that hope wasn't as bright as it might have been because I was worried about Indi. I'd texted her several times with no response.

Hudson: I hope you're feeling better. Call me when you can. I have a lot to tell you.

INDI

I'd had no plans for the day except to study hard for my EDT exam. Ever since I'd started seeing Hudson, the study habits I'd honed my whole life had fallen by the wayside. I'd gotten behind with both my homework and my MCAT prep and I had no one to blame but myself.

I didn't bother putting my face on because that way I would stay in my room until I'd caught up. I didn't even need to go out for food because I took the last few dumplings out of the freezer and by the time I was hungry and ready for a break, they'd be defrosted enough to cook.

When the knock on the door came, I'd thought it was Ruby. She was always forgetting her keys. It happened often enough that we talked about keeping an extra outside the door, but there wasn't any place to safely hide one.

Unfortunately, it wasn't Ruby.

I had always prided myself on remaining calm in emergency situations. Once when I was little, I'd slept over at a friend's house and we'd gotten up before everyone else, determined to surprise everyone with breakfast the next morning. We were cooking bacon when the pan caught fire. My friend freaked out and rushed to fill a glass with water, but I stopped her. As the daughter of a restauranteur, I knew you extinguished grease fires by either cutting off its oxygen or dousing it with baking soda. The fire went out soon after we slapped the lid on the pan.

But opening the door and seeing Hudson there induced a panic in me that no fire ever would.

My heart went into overdrive as I slammed the door. He was talking to me, but I couldn't focus on what he was saying. All I could hear was the deafening tympanic drumbeat of my pounding heart.

Had he seen my birthmark?

Of course he had. I had my hair up in a ponytail and it was broad daylight.

He was probably standing there, a look of horror on his face, and maybe thinking he'd knocked on the wrong door or entered some alternate reality where an alien had abducted me and left a monster in my place.

I could only blame myself. I should have told him about my birthmark ages ago. After he tried to touch my face and I'd freaked out would have been the perfect time to explain. With a little warning, he might have been okay with how I look without my makeup on. But now…now he knew I'd been lying to him all this time, pretending to be something I'm not—a normal, pretty girl. He was one of the stars of the hockey team. All he had to do was snap his fingers and ten girls would jump at the chance to date him, girls with normal looking faces who didn't hide who they were.

Ruby came home about an hour later.

After one look at me, she exclaimed, "Indi, what's wrong?"

Sick at heart, I told her what had happened. She was sympathetic, but she'd also told me time and again that I needed to tell Hudson about my birthmark. She'd told me exactly how to do it too.

"First you say, 'Hudson, I have something I've been afraid to tell you.' He'll immediately think it's something really horrible—like you were abused as a child or your uncle is a member of the Klan. So when

you tell him you were born with a birthmark on your face, he'll actually be relieved."

"If only I'd taken your advice," I said, after recounting to her what had happened. "Now, it's too late."

"Stop that. It is not too late," she declared.

"Yes, it is. This face is too scary to take if you're not ready for it."

"I love you like a sister, but right now? You're being a grade-A drama queen. Your face is not scary. What's scary is your refusal to give the guy a chance. You think it's a foregone conclusion that he's going to reject you, but I see no evidence that that's true."

"Austin did."

"Who's Austin?"

"Austin was my first boyfriend. We went together in high school."

Ruby winced. "This story is going to have a tragic ending, isn't it? Never mind. Don't answer that. I already know it is, but I want to hear it anyway."

"I was a senior and feeling some social pressure to get things rolling in the sex department. He knew I was a virgin and been really patient. So, we planned to do it a week before the prom. But...it didn't go well.

"I admit it was partly my fault for deciding, after keeping my birthmark a secret from him, to bare everything to him on the big night. It made perfect sense to me then. I thought we were in love, that he loved me and if he loved me, he'd be okay with my birthmark."

"Oh, Indi," Ruby murmured.

"I know. I was so incredibly stupid. If I hadn't sprung it on him without warning, things might have turned out a lot differently. As it was, he was horrified. We never had sex. He never talked to me again."

"Listen to me, Indi. You were not stupid. You are not at fault. The only thing you did wrong was choose a loser to sleep with. There are a lot of dicks out there who aren't worth five minutes of conversation, let alone sex, and Austin was one of them. But that doesn't mean that Hudson is a dick. From what I've seen of him, he's the exact opposite, but I don't know him like you do. What do you think? Is Hudson a dick?"

I sniffed. "No."

"Do you think he only likes you because of what you look like? Or—don't interrupt me—or do you think you have other qualities that he's attracted to, like your intelligence, your wit, your sense of humor?"

"Ruby, stop it. I get it. Yes, of course he likes other things about me other than the way I look, but that doesn't negate the fact that the way I look is a factor."

She stared at me with narrowed eyes, but I knew I'd made a point.

"I will concede it's a factor, but not as big a one as you think it is. Remember when you first showed me?" She reached out and clasped my hand, squeezed it. "I'll admit now that I was shocked. I'd never seen anything like your birthmark before, but I got used to it."

"Thanks a lot."

"You know what I mean. You've told me yourself that the kids you went to grade school with were so used to it, they didn't even see it anymore. You gave them the chance to get to know the real you. Doesn't Hudson deserve that same chance?"

"Yes," I said, my voice trembling. I looked outside at the gray skies. A storm seemed to be gathering.

"Then what are you waiting for?" She glanced at the wall clock. "The game's over by now. If you hurry, you can catch him at the rink."

I left Carter Hall with every intention of going to the rink, but as I approached the still full parking lot, I decided against it. Ruby hadn't let me put on any makeup, saying that horse already left the barn, and I had enough anxiety about facing Hudson barefaced, let alone thousands of hockey fans. Instead, I drove to his apartment, parked and waited.

I woke up some time later, disoriented and freezing. It was raining hard. The streetlights reflected off the wet streets. Teeth chattering, I checked my phone, still a little groggy. I'd somehow slept through another text from Hudson, sent about an hour ago.

Hudson: I hope you're feeling better. Call me when you can. I have a lot to tell you.

A wave of guilt rolled through me. It was midnight, but I tapped out a reply anyway.

Indi: I'm freezing, but I'm okay.

His response was almost immediate.

Hudson: OMG. I've been worried sick. Why are you freezing? Is the heat out in the dorm?

Indi: No. I'm in my car outside your apartment.

A light went on in his unit and he appeared at the window, peering out. By then, I was out of the car and running across the street. No umbrella. The rain was coming down in sheets and I was instantly drenched.

I got to his front door just as he was coming out.

"Indi, you're soaked to the skin," he exclaimed, pulling me inside. "Are you crazy coming out in this without an umbrella? Jesus, you're shivering."

He hurried to his bedroom and came back with a T-shirt, some sweatpants, a towel and a woven blanket which he gave to me. "Go dry off and put these on. I think we have some tea somewhere. I'll make some."

A few minutes later, I came out of his room, dry but still frozen. He must have found tea because there was a pot of water on the stove and two mugs on the counter.

Setting the towel aside, I curled up in a corner of the sofa with the blanket wrapped around my shoulders. A short while later, he came over with the tea. I curled my hands around the steaming mug, grateful for the warmth.

"It's a good thing for you AJ's sleeping," he said sitting next to me, "because I'm tempted to read you the riot act. What the hell are you doing coming out in this weather when you're sick? For someone studying to be a doctor, you should know better."

Biting my lip, I said, "I lied to you. I'm not sick."

He frowned. "I don't understand."

Closing my eyes, I took a deep breath and, all the words exploded out of me in a rush, like I was a piñata that had just been dealt the last blow.

"As you can see, I have a…thing on my face." I kept my gaze averted as I spoke. "It's a birthmark called a port-wine stain and I've been covering it up with makeup because I didn't want you to see it. That's why I slammed the door in your face. That's why I pretended to be sick today."

He leaned forward and slowly, carefully tucked my hair behind my ear so my entire face was revealed.

"I was wondering what this was."

Despite my best efforts, I felt tears gathering.

"Is this why you wouldn't let me touch your face?"

I nodded.

"Can I touch it now?" he asked in a soothing voice.

I nodded again and a moment later felt his warm hand on my cheek, cupping my jaw. His thumb stroked my skin ever so gently.

"Tell me something. Were you the girl I collided with in the cafeteria last month?"

Taking in a shaky breath, I nodded.

A few more moments ticked by as he continued to study my face. This was how I imagined zoo animals or circus freaks felt.

"I'm sorry, Indi. I can't stop looking at you."

I scoffed. "Because I'm grotesque."

"Don't put words in my mouth. Look at me, Indi."

I met his gaze and through the blur of fresh tears, I saw an acceptance that warmed me from the inside out.

"I can't stop looking at you because I've wanted this for a long time. I can't tell you how often I wondered what you looked like when you weren't all made up. I wondered when you'd feel comfortable enough with me that you'd let me see the real you, the private you. And I'm sorry that it came about the way it did, that I freaked you out this afternoon, but I'm glad at the same time. You're beautiful. You're so, so beautiful."

It took a while for his words to sink in but when they did, they wrapped around me more snugly than the blanket.

He moved closer, still cupping my face, and brushed his lips against mine. I could taste his toothpaste, smell the soap he'd used and the unique scent of his skin. It was the most tender kiss I'd ever had because it was more than physical. This wasn't just nerves and synapses firing. The knowledge that he accepted my face and thought it was beautiful opened me up inside. This was what I'd hoped for but was afraid would never happen. This gorgeous, amazing hockey god had seen me, seen my birthmark, and hadn't rejected me or recoiled.

I sighed as he rained gentle kisses on my lips and cheeks, paying special attention to my birthmark. All the while he told me again and again how beautiful I was and each time he said it, I believed it a little more strongly.

As he slipped his hand under the T-shirt and closed over my bare breast, I moaned. It felt so good, especially when he slowly circled the nipple with his fingers, making it tighten into a hard point of sharp sensation.

In a matter of moments, I was nothing but need and wanting. When he pushed his knee between my legs, I opened them.

Almost immediately, he moved in. I felt the hardness of his erection right where I needed it. I lifted my hips and he ground himself against me. It felt so good. I never wanted it to stop. There was no place I'd rather be than pinned under Hudson's hard body with his hips thrusting and rubbing me where it counted.

We were panting. My lips were throbbing from his kisses and I felt lightheaded. I was only dimly aware of the rain pelting the windows.

With a groan, Hudson stopped and raised himself on his elbows.

"Indi," he said, breathing hard. "Let's go to my room." His hair was disheveled and his eyes blazed with heat.

I couldn't answer, but when he stood up and took my hand, I went along, eager, scared, my heart pounding.

The desire I felt right now was ten times sharper and more intense than it had been the other times I'd made out with him. My legs were literally shaking as we made our way to his bedroom and I could only surmise that we'd crossed a threshold, or maybe just I had. By being honest and open with him and exposing my most vulnerable self, I'd unlocked something inside and now my body *and* my mind were synced, aroused, *hungry*.

Except I still had one thing I was keeping from him.

And that had to change.

Tonight.

22

INDI

Secrets suck. The longer you keep them, the more difficult it is when you finally have to give them up.

I hadn't come over intending to lose my virginity and I wondered if, rather than confess to him that I'd lived twenty-one years on this earth and never had sex, I should pretend I knew what I was doing. I would get him all hot and bothered—not a difficult task—and in his frenzy of lust, he wouldn't notice that the only sex I'd ever had was in my mind. I mean, sex wasn't like playing a musical instrument. If I picked up a saxophone and tried to play something, it would in no way resemble music, not without practice. But sex? Sex didn't seem that complicated. There were two moving parts. How hard could it be?

And yet, hadn't this whole shitty day come about because I hadn't been honest with him? I could have saved myself so much grief if I'd told him about the birthmark right off the bat. I already embarrassed myself a lot today, so a little more wouldn't make that much of a difference. It was as if I'd sloshed my coffee drink on my white T-shirt and was worrying about dripping some chocolate sauce on it too.

Hudson was busy shoving the huge pillows off the bed, scattering them like a thief in a heist movie who needed a tabletop to spread the blueprint on.

"Hudson, wait. Stop."

He paused slightly before turning around with a carefully neutral expression on his face. I, frankly, wouldn't have blamed him if he was irritated. I was irritated with me too.

"I need to tell you something. Something else I probably should have told you earlier."

His expression didn't change, but his brows rose and I could almost hear him thinking, *Oh, God, what now,* and all of a sudden, I was sure he thought I had an STD. What else could a woman possibly need to tell a guy before they had sex? Luckily, fear that he thought I was diseased prompted me to just blurt it out.

"I'm a virgin."

His eyes widened. "You are?"

"Yep." I shrugged in what I hoped was a carefree manner.

A nervous laugh escaped him. "I...wow." He ran his hands through his hair. "I wasn't expecting that."

"Sorry."

"No, no, don't be sorry. There's nothing to be sorry about."

We stood there staring at each other from opposite sides of the bed. The pillows lay discarded on the floor and I wondered if I should go home after all.

"You're a virgin," he said. "So if we..." He gestured haphazardly toward the bed. "I'll be your first time."

"If you're willing," I said, half-jokingly.

But even though he'd been ready, willing and able a few minutes ago, now he seemed hesitant.

It would serve me right if he wanted to kick me to the curb. If a guy had kept dumping secret after secret on me, there would be a tipping point where I'd be like, nope. I'm done.

Maybe Hudson had reached that point.

"I...Jesus. Sure, I'm willing. I'm just...a little wigged out is all. I mean, that's a lot of pressure, a lot of responsibility, you know? I don't have any idea what to do... I mean, there have got to be certain things you do with virgins."

"Maybe you can google it," I said in a lame attempt at humor. "Top Ten Things to Do When Breaking in a Virgin."

He laughed nervously. "I don't doubt a list like that exists," he said, sitting at the foot of the bed. I perched next to him, my hands clasped in my lap, my knees pressed together. When he heaved a deep sigh, my heart sank.

He was going to reject me, just like Austin had. The only difference was Hudson would do it with kindness, which in a lot of ways would be worse. I sat up straighter and tried to prepare myself.

"First of all, thank you," he said.

Thank you?

"For what?"

"For the honor of wanting me to be your first." He smiled and the tension drained out of me. "Unless there wasn't any special consideration given and I happened to be the most convenient candidate."

"No, not at all," I assured him. "I mean, I haven't been 'saving myself' all this time for that special someone, no offense."

"None taken," he said, still smiling.

"But my virginity isn't a nuisance that needs to be taken care of either, like an item on my daily calendar. It's a milestone that doesn't deserve fanfare, but some consideration would be nice. Does that make sense?"

"It makes perfect sense. Can I ask a question?"

I nodded, suddenly nervous.

"You don't have to tell me, obviously, but if you weren't saving yourself, then why do you think it hasn't happened yet?"

I sighed and lay back on the bed. "You really want to know? Because I guarantee you, by the end of my story you'll be on emotional baggage overload."

"I don't mind," he said, lying down next to me and taking my hand. "Honestly."

"Senior year in high school, I was seeing this guy named Austin. Things were going well. I told him I was a virgin and he was incredibly patient with how slow I wanted to go and it had finally gotten to the point where I was finally ready."

"I sense a 'but' coming."

I nodded. "But when he saw my birthmark, he…couldn't go through with it."

"What an utter fucked-up fuckhead," Hudson said, outraged.

"He also stood me up for prom."

"That's it."

Hudson jack-knifed up so fast, it was clear his abs weren't just for show. His lips were drawn tight and he seemed to be trying to control his breathing.

"Indi, I want you to tell me that fuckhead's full name and address, if you have it. I'm going to track him down and teach him a lesson."

I'd never confronted Austin, so it would have been oh so satisfying to see him have to face the music for what he'd done. But this was ancient history. I'd long ago decided to put that on my list of "What Doesn't Kill You" things.

"Come on, Indi," Hudson said. "I know you come from Brattleboro. There can't be that many high schools or Austins there. It wouldn't be that hard to find him."

"No, Hudson. I appreciate the offer. Really. But that wouldn't do any good. I believe in what goes around comes around. Someday, some girl will break his heart as cruelly as he did mine and I'll have to be satisfied with that."

"You're a better person than me," he said. "I'd rather someone, preferably me, broke his face than his heart."

"Again, no."

He lay back down, this time on his side, so I turned to face him.

"I'm glad you didn't sleep with him," he said, clearly still angry.

"Me too."

"*I* want to sleep with you. You have no idea how much," he said. "Do you want to sleep with me?"

"I do."

I wanted that more than anything.

23

HUDSON

After our emotionally fraught conversation, the rain was still coming down in sheets and since Indi had already been soaked once, neither of us thought it was a good idea to go out there again.

I scrounged up a spare toothbrush for her from the three-pack I had under my bathroom sink and after we'd both brushed our teeth, I'd put on a T-shirt and some shorts and we got into bed. I was on my back and she tucked herself up under my arm, laying her head on my chest and moments later, she was fast asleep.

I, on the other hand, wasn't the least bit sleepy. My day had been a topsy-turvy emotional rollercoaster.

I'd gotten valuable advice from Mac and assurance that he was there for me whenever I needed him and that no one would hear from his lips what I was going through. I was hopeful that if I adopted his pregame routine, I would soon be done with my anxiety attacks. I'd be able to eat normally again, the dizziness on the ice would disappear and I'd be back to my old self, the man the Dragons drafted. It was a huge relief, but I had worried about Indi all day.

Then she'd shown up in the middle of the night, soaking wet and full of revelations.

She was the girl in the hoodie from the cafeteria.

She had a wine-colored birthmark on her face.

She was a virgin.

Fuck. I could have used a drink. We had a bottle of vodka in the freezer, but Indi was sleeping so peacefully, I didn't want to move her. She'd been through more than I had.

I sincerely hoped I'd convinced her what a non-issue her birthmark was for me. Granted, it was unusual and striking, but not any serious impediment to my feelings about her. Indi was still Indi—the smartest, sexiest most fun, complex girl I'd ever dated, with or without makeup. It was like when my dad had lost that front tooth during a game. At first it was a shock, but eventually I didn't even notice it. Pretty soon, the newness of her birthmark would wear off like just like it had with the hole in Dad's smile.

Her secondary issue presented more of a problem, because the literal last thing I needed was additional pressure to perform. And yet, there were worse things in the world than a beautiful woman trusting you to show her all about the wondrous pleasures of sex. If I'd complained about this to my teammates, I'd have gotten laughed out of the locker room. And yet, I had legitimate concerns. She said she wasn't expecting fanfare, but I did need a carefully considered plan of action. Winging it wasn't an option.

And honestly, it was great. So many curveballs had been thrown at me, I needed the rest.

But it was a while before I felt asleep because every time I thought about what that guy had done to Indi, or more accurately, what he *hadn't* done to her and how it had destroyed her self-esteem, I became incensed. I had meant it when I said I wanted to track that ass wipe down and teach him a lesson. Call me a Neanderthal, but nothing would have made me happier than to use my fists to pay that guy back for all the hurt he'd caused her.

But as cruel as he'd been, I realized I had the opportunity to teach her that not all men were shallow sons of bitches. And I wanted that more than anything. I wanted to be that man for her and to hopefully repair some of the emotional damage Hurricane

Fuckhead had wrought. Luckily, one of the best ways I could think of to accomplish this was to make love to her. I was going to worship her body with everything I had and show her just how sexy and gorgeous she was.

I just needed to figure out exactly how I was going to do that.

When I asked Indi for some time to formulate a plan, she agreed, but not without some teasing.

"I had no idea what I was asking was so *hard*," she said, gazing up at me with a wide-eyed innocent expression.

"Very funny," I said. "It's *not* that hard. I just want to make sure I do it right."

"Oh, I see. You need to *bone up* on the basics."

Smiling, I rolled my eyes.

"Because I'm pretty sure tab A goes into slot B."

Compared to the chirps I got on the ice and in the locker room, her jibes did as much damage as a pillow. It was absolutely adorable.

"You know," I reminded her, "we're supposed to be looking for a 'Human of Burlington.'"

We were walking in Waterfront Park for a photography project modeled after the work of Brandon Stanton's Humans of New York project. Stanton had set about posting portraits of New Yorkers along with interviews with them for a blog that drew millions of followers. Along that vein, we were to photograph a citizen of our fair town and include a quote from them or a story about their lives.

"You want a good grade, don't you?" I asked.

She immediately sobered, as I'd known she would. To Indi, school was serious with a capital S, even a throwaway class like photography.

Finding a subject for this kind of project wasn't as easy as it seemed. Professor Larkmont instructed us to choose someone with a "visual story to tell," whatever that meant. I'd asked her for clarification, but she said, "You'll know it when you see it. Like porn."

To be honest, I wasn't too concerned. I only took the class to fill out my schedule and even though I was really enjoying the class, getting a good grade in photography wasn't high on my priority list. I had a lot of details to nail down for The Big Night. Both AJ and Ruby were helping, although AJ's part was just finding somewhere else to be for twenty-four hours.

Indi and I had been wandering for about fifteen minutes when I spotted a little girl going down the playground slide. Miraculously, she had a birthmark like Indi, but it spread across her eye all the way down to her lip with an almost straight line down the median of her face.

"Indi. Look." I inclined my head toward the little girl.

A broad smile broke across Indi's face and she went right over.

"Hi, I'm Indi. I like your birthmark."

The little girl beamed. "Thank you."

"What's your name?" Indi asked.

By then the mother had approached and put her hands on her daughter's shoulders in a protective gesture. "Excuse me, who are you?"

"My name is Indi Briscoe and this is Hudson. I was telling your daughter that I like her birthmark."

"It's not often that people realize it's a birthmark," the mom said, warming up slightly.

"Well, I have one too," Indi said.

"You do?" the little girl exclaimed excitedly. "Where?"

"It's on my face, but you can't see it right now because I have makeup on."

"I'm Denise Snow," the mom said.

"And I'm Leah! I'm seven and a half."

"You're practically a teenager," said Indi.

Leah giggled.

"Mrs. Snow, do you mind if I take her picture for my class project?" Indi asked.

She produced the form letter Professor Larkmont had given us that outlined the project parameters and gave both her phone number and the website address where the photographs would be displayed.

After reading the letter, Denise said, "It's all right with me if it's all right with Leah."

"Is it okay, Leah?" Indi asked.

Leah nodded.

"I'll be right over here watching, sweetheart."

While Denise and I made small talk, Indi snapped shots of the little girl, who seemed like a natural. I could hear their laughter as Indi pushed her hard on the swing and then ran around to the front so she could take pictures. Denise was a bookkeeper who worked out of her home. Leah was her only child so far.

"But there's a baby sister or brother on the way," Denise said, her hand on her stomach. She didn't look pregnant at all, but I was certainly no expert.

"When are you due?"

"March. We have a while yet, but Leah's so excited to be a big sister."

"I can imagine. I was an only child and I'd always wished for a brother or a sister," I said. "Do they know if port-wine stains are hereditary? Will your new baby have a birthmark too?

"There's a one in three hundred chance the new baby will have a port-wine stain, but if he or she does, it won't matter much. We'll have a matched pair. That's all."

Leah came running up. "Mommy, the monkey bars are empty now. See? Can I go play on them?"

"Of course, honey."

"Can you come help me reach, Indi?" Leah asked.

"I was going to show your mom the pictures I took…"

"I'll help you," I said. "I love the monkey bars. Race you!"

I loved kids. Being with them made me feel like a kid again

myself, especially the younger ones, like Leah. They always made me laugh.

I let Leah win the race and then helped her reach the first rung. She weighed practically nothing.

"I want to make it all the way across today," she said, her face screwed up with the effort it took to hang on. She swung her legs back and forth and managed to grab the next rung.

"Atta girl!" I exclaimed. "Keep it up."

After hanging there a while gathering her strength, she reached out but missed the third rung by an inch before dropping to the ground.

"I'm going to try again."

We went through the same routine again, and again she missed that third rung. This time, she flopped onto the rubber mat below.

"My arms are tired," she said dejectedly.

"You know what would help?" I asked.

"What?"

"Once you get going, don't stop. Keep going. Like this."

After grabbing the first rung, I bent my knees so I was off the ground and swung for the second and then the third. "See that? You've got to keep up your momentum. Don't stop. Don't stop. Don't stop." I kept this up until I reached the other side.

I glanced over to see if Indi had seen me. She was still talking with Denise but she was frowning. I wondered what they were talking about.

Leah regarded me with wide eyes. "You're strong."

"Thanks. Now try again. Let's see if you can make it to the third rung."

I boosted her up again with one eye on Indi. As before, Leah successfully grabbed the second rung but this time, she didn't hesitate before reaching out again.

"You did!" I exclaimed as she grabbed the third. "Keep going, girl!"

Despite a valiant effort to make it to the fourth, she missed and dropped to the ground. Her face was red from exertion, but she was beaming.

"Did you see me?"

"I sure did. You did a great job."

She took off running back to her mom. "MOMMY, I MADE IT TO THE THIRD BAR!"

As she recounted what she'd done, Indi strode toward me at a quicker than normal pace.

"Let's go," she said, passing me by.

Waving, I called out a goodbye to the mom and daughter then turned to catch up with Indi.

"What's going on?" I asked.

Stopping abruptly, she made a hand gesture toward where Denise was still sitting and made a frustrated sound. "That woman!" she exclaimed then started off walking again. "She suggested that because I wear makeup, I'm ashamed of my birthmark. I'm *not* ashamed."

I wasn't sure this was one hundred percent true, if only because she'd been so afraid to show it to me. Then again, I'd been blessed with a fair amount of good looks and had zero body issues, but I could see that Indi might have had a rough time of it, growing up Asian in an all-white community *and* having the birthmark front and center on her face. If she was hesitant about going out without makeup, I could understand why.

"I just don't see the point in flaunting it all over the place," she said. "I mean, makeup was invented for a reason. And she'll see." Indi waved her hand again so violently, I ducked instinctively. "My parents tried to convince me my birthmark was a beautiful part of me, just like Denise is trying to do with Leah, and that's a nice sentiment, but it's not real life."

We had been walking on the wide boardwalk along the edge of Lake Champlain. It was a sunny and slightly warmer day, and plenty of people were taking advantage. Bikers galore, parents with strollers, joggers. But they were all giving us a wide berth, maybe because my girlfriend looked like she was ready to take someone out.

"Sooner or later," Indi said, "probably in junior high, she'll want to cover it up with makeup, I guarantee you." She gave me a piercing stare. "When I went to a new school where people didn't know me, they weren't aware that it was a birthmark. That's when they started in on me."

As we walked, she began to tell me some of the ways kids at school bullied her or made her feel shitty. The more she talked, the more my heart broke for her. Sometimes it had been as easy as stuffing a note into her locker that said "Why are you so ugly?" or "You should just go kill yourself." or "I hope you're not contagious." One particularly motivated person graffitied a face on the wall of one of the buildings. The face had a bright red splotch on it and in all caps, "INDI = UGLY."

"That is seriously fucked-up."

"That was my life. In fact, remember the interview question, 'What do you strongly suspect but have no proof of'?"

I nodded.

"When I was in seventh grade, people spontaneously started calling me Juicy. They said it was because I looked like I fell asleep in a puddle of grape juice. And I strongly suspect, but have no proof, that Jessica, the girl who came up to us when we were having dinner with my parents, was the one who got people doing it."

Hudson frowned. "See? I knew there was something off about that girl. She seemed like one of those people who are uber-polite to the parents but are actually little shits behind their backs."

"You nailed it. That's exactly what she is. I mean, we were never friends; she could have just ignored us that night. But she didn't. I'm pretty sure she came up to us specifically to call me Juicy."

"I gotta tell you, Indi, you went to school with a lot of winners. It's easy to see why you started wearing makeup. I would have too just to shut those people up."

"Exactly. Thank you. So that's why what Denise said really frustrated me. It's admirable to teach Leah that her PWS is nothing to be ashamed of. My parents did that too. They told me I should display it proudly as something that was uniquely me. And I did for years, but eventually I just got so tired of the stares and the whispers and the bullying."

Indi went to stand near the gray railing which stood between the boardwalk and the lake. I came to stand next to her. The water was a good five feet below the level of the walking path and there was foliage and rocks. No beach to speak of.

"Did everything get better once you started using makeup?" I asked, wrapping an arm around her shoulders. She put her arm around my waist and snuggled closer.

With a small smile, she nodded. "Yes. For the first time in my life, I looked normal, like everybody else. I could go to the mall or to the movies or wherever and not draw any attention."

"That must have been incredible."

"Honestly? It felt like I'd been stuck in a chrysalis and finally emerged as a butterfly."

INDI

When I got home after my last class on The Big Night, Ruby leapt up from the couch.

"Finally!" she exclaimed. "A package came for you from Hudson and I'm dying to see what's inside."

On the kitchen table was a box about a yard long and a foot and a half wide. I picked it up and shook it. It didn't weigh much and a rustling noise came from inside.

"What do you think it is?" I asked, going to get scissors from my desk.

"I don't know for sure, but I've spent the last three hours imagining. Hurry up!"

Inside the plain ordinary brown cardboard box was another box, this one white with the words "One Night Only" in an elegant script on it.

Ruby squealed. "One Night Only is a company you can rent designer formal wear from and it's about time too. Men have been able to rent tuxes for like forever."

Intrigued and excited, I opened the white box inside of which was a two-layered, long sleeved black cocktail dress. I gasped as I shook it out then went to the mirror and held it up in front of me.

The inner layer was an opaque black silk. The outer layer and the sleeves were made of a sheer fabric covered with gold embroidered cranes.

I slanted her a look. "You knew about this."

She didn't even try to deny it.

"I helped him pick it out too. You need to try it on with the proper shoes."

Ruby left the room and returned with a pair of black high heels dangling from her hand.

The dress fit perfectly. The hem hit just below the knee and there was a sexy cut out in the back I hadn't noticed before. With Ruby's strappy heels on, I looked pretty good. Elegant and, well, grown-up.

A couple of hours later, Hudson arrived to pick me up. I knew I shouldn't compare, but the night Austin and I had planned to have sex, he hadn't taken me anywhere. He'd just come over one evening while my parents were at Slice. He'd been wearing a T-shirt, jeans and athletic shoes. I think the one choice he'd made for the "occasion" was to take a shower.

Hudson, on the other hand, looked like a dream in a tailored gray suit. His tie had black and gold stripes to match my dress and his black shoes were polished to a high gloss. Hudson in casual clothes was sexy personified. Hudson dressed up in a suit blew every standard for sexy out of the water.

"Hello, gorgeous," he said, kissing me.

"Back at you," I replied. "Thank you for the dress."

"My pleasure. You look...almost perfect," he said.

"Almost?" I said in mock indignation.

"You're just missing one tiny detail." He whipped a corsage out from nowhere and presented it to me.

As I opened the box, I caught the sweet scent of gardenia. I held the delicate flowers up to my nose to inhale deeply before sliding it onto my wrist. When I looked up, he had a matching boutonniere pinned to his lapel.

"It's beautiful. Thank you."

"You guys look so great together. Let me get some pictures," Ruby said.

After the mini photo shoot, Hudson thanked Ruby.

"Anytime. Where are you going?"

"That's for me know and her to find out," he said smiling at me.

Ruby scoffed. "Are you really not going to tell me?"

"I'll let Indi tell you tomorrow."

"I officially hate you, Hudson Forte," Ruby said.

He took me to one of the nicest restaurants in Burlington, Hen of the Wood. It was a farm-to-table place with a menu that depended on whatever was the freshest or ripest. Inside, the ceiling was especially striking. Beams intersected to create deeply recessed triangles that housed the warmly glowing lights. The large bar was crowded and the delectable aromas of food made my stomach growl.

People glanced at us curiously as we entered. Although Hudson wasn't the only man wearing a suit, no woman was as dressed up as I was. But as my mom always said, better to be overdressed than under.

"Reservation for two. The name is Forte," Hudson said.

"Yes, Mr. Forte. Right this way," the hostess said. "Prom?"

Hudson chuckled. "Yes. Prom."

"I didn't know they held proms in the fall," the hostess said.

"This one's special."

"Hudson," I said as he pulled my chair out for me. "why did you tell her it was our prom?"

He lifted one shoulder. "Maybe they'll give us a free dessert."

We drank some excellent champagne, ate amazing food like their signature mushroom toast, wood-fire roasted broccoli, hanger steak, and crushed potatoes with a tarragon aioli. For dessert, he ordered the ice cream trio and I got the honey tart and we shared. At the end of the meal, he refused to let me even look at the bill, and although it had to be the most expensive meal I'd ever consumed, I didn't put up much of a fight.

The drive back to his apartment only took three minutes, but that was long enough for butterflies to show up in my very full stomach. After he put the car in park, he turned to me and said, "I need you to wait here while I get some stuff ready. I'll be right back. Close your eyes."

"What?"

"Don't argue. Just close your eyes and keep them closed until I tell you. No peeking."

Even though I was dying of curiosity, I closed my eyes. A couple of minutes later, he was back, opening my door and leading me by the hand up the stairs to the door of his apartment. I stood at the threshold vibrating with excitement and nervousness.

"Okay…on three, open your eyes. One…two…three."

A confusing curtain of colorful crepe streamers blocked my entrance. I bit my lip as I crossed the threshold then gasped in amazement. A reflective, rotating disco ball hung suspended from the ceiling, creating a kaleidoscope of dazzling color and light. More streamers arced across the room from corner to corner. A moment later, some upbeat music began to play and I saw he'd cleared a space in the center of the living room.

"What is all this?" I asked, still agape in wonder.

Smiling, he gestured with his finger for me to turn around.

On the wall behind me was a big, hand-painted sign that said, "Indi's Prom: The Sequel." Below that was a photo booth station with glittery props—his and her crowns, wacky eyeglasses, moustaches and beards and "My prom date is a hottie!" and "A Night to Remember" signs.

The corsage suddenly made sense. So did the prom comment at the restaurant. I turned in a slow circle, staring at it all, unable to speak. He'd gone to so much trouble to try and fix one of the most horrible nights of my life. I remembered the Monday after the prom having to lie to everyone at school and say I was sick. And when I'd returned the dress to the store, they gave me dirty looks.

Hudson came to stand beside me, a worried expression on his face. "Indi, say something. Do you like it?" he asked over the music.

I threw my arms around his neck. "It's the most wonderful thing anyone's ever done for me."

Then I couldn't help it. I started crying.

"Hey, hey, don't cry," he said, laughing.

"They're happy tears," I told him. "Very happy tears. My first ever."

"I guess it's a night of firsts. How about this song?" He raised his index finger. "I thought it was particularly appropriate."

As I listened, he started dancing, snapping his fingers, kicking his feet out and singing along with "Wake Me Up Before You Go Go." Laughing, I took my shoes off and joined him. Dancing with him was free and easy, mostly because no one was watching, but also because he inserted silly moves, naming them as he performed them.

"Target!" He pranced forward and back pretending to put items into an invisible grocery cart. "Come on, do the Target."

Laughing, I followed his lead.

"Pepper grinder!" We both ground imaginary pepper to the beat.

"Lasso!" We made like cowboys twirling ropes above our heads. "And *double* lasso!" Two ropes and goofy grins.

Each time he called out a move, I tried to copy him but it was hard to breathe because I was laughing so hard.

I honestly had never had so much fun dancing. We made full use of the photo station and danced a bunch more but then a slow song came on. With a relaxed smile, he took me into his arms and held me close as we swayed to the music. I could feel his heart beating against my cheek. The deep bass of it comforted me, calmed me.

"Hudson, this...you..." I looked up, unable to express my feelings. As a child, I'd received a bounty of love from my adoptive parents. The home they provided me, their guidance, their attention...it was all for me. I had no siblings. But what Hudson had done tonight made me feel cherished in a completely different way. He'd done all this of his own free will, out of a desire to give me a special experience. He'd been worried about tonight not living up to my expectations, but he needn't have been. He'd already far exceeded anything I could have imagined.

He smiled down at me and kissed me. The moment our lips touched, my body seemed to wake up. I was suddenly very aware of the very hard, very male body touching mine. Crazy how I'd forgotten that tonight wasn't just about dancing or taking silly selfies. It was about sex.

I was going to finally have sex.

His mouth moved over mine and I gave myself up to the kiss. Surrounded by the slow tempo song and the swirling lights, we stood there kissing and swaying. His hands roamed over my back down to my butt and I made a breathless noise.

With a groan, he slid his tongue inside to deepen the kiss. He took his time exploring my mouth, the kiss a tantalizing slide into a place where nothing mattered except Hudson. I felt a sweet insistent ache between my legs and when he pulled me closer, his erection pressed against my belly and that got me even more excited.

"God, Indi," he said against my lips as he hiked my dress up. "I want you so much."

A moment later, his hands were sliding into my underwear and over my butt again. My body arched and I found myself fumbling with his zipper, pulling it down and pushing my hand inside to find him hot and hard. He groaned loudly and, not to be outdone, he cupped me with his palm then stroked me softly. Pleasure surged through me, hot and intense, better than anything I'd ever felt before, but I wanted more. I wanted his hands on me, everywhere. I wanted us naked and horizontal, skin to skin, no barriers.

The only problem was, I really liked what he was doing with his fingers. I didn't want him to stop, not even for the two minutes it would take to get naked and in bed, but he withdrew his hand and took a step back. He was breathing hard and his eyes were blazing with hunger. For me.

"Ready?" he asked. "Obviously, I am."

His cock stuck out of his pants at a sharp upward angle. I imagined him pushing it inside me, thrusting and thrusting, and another surge of agonizing want swept over me.

"I'm more than ready."

He took my hand and led me to the bedroom. Here, too, he'd worked some magic. Lit candles flickered, bathing the room in a golden glow. All the decorative pillows were gone and the bed was turned down like at a fancy hotel, but unlike any hotel I'd ever been to, there were delicate pink rose petals scattered across the sheets.

He smiled as he reached for the hem of my dress and pulled it up over my head. I hadn't worn a bra because of the cutout on the back of the dress and the sudden chill made me shiver. I stood there in nothing but my black lace panties, panties I'd bought just for tonight.

"God, Indi, you're beautiful."

My face flushed as his eyes roved over me, drinking in every detail, and I reveled in his attention. Somehow his words felt true and real in a way that they never had when my parents had uttered them. Truthfully, it didn't matter if my parents thought I was beautiful. It meant everything that Hudson did.

Intoxicated with confidence, I turned around for him, spinning slowly so he could get the full 3-D Indi experience. He stared at me reverently and I could hear his labored breathing. As I finally completed my turn and faced him again, he pulled his tie off and let it fall to the floor. His fingers undid his shirt buttons like they were white hot. In moments, he was bare-chested and all his gloriously defined muscles were on display. As he shucked his shoes, pants and boxer briefs, I stepped out of my undies and when I looked up, he was naked too.

Our eyes met. His lips curved in a slow smile as he cradled my head in his hands and kissed me again. This time, our bodies pressed together too. Again, I was lost in this entirely new sensation. There was so much to take in. His skin was hot, his body incredibly hard and solid. I felt the hair on his chest against my breasts, his big hands caressing my waist, my back, my hips, my butt. But most of all, I felt his cock burning against my belly.

He bore me down to the bed his body on top of mine. I started to spread my legs, but he didn't seem intent on getting between them, so there was a moment of awkwardness as our legs bumped, but I got over it quickly, because he was kissing his way to my breasts, one of which he was caressing with his hand. He brushed the nipple with his thumb, sending sparks of pleasure to my sex. Then his mouth descended.

I got dizzy as he swirled his tongue around my nipple. He flicked and teased the hard tip and the scientific part of my brain wondered how many nerve endings were centered there but then he closed his lips around it and sucked and all rational thought left my head. The rhythmic pull of his mouth made me restless. I grabbed handfuls of his hair and rubbed my leg against his flank. When he moved away from my breasts, I whimpered until I felt his lips on my stomach where he laid a path of warm kisses as he parted my legs.

My heart pounded and I rose up on my elbows. Was he going to…?

Then I felt his hot mouth on me.

Yes. Yes, he was.

25

HUDSON

My dick was literally aching and all I needed was a soft breeze and I'd go off like a Roman candle, so I decided to cool off a little by going down on her.

I kissed my way down her stomach, going slowly and watching for any signals she didn't want this. As for me, I was always up for a BJ, but I'd been with girls who didn't want my face anywhere near their pussy.

Indi didn't seem to be one of them. When I put some gentle pressure on her thighs, she parted them for me and her spicy scent drew me closer. She was perfection from the soft thatch of black hair to the plump lips that I parted gently with my thumbs. Inhaling deeply, I put my mouth on her and licked.

Fuuuuuck. The taste of her intoxicated me—smoke, musk, and a salty sweetness that I couldn't get enough of. I lapped at her lazily, exploring her with my tongue while she lay here panting.

"Does that feel good?" I asked between licks. Her clit had stiffened and I circled it with the pad of my finger.

"Yes. It feels so good that if you stop, I'll have to kill you."

I laughed softly and used my tongue to stroke that small nub until she started moaning and rocking her hips, silently asking for more. I kept it up, sucking, nibbling, laving her. I could tell from the noises she was making that she was close. That's when I went at her harder, when she shifted away, I followed.

That's it, Indi, let it come, I thought. *You're almost there.*

Then with a sharp gasp, she grabbed my head and shuddered against my mouth. Her pussy pulsed against my tongue and her panting cries were muffled because her thighs were clamped over my ears.

Triumphant, I stayed with her until her orgasm faded and she relaxed onto the mattress, then I reached for one of the condoms I'd left on the nightstand. After sheathing myself, I lubed it up too. Every article I read said this was a good idea for a girl's first time. It made sense to me. But, fuck, she looked plenty wet. My cock was so primed, I was literally gritting my teeth and thinking about face-off strategies to keep myself from coming before I even got started.

Her silky black hair was spread against the pillow. She was flushed and a little sweaty, still breathing hard. A few rose petals were stuck to her skin.

"You look so beautiful right now," I said, sitting back on my haunches.

"You keep saying that."

"Because it's true." I ran a hand down her stomach and stroked her pussy. "Are you ready?"

She nodded. "As ready as I'll ever be."

"If you feel any pain, don't be shy. I want you to tell me. We do this at your pace."

I reached between us and nestled my cock against her entrance.

"Fuck," I swore. Her pussy scorched me and the fear that I'd go off too early reared its head again.

She tensed. "Did I do something wrong?"

"No. You're fine. I'm fine. Everything's fine."

Maybe if I said it enough times, I could make it true.

Smiling through the torture, I got myself in position again and swallowed a groan as I pushed the head of my cock in, slowly but steadily.

"Are you okay?"

She nodded but had a slight frown on her forehead. "It's... uncomfortable, but not painful."

I got the head in but then met with some resistance. She was incredibly tight, tighter than I'd expected and as I worked my cock inside her with short probing strokes, every moment that passed I got one step closer to blowing my wad.

It was the most excruciating exercise in control ever devised.

Eventually, I felt the vise grip on my dick loosen. I was making headway now with each tentative thrust.

"Indi, are you okay? How does it feel?"

She didn't answer, so I just kept rocking my hips, inching inside bit by bit until finally, I was fully sheathed, balls deep. I was panting like I'd just run a mile.

The urge to thrust was intense. Everything inside me demanded action. Suddenly I knew what a horse at the starting gate felt like. But I took it slow, keeping my movements relaxed and easy. I was determined to make it good for her and wasn't going to ruin it by losing control now.

When she started rubbing my back and the line between her eyebrows disappeared, I knew she'd turned the corner.

I kissed her deeply as I started pumping in earnest. She moaned into my mouth and started to meet my thrusts. The moment she started responding was the moment my orgasm decided it was tired of waiting. I broke into a sweat trying to stave it off. I couldn't come yet, not until she did.

I shut my ears to the desperate mewling sounds she was making, the way she was writhing beneath me. I tried not to think about how her hot velvety pussy opened for me as I drove myself into her again and again. I just needed to last another minute...

On my next thrust, Indi suddenly scissored her legs together, keeping me buried to the hilt inside her. She bucked off the bed, hands fisting in the sheets as her pussy contracted around my cock. I came harder than I'd ever come before. The pleasure blew the top off my head and my balls erupted for what seemed like an eternity.

INDI

I'd done it. I'd literally done it. I was now a sexually active woman.

I couldn't have planned a better first time if I'd tried. Hudson had made it a perfect night. He'd been so patient and careful, and talk about skilled... I really hadn't expected to come once, let alone twice. I mean, talk about starting with a bang.

The next morning, we had sex again, and even though it was great, I did regret it a little because the soreness between my legs lasted until the afternoon. Ruby recommended a hot bath with Epsom salt and our apartment only had a small shower.

But Hudson's *en suite* bathroom had a tub, so I returned that night.

Of course, we couldn't keep our hands off each other, especially when he saw me naked in the steaming hot water, my hair pinned up, my breasts just breaking the surface.

"God, you look so sexy," he said.

Smiling, I tickled my nipples with my fingertips.

He swallowed hard, his eyes glued to my breasts. "I'd better leave. I promised myself I wouldn't have sex with you. You came here because you were sore."

I could see a prominent bulge in his jeans and just the sight of him hard and ready caused a heat to bloom between my legs.

"I'm not that sore," I said.

He stared at me a while, gauging my seriousness. "Don't toy with me, Indi."

"I'm not. I want it. I want it as much as you do."

With a groan, he stripped off his clothes in nothing flat. I stood up and even though I was soaking wet, he picked me up in his arms and deposited me on top of the bed. As he fumbled with the condom, I urged him to hurry.

"I'm moving as fast as I can," he said with a laugh.

That moment when he pushed into me...the pleasure was so intense my eyes rolled back into my head. It hurt a little, but I didn't care. I wanted it hard. I wanted it fast. He seemed to understand that without me telling him, or maybe he was just as worked up as I was.

It wasn't long before I was coming apart, intense pleasure flooding me as Hudson came with a prolonged groan. We lay there, limp and wrung out until that inevitable moment when he pulled out and went to dispose of the condom.

"Want a cold pack again?" he asked.

I shook my head. "I'll be fine. I just want to cuddle in bed."

He slid between the sheets and spooned me. I loved the feel of his big hard body cradling me. His breath sifted through my hair and I couldn't have been more content.

"Thanksgiving is coming up," he said.

"I know. Are you going home too?"

"I think so."

I sighed. "I don't want to be apart for a whole week."

"Can't get enough of my amazing bod?" he joked.

I reached back and gave him a light smack on the behind. "That's the pot calling the kettle black."

That's when I got the idea.

"What if we spend it together?" I asked. "We could spend a few days with your family and a few with mine. My parents have been hinting around that we should come for a visit and I keep telling them you have hockey games on the weekends. Thanksgiving break is the perfect solution."

"I don't know, Indi. My family's pretty intense. Sometimes there's drama." He scoffed. "Who am I kidding? There's usually drama."

"I'm sure I can handle it. What I *can't* handle," I said with a sly smile, "is being separated for a whole week. I mean, think about it. If we take this trip, we could have sex every single night." I wiggled my butt against him in case he needed more encouragement.

His arm tightened around my waist and he growled into my hair. "Woman, you don't realize what you're getting yourself into. How about this? We spend the first few days with your parents, go to my house for Thanksgiving and come back here Friday? That way, we spend a minimal amount of time with my crazy family and you'll still have the weekend to study."

I loved that he knew me well enough to know that I couldn't ignore school, even during Thanksgiving break. So what if his family was intense? So were my parents. I was convinced this little mini vacation would be dreamy.

The trip to Brattleboro only took a couple of hours. We took his Jeep because it was far more reliable than my car and would handle better if it started snowing. We'd just pulled up to my parents' house when I laid a hand on his arm.

"Before we go inside, I want to warn you about a couple things," I said.

"That sounds ominous," he said with a laugh as he engaged the parking brake.

"My parents like to greet me with a group hug when I come home for a visit and...I'm not sure if they're going to pull you into it or not."

"No worries," he said. "I'm not opposed to a group hug."

"Well, this one lasts a while." I glanced at the house. "Like almost a full minute. I'm not exaggerating."

"Bring it on," he said.

We got our bags from the back and headed up the concrete front walk. The home I grew up in was a plain two-story house with a garden that was spectacular in any other season, but now was nothing more than a collection of empty dirt plots and leafless shrubs and trees. My parents had grown vegetables for the pizzeria long before farm-to-table became a thing, so the entire backyard was like a mini farm.

We didn't even get to the front door before it swung open and my mom and dad tumbled out of the house, arms outstretched.

The welcoming hug started out with just me and my parents, but after several moments, my dad waved an arm at Hudson, who joined in for the latter half of it.

"It's so wonderful to see you again, Hudson," my mom exclaimed as we finally made our way inside. "You and Indi will be up in her old room. Why don't you go up and get settled? Kevin and I have some work to do but we can all head over to Slice around eleven thirty, if that's okay."

"Pizza for lunch sounds good to me" Hudson said.

I led the way up the stairs and down the hall to my room. Even thought it was larger than my room at Carter Hall, it seemed smaller. Maybe that was because, with his large frame, Hudson seemed to fill up all the empty space.

"This is so embarrassing," I said, looking at the posters, the purple walls, stuffed animals, and flowery comforter.

"Don't be embarrassed. I love this. I didn't know you were a reader of anything but textbooks and prep manuals." He knelt to peruse my bookshelf which held everything from Dr. Seuss and Harry Potter to Julia Quinn and Anne McCaffrey.

"It's hard to find time to read for fun these days. Someday, I'll get back to it."

"I hear you. Same, except I've got studying *and* hockey. I sometimes listen to books while I'm working out, but I like reading actual books better."

We spent the next two hours sitting cross-legged next to my bookshelf talking about our favorite books. My parents were avid readers too, so lunch at Slice was spent discussing even more books and then books that had been turned into movies.

Hudson was fascinated by the restaurant, so before the dinner rush, we took him into the back and showed him how to make a pizza. It was pretty hilarious to watch. He got cheese everywhere and his crust was comically uneven and misshapen, but it was a testament to our ingredients and the recipe for the salami and hot honey creation my parents had recreated that his pizza still turned out delicious.

"Since we saw you last, we tested, what, Bonnie?" my dad asked. "About a dozen different honeys?"

"That sounds about right. All from local honey producers."

"And how many salamis?"

"Six or seven. We settled on *finocchiona* sourced from Tuscany. The fennel in it really complemented the honey."

I had to agree. The version we'd had in Boston had been tasty, but you could get Genoa at the grocery store. My parents preferred higher end ingredients.

"So it's going on the menu?" I asked.

"It's going to be launched as our Black Friday special," my mom confirmed. "People will be able to get it at half price for one day only."

"Nice," Hudson said.

"What are you going to call it?" I asked, because while we had no problem using other people's recipes, for some reason, we didn't poach the names people came up with.

"We decided to call it the Bee-licious Special," my mom said.

"Love it," I exclaimed.

Hudson and I ended up staying to help with the dinner rush. Hudson wanted to "perfect" his pizza prep skills and to everyone's surprise, it didn't take him long to get proficient. Before long, he was speedily rolling and stretching out the dough, then adding the toppings like a pro. Several times during the evening, I got meaningful looks from my parents that said they were impressed with him.

"You know what it means if you serve a pizza in hockey?" Hudson asked, spreading tomato sauce with the small ladle.

None of us did. In the kitchen, there was me, my dad, and four other cooks.

"It means your pass went right up the center of the ice only to be intercepted by the opposing team. If you're serving up pizzas on the ice, your teammates aren't going to be happy with you."

"Hey, that reminds me," my dad said. "I saw on the news that the Zamboni driver at the local rink is missing."

"Really?" Hudson said. "I hope nothing's wrong."

"Well, last I heard, they think he'll resurface."

A pause and then Hudson laughed. "Good one, Kevin."

"Oh no," I said. "Now you've done it."

"Done what?"

"Dad loves telling bad jokes."

"Hey!" my dad protested. "That Zamboni one was good!"

"And if you encourage him," I continued, ducking the piece of pepperoni my dad had thrown at me, "it's like throwing fuel on the fire. Don't waste the product, Dad!"

"I'll show you fueling the fire," he said, then yelling, "Team, why do hockey rinks have rounded corners?"

Everyone in the kitchen, including Hudson, said, "WHY?"

"Because if they were ninety degrees, the ice would melt!"

I gave Hudson a look but he was laughing with everyone else and thus, we were rewarded with several more minutes of hockey jokes that I knew my dad had looked up and memorized just for our visit.

When we got home around midnight, my parents said good night and went to their room while Hudson and I went to mine.

"My parents were so impressed with you. Everyone was. In fact, my dad said if you ever flunk out of hockey, you could have a job at Slice."

"God forbid," Hudson said. "I mean, it was a lot of fun, but night after night? I couldn't hack it. I had no idea how much work was involved in running a restaurant," Hudson said. "It was nonstop for *hours*. And then when all the customers are finally gone you have to clean everything." He shuddered for emphasis. "And the heat! I finally understand that saying about it being too hot in the kitchen."

"I'm convinced that's why so many restaurants fail. People don't realize how hard it is."

He took me in his arm and nuzzled my neck. "You smell like pizza," he said.

"You do too. It's an occupational hazard. I usually take a shower after I work a shift there."

"Sounds like a plan."

He started undressing, but I hesitated before I began rubbing my face with one of my makeup-removing wipes. When I finally joined him in the shower, he greeted me with a broad smile.

"There's that beautiful birthmark," he said, brushing a thumb over it.

I glanced away. "It still feels weird, letting you see it."

"The more you do it, the easier it'll get. Pretty soon, it'll be second nature." He caressed my backside and kissed my shoulder. "You feel like fooling around?"

"Why do you think I got in here with you?"

He grinned as he pulled me to him and covered my mouth with his. We'd never had shower sex before, but I had to say, anything that involved Hudson's body, wet and naked, was worth doing.

27

INDI

The next morning, the smell of coffee woke me up. Hudson was still out like a light so I snuck out of the room in search of caffeine. My mother loved flavored creamers and so did I. She usually dedicated a whole row of the fridge door to them.

"There's my beautiful girl," my mom said as I entered the kitchen.

Unlike the commercial kitchen at Slice, which was all industrial stainless steel and white subway tile, our family kitchen was small and cozy, with moss green walls and antique wooden cabinetry. The fridge was covered with pictures of me at various ages, coupons of every sort and take-out menus.

I got myself a mug and filled it with coffee and a liberal amount of pumpkin spice creamer while my mom pulled ingredients out of the fridge.

"I thought I'd make breakfast pizza this morning," she said.

"Breakfast pizza. Trying to impress Hudson?" I asked.

She smiled. "I'm certainly not going to toss cereal boxes on the table."

"Honestly, he'd be fine with that."

"Well, it's not every day my daughter brings home a boy who could star in his own season of *The Bachelor*."

"That's not too far from the truth," I said. "He's one of the stars of the hockey team and girls fall all over themselves to talk to him. After games, especially."

"But he didn't go on a week-long road trip with any of them," my mom pointed out. "Are you two serious?"

"Mom, don't. We're just enjoying each other's company right now. Hockey keeps him very busy and I'm scheduled to take the MCAT at the end of January. Neither of us have a lot of time."

As she mixed frozen shredded potatoes, shredded cheese and eggs together in a bowl, my mom shrugged. "People make time for what's important to them and if you ask me, you're very important to Hudson." She sprayed a sheet pan with olive oil, dumped the mixture onto the tray and began shaping it into a circle. "He's head over heels with you."

"He is not."

"Oh, really? Last night was all about impressing you."

"No, it wasn't. It was about impressing you and Dad."

My mom shook her head. "We'll have to agree to disagree on that one. He kept stealing glances at you while you were working, and when you and Walt were talking about that music video, he quietly glowered. In fact, if memory serves, that was right before he started spinning the pizza pan on his finger and singing 'That's Amore.'"

Out loud, I poo-pooed that, but the idea that Hudson had been jealous last night amused me. I was so in love with him, I could barely think of anything else, but I had no idea if he felt the same way, so any evidence he did was more than welcome.

"Well," she said, popping the pan into the oven to bake, "I can think of worse things than being married to a professional athlete."

"Mom, shhh!" I glanced toward the stairs, terrified Hudson had come down unnoticed.

He hadn't, thank God.

"We haven't even talked about being exclusive." I wrapped my hands around my coffee mug.

"Do you want to be exclusive?" she asked.

"Maybe," I hedged, but at her arched eyebrow, I gave in. "Okay, yes. I absolutely hate the idea of him dating anyone else but me."

"Then you should have a conversation with him, let him know where you stand." She chopped some bacon and tossed it in the hot cast iron skillet. The tantalizing aroma filled the room.

"But I don't want to scare him off," I said, still keeping an eye on the stairs.

"Indi, honey, I understand that, but you owe it to yourself to be with someone who recognizes how wonderful you are and wants to be with you as much as you want to be with him."

Of course, I agreed with her in theory. It was obviously a bad idea when one half of a couple was wildly in love, while the other was indifferent. But when, against all odds, you ended up with someone completely out of your league, better safe than sorry. That way, when they took off looking for greener pastures, you weren't taken by surprise.

After the crust had cooked for a while, my mother cracked four eggs over it, tossed on more cheese and finished it with the bacon before putting it back in the oven. My dad and Hudson wandered downstairs just as the timer went off.

"Good morning," Hudson said before leaning down to give me a kiss.

"Good morning. There's coffee there on the counter," my mom said, pointing with the oven mitt on her hand. "Hudson, how did you sleep?"

"Coffee sounds great. Thank you. I slept like a baby. Is that… are we having pizza for breakfast?"

"Yes we are," my dad said as he took a seat at the table. "Bonnie makes the best breakfast pizza. She always gets the hash browns really crispy. I like to dump ketchup and sriracha on mine."

"Don't take this the wrong way, but do you have pizza at every meal?" Hudson asked.

"It sure seems like it sometimes," I quipped.

"Funny story," my dad said, "when I was a kid, I loved pizza day at school and I would often say, 'I'd eat pizza every day, if I could,' and look at me now."

"I'd probably eat pizza every day if it was pizza like you make at Slice," Hudson said. "I have to tell you, I don't usually eat all the crust on my pizza, but yours is so good. Crispy on the outside and chewy on the inside."

"It's the oven. It's an antique, imported from Italy."

"Really?"

My dad laughed. "No. The oven was from a kit we got from a company in Salinas, California. But it really does make the best crust."

My dad then talked about his beloved pizza oven, Marge, short for Margherita for the next fifteen minutes—the eight-hundred-degree temperatures necessary for cooking the pizzas, how the draft and ventilation system created and maintained those temperatures, how we could bake one hundred pizzas per hour in it…

Poor Hudson. I'd warned him my parents could be a little much.

Eventually, my mom said, "Enough about Marge, Kevin. I want to find out how these two met. I meant to ask you when we were in Boston but I forgot."

I glanced at Hudson and my cheeks warmed. There was no way I was telling my parents about walking in on Hudson and my ex-roommate. Or about how I crashed into him and turned his shirt into a Jackson Pollock painting.

Luckily, Hudson said, "We are taking the same photography class and we paired up for a project."

"Oh, something creative. How nice," my mom said. "What was the project?"

We told them about the interviews we had to conduct and showed them the results, and my mother noticed the photographs I had from the dumpling-making day.

"What are those?" She peered closer. "It looks like you're cooking something."

"They're dumplings," I said.

"Really? Those are the weirdest shaped dumplings I've ever seen," my mom said, having enlarged one of the photos.

"They may be weird," Hudson said, "but they taste like heaven." He kissed his fingers in appreciation. Ruby and I had made a couple of batches since then. They were handy to keep in the freezer and cheap to make.

"One of Ruby's old professors is Chinese and she invited me and Ruby over to make dumplings," I explained.

My parents exchanged a glance.

"What's that look?" I asked.

"We're just...surprised," my dad said.

"Ever since I can remember," my mom said, "you've been adamantly opposed to anything Chinese. We tried to introduce you to all sorts of things, but you refused to cooperate. We even signed up for a summer camp for families with children adopted from China, which we thought sounded perfect. The kids had activities—dancing, crafts and games and the adults had their own sessions about the phases of adoption and our children's heritage. But you cried for hours and begged us not to make you go."

"You actually screamed at the top of your lungs," my dad said. "It was a fit like you'd never thrown before so, against our better judgement, we cancelled the trip."

"I...don't remember that," I said. I searched my memory and found nothing, but that didn't mean anything. There was a lot about my childhood that was a blur.

"How old was I?"

"About six, I think," my mom said.

My dad nodded in agreement. "So, even though we didn't go to the camp, we tried to teach you about your heritage, but you made it clear you didn't want anything to do with your birthplace, so eventually, we gave up."

I sat there, stunned and speechless at this revelation. I'd been harboring a grudge against China since I was a little girl and forced my parents to go along with it.

"I had no idea," I said. "All this time, I thought you were just, I don't know, trying to make me assimilate more fully as an American."

"You thought we were racists?" my dad asked, looking hurt.

"No! No, I didn't, honestly. If you were racist, you would have adopted a white girl."

"But you thought we valued our culture over yours," Dad said.

"I did, yes, but I know now that isn't true."

Hudson cleared his throat. "You know what this means, right?"

"What?" I asked.

"It means you've got to make us dumplings for dinner," he said.

My parents agreed wholeheartedly. "That sounds wonderful!" my mom exclaimed.

"Can you make enough for staff meal?" my dad asked.

"I can. We can," I said, glancing at Hudson. "The recipe makes a lot."

As I got a piece of paper to write down a list of what we needed to pick up from the grocery store, I was filled with a relief I couldn't even describe. I'd come to think that part of my reluctance to explore my Chinese side came from the mistaken belief that my parents wouldn't like it. I owed them so much and I tried never to displease them out of respect and love. But now that I knew the truth—that they *wanted* me to embrace my heritage—I was free to be as Chinese as I wanted. What a revelation.

28

HUDSON

I hadn't understood until this road trip how much it took for Indi to "make herself presentable"—her words, not mine. I'd thought she put on something to cover up the birthmark and then regular makeup on top of that. Boy, was I wrong.

I know this because on the day we were setting out for Brooklyn for part two of our Thanksgiving road trip, I convinced her to let me watch her do her face and it took a long time and a bag full of products—stuff to moisturize, stuff to prime, stuff to cancel out the purple, stuff to conceal. And there was so much blending. I swear, she spent half the time dabbing at her face with a sponge so it looked smooth. Eventually, she put on stuff I was more familiar with—mascara, eye shadow, blush.

When she was done, she turned and smiled at me. "Here it is. Totally worth the effort, right?"

"You look beautiful, as always," I said in a tone that must have pinged her radar in some way.

Narrowing her eyes, she put her hands on her hips. "But…?"

I hesitated to tell her what I really felt, but in the end, decided honesty was the best policy. All I wanted was for her to realize, to me and her parents and everyone who loved her, she was perfect the way she was and nothing extra was required.

"But...is it all or nothing?" I asked. "There's no middle ground? Because with girls I know, even my mom, there's like a sliding scale of stuff they do to their face...like a light version for like just going to the grocery store or wherever. Like just mascara and blush, you know?"

I knew from the frosty expression on her face that I'd stepped in it.

"Oh my God, Hudson, it's like you didn't just watch me go through my whole routine. No, I don't have a light version of my face to fall back on. I wish I had the choice, believe me, I do, but I can't just go out with mascara and blush like other women."

"When was the last time you went out without makeup?" I asked.

She scowled at me. "Not counting that time I ran into you at the Marketplace, eight years ago."

"And you were how old?"

"Thirteen. We've been over this. I told you that day at Waterfront Park how much I was bullied, that my life was a misery before I started wearing makeup."

"I remember. But you were just a kid back then. At that age, we're all fucked-up and insecure, surrounded for seven hours a day by other fucked-up insecure little pricks. But it's got to be different now that you're older. Plus, society has made a little progress too, hasn't it? I mean not too long ago, hockey players slung homophobic slurs around as a matter of course. These days, at least on the ice, there are fines and punishments. People in general are more sensitive, aren't they?"

"You know, if I'd known when you asked to see my makeup routine I was going to get lectured afterward, I would never have said yes."

"Indi, I'm sorry. I didn't mean to lecture you."

"Damn straight. You have *no* idea what I've been through or what it's like to look like me. You look like a Greek god, for shit's sake. You do realize that, don't you? Unless something major happens to your face—God forbid—you'll never know what it's like. You'll never be told your face would make a great Halloween costume or watch people back away from you because they're afraid they're going to catch whatever disease it is you've got. So do me a favor. Until you've experienced that firsthand, keep your suggestions to yourself."

Then she announced she was going for a walk, alone, and left the house.

In the aftermath when I went downstairs, Bonnie said, "How about a nice cup of hot cocoa?"

"With marshmallows?"

"Of course with marshmallows."

"That sounds perfect," I said, sitting down at the table.

She put some water into her electric kettle and turned it on then got out two mugs and two packets of instant.

"You heard, I take it?" I asked.

"I heard some kind of argument going on. Indi gets loud when she gets angry."

"And boy, was she angry."

"But I don't know what it was about."

I told her.

"Her birthmark is a touchy subject, that's for sure," Bonnie said. "Always has been. I will tell you, though, it's a sign of how much she trusts you that she lets you see it."

"Yeah, but that doesn't negate the fact that I royally fu—er, messed up. She's probably out there right now buying a bus ticket back to Burlington so she won't have to come to Brooklyn with me."

Bonnie shook her head. "Trust me. I know my daughter. Indi's crazy about you. And for the record, so are Kevin and I. You're exactly what she needs, Hudson."

"Oh? What's that? A guy who can't seem to resist pushing his girlfriend's buttons?"

"From what you told me, you didn't push any buttons on purpose and Indi will realize that. Eventually." Bonnie poured the boiling water into the mugs and brought them to the table along with two spoons.

I cleared my throat. "I believe I was promised marshmallows."

"Oops!"

She jumped back up, dug out a bag of mini-marshmallows and laughingly shook some into our mugs. I stirred mine a little longer to get the marshmallows all gooey, then took a sip.

"Man, this hits the spot. Thank you."

"Not at all," she said, sipping her own cocoa with her spoon. "Now as I was saying, Indi will realize she overreacted and when she comes back, she'll apologize."

"And I'll apologize right back. She was right. I *don't* know what it's like to have a birthmark on my face. I should have just kept my mouth shut."

"I disagree."

I blinked at her in surprise.

"If you ask me, the makeup is a crutch that she's been using far too long. Don't get me wrong. I have nothing against makeup. I really don't. It helped her get through a very rough time, but at the risk of mixing metaphors, it's time she started riding without the training wheels. It's always been her dad's and my hope that she wear the makeup to enhance, not to hide."

"Yes, exactly! That's exactly what I want too, I just didn't know how to put it into words. But how can we do that?"

She smiled ruefully. "I think *we* can't to anything. This is something Indi has to figure out for herself. All we can do is support her."

Bonnie did indeed know her daughter. When Indi came back, she immediately walked up to me and hugged me fiercely. It wasn't until that moment that I realized how on edge I was. On some level I had been afraid I'd ruined everything and destroyed her trust and that when she came back she'd break up with me. But now, with her face pressed into my chest and her arms around me, those fears flew away.

"I'm sorry I blew up at you," she said, her voice muffled. "You didn't deserve it."

"And I'm sorry I was an insensitive jerk."

She stepped back and looked up at me. "You weren't being insensitive. I was the one being *over*sensitive. I just…" She shook her head. "I thought you understood why I wear makeup."

"I do. I do understand."

"Good. Then we never have to talk about it again. It's my choice. Mine. You don't get a say."

"Of course not. It's your face."

"Exactly."

We were about fifteen minutes away from my parents' house when I said to Indi, "Remember how you had to warn me about your mom and dad's group hug?"

"Yes."

"Well, I wanted to warn you that my parents like extravagance, they like to spend money. Understated is a four-letter word."

"I don't care. I just want to see where you grew up."

"I actually only lived a couple of years in the State Street house. I was born in Philadelphia where my dad played for three years. Then he was traded to Boston. We spent five years there. Then the rest of his career, eleven more years, we've been here in Brooklyn but in three different houses."

"That's a lot of moving," she said. "Occupational hazard?"

"Yep," I said, wiggling my finger in my ear. "One that's a lot more disruptive than smelling like pizza."

"Still hearing that noise?" she asked.

I'd noticed a high-pitched ringing when we were driving from Burlington to Brattleboro and thought something was going on with the Jeep, but then I'd heard it again yesterday afternoon when we were in the Briscoes' living room.

"Yeah," I said, frowning. "It comes and goes."

"It's called tinnitus. I get that too once in a while. I happen to know that it can be caused by a build-up of ear wax. There are kits you can get at the pharmacy to clean out your ears. We could get you one if you want."

"Look at you, getting your doctor on," I teased.

She laughed and punched me in the arm playfully. "Stop it. I'm a long way from being a doctor."

"Let's give it a try. This is three times in the past few days."

We stopped at a drug store to get the ear wax kit and a decongestant. My head was feeling a little stuffy and I wondered if that could be a factor too. I made a mental note to do more research on tinnitus if cleaning my ears didn't make it go away.

"Do me a favor. Don't mention the tinnitus to anyone, okay?"

"Why?"

I sighed. "I might as well tell you. You're going to see it first-hand as soon as we get there."

"See what?"

"My family has no boundaries when it comes to me. I told you all about how I'm the only one of my generation to be drafted…"

"No, you told me you'd been drafted, but not that you were the only one. How many of your cousins play hockey?"

"Three."

"And you're the only one who was good enough?"

I shrugged. "Anyway, the family has a reputation to uphold, which means *I* have a reputation to uphold, so everyone feels like they have a stake in my career, which means they all think nothing of sticking their noses into every aspect of my life."

"How annoying. Can't you tell them to stop?"

"I've tried, but it doesn't work. It's better to just not give them any ammunition in the first place. Trust me."

29

HUDSON

"Hudson!" Tears in her eyes, my mom embraced me with a squeal then leaned back.

She was a beautiful woman, my mom—tall and lithe with loads of blond hair and a body she worked hard to maintain. She was gracious and warm and loving, generous to a fault and loved company, but she was no pushover. She couldn't be, not and be married to my dad.

"Smile," she commanded me.

I obeyed and, as per our ritual, she inspected my mouth, saw that I still had all my teeth, then patted me on the cheek.

"Where's Dad?" I asked.

My mom waved a hand. "He had something to go to in Minneapolis. He promised he'd be back tomorrow in time for dinner. Indi, darling. I'm so glad you could come."

"Thank you for having me," Indi said after the obligatory hug. "You have a beautiful home, Mrs. Forte."

"Call me Marlene. Would you like a tour?" my mother asked.

"I'd love one," Indi replied.

Even though I'd told Indi to expect lavishness, I could tell she was still awestruck. I didn't blame her. I should have told her about the temperature controlled 1500 bottle capacity wine cellar in the basement; the rooftop terrace where the hot tub was, the third-floor terrace off the second kitchen (yes, *second* kitchen) that was part herb garden, part lounge area; and the phenomenal view of the Manhattan skyline, visible from the fourth and fifth floors.

I worried she was going to look at me differently after she saw, in person, how wealthy we were. It had happened before. Friends who had been perfectly comfortable around me before became suddenly awkward once they realized either who my family was and/or how much money we had.

"I made reservations for the three of us at Alec's at seven thirty. Indi, that's a steakhouse, but if you don't eat red meat they have other options. Personally, the truffle fries there are to die for. So is are the mashed potatoes with truffle butter. It's like truffle heaven for me every time we go there."

"Sounds delicious."

"Indi's parents own a pizzeria in Brattleboro," I said.

"Really? How wonderful. Dom wants to open a restaurant but I don't think it's a good idea. It seems like a lot of work."

"It *is* a lot of work," Indi said. "The hours are insane and you're almost never able to take a vacation."

"Do me a favor," my mom said. "Tell Hudson's father about the nitty-gritty reality of restaurant ownership. I think he has this grand idea that he can just breeze in whenever he feels like it, schmooze a little, eat for free and leave."

"I suppose he could do that, if he had good people working for him," Indi said. "But honestly, it's a tough business and if he has no restaurant experience…"

"Just eating in them," my mom said.

"Then he's probably better off just investing in someone else's restaurant. That way, he can say he's an owner, but doesn't actually have to do the work or know what he's doing for that matter."

My mom looked at her smart watch. "I'm afraid I have a spa appointment I have to go to now, a facial." She pursed her lips.

"Indi, would you like to come along? I'm sure Brayden could fit you in."

"Marlene, thank you so much for the offer," Indi said, "but I'm beat. I'd like to just lay down and rest until dinner."

"There's nothing more relaxing than a facial," my mother said.

"Maybe next time," Indi said. "I've got studying to do too. I only have two more months before the MCAT."

"All right, I understand. I'll be back in a couple of hours, you two. In the meantime, there are a few snacks and a bottle of Chardonnay in your room to tide you over."

After my mom left, Indi said, "Oh my God, Hudson. I feel like I'm staying at a resort. Did you see the shampoo and stuff?" She went into our *en suite* bathroom. "Your mom told me to take all of this home. Oh my God, this smells so good. Smell this lotion. It's grapefruit and ginger."

"It does smell good."

"And the flowers! They're gorgeous. Almost as gorgeous as this view. I can't believe we can see Manhattan *from our room!*"

There was a large vase of blooms on a small table by the window along with a charcuterie platter. I opened the wine and poured us each a glass.

"Hudson, I'm trying really hard not to be overwhelmed, but…"

"I know," I said with a rueful smile. "It's too much. I'm sorry."

"You have nothing to apologize for. Your dad was a professional athlete who worked hard and made a lot of money. This is the result. Now what do you say to…damn. Never mind."

"What?"

"I was going to suggest we take the wine and the snacks and soak in the hot tub, but I didn't bring a suit. Why didn't you tell me to bring a bathing suit?"

I scoffed. "Who needs a suit?"

On Thanksgiving Thursday, Indi was extremely nervous. My two uncles were coming with their families, which meant a total of thirteen family members she had to meet. I told her she had nothing to worry about, but truthfully, I'd never brought a girl home for Thanksgiving before and everyone was bound to be curious.

As a result, Indi took forever to get ready. She dithered about every aspect of her appearance until I almost ran out of patience. Eventually, she settled on a red sweater (not the yellow blouse with the tiny white flowers) and brown plaid skirt (not the black slacks or skinny jeans) over tights and high-heeled leather boots (not loafers or Uggs).

"It's not too casual?" she asked.

"No. It's perfect. Even though it's catered, everyone's going to dress fairly casual."

It didn't take long for her to relax. My family was pretty down to earth, but the free-flowing champagne helped. Along with the bubbly, the caterers offered platters of appetizers—creamy Brie and apricot puffs, deviled eggs with applewood smoked bacon, along with mini leek, mushroom and Gruyere quiches.

Indi said something to me under her breath.

"What was that?"

"I said everything is so good. And so fancy."

"It's Thanksgiving, Forte-style," I said. "We've used this company for the past several years and they're top-notch. One of the servers told me they've catered for some real top-tier celebrities. Taylor Swift, Kevin Bacon…"

"Wow."

"Save room for dinner and dessert," I told her. "There's a lot more where this came from."

A commotion took place at the front door as my dad finally arrived.

"Sorry I'm late," he said in his booming voice as he trudged up to where we were gathered on the second floor. "Mother Nature wasn't cooperating in Minneapolis. I'm lucky I got here at all."

He brought his luggage upstairs and came back down about fifteen minutes later wearing a sport jacket and slacks. After someone put a drink in his hand, I brought Indi over to him.

"Dad, this is Indi, my girlfriend."

He gave Indi a once over. "I didn't know you had a girlfriend."

"Yes, you did, Dad. I told you about her."

My dad shrugged and shook her hand perfunctorily. "Glad you could come, Mindy."

"It's Indi and I'm happy to have been invited. Your home is beautiful."

"Thanks. Sorry, but I have to talk to my brother about something." And he walked away.

"I don't think he likes me," Indi said, looking worried.

"He just needs time to warm up to you. He's always a little bristly at first."

But I only said that to make her feel better. My dad usually turned on the charm with women, but apparently, he still thought I needed to concentrate on hockey to the exclusion of all else and he wasn't above being rude to Indi in order to get his point across to me.

Dinner was more traditional, but still souped up. With truffles, of course. Black truffle butter turkey, green bean casserole with thyme and cremini mushrooms, herb and fennel dressing and several other gourmet sides.

For Indi's sake, I tried several times to introduce non-hockey topics, but the conversation always circled back to hockey. Everyone in the family was either a hockey player or a hockey fanatic.

"Hudson, you sound a little stuffed up," Uncle Rick said. My dad's youngest brother played for the Rangers.

"You're not getting sick are you?" my mom asked.

Conversation stopped. All eyes zeroed in on me.

"Me? No. I'm fine. It's allergies."

Which didn't stop the horde from spouting off their

suggestions, because God forbid I fall ill, not be able to play and thereby lose a chance to rack up points.

"I swear by this organic tea," one of my aunts said. "It's made with ginger and gingko biloba. I'll text you the brand."

"The best thing to do when you feel a cold coming on is to suck down that Airborne stuff like crazy." This came from Uncle Matt.

Uncle Rick scoffed. "That doesn't work, but I'll tell you what does. Close yourself in the bathroom and run the shower at maximum heat until the hot water runs out. Breathe the steam way down deep into your lungs and drink a half gallon of orange juice that day."

Uncle Rick had a reputation for kooky home remedies and I suspected his miracle cures were cousins of the many idiosyncratic superstitions hockey players were known for.

"Thanks for the advice," I said. "I'll keep all that in mind."

"Except that sounds like it wastes a lot of water," my little twelve-year-old cousin said. "You should save the water in pots and water your plants or cook pasta with it. Or you could put it in your washing machine and turn the dial directly to 'agitate.'"

"That's a very smart idea, Megan," I said. "The world needs more socially responsible problem solvers like you."

"What about me?" Megan's little brother demanded. "I want to be needed."

As several members of the family reassured him about his own individual strengths, my organic tea swilling aunt asked Indi about her major and plans for the future.

"I'm planning to apply to medical school," she answered.

"Indi's going to be a surgeon so she can go abroad and repair cleft palates and cleft lips on children," I said proudly.

"Like Doctors Without Borders?" my mom asked.

"Yes, like that," Indi said. "I'm taking the MCAT at the end of January so right now it's all about the studying."

My dad nodded. "Exactly. When you have important career

goals, you need to keep your priorities straight. You need to study, study, study just like Hudson has to focus on hockey."

"Dom, don't," my mom said.

"Don't what? I'm just talking big picture. She needs to understand what's what. Hudson has an amazing career ahead of him, *if* he keeps his nose to the grindstone. Even though he was drafted in the first round, that doesn't guarantee him an NHL contract and no son of mine is going to molder in the farm league because he lost his head over a pretty face."

No one spoke. Uncle Rick poured himself another glass of wine. My mom was glaring at my dad.

"Jesus, Dad," I said. "First of all, Indi is so much more than a pretty face. She's smart, she's organized, she's disciplined. She's the kind of person who doesn't just talk the talk, she walks the walk, and when she becomes an MD, there are going to be a lot of little kids whose lives will be changed because of her."

Indi's hand found mine and I squeezed it.

My dad sucked at his teeth, plainly unimpressed. "A regular Mother Theresa in the making. Except nuns take a vow of poverty and this young lady will be raking in the dough as a plastic surgeon. That's the specialty needed for cleft palates, right? Same as boob jobs, nose jobs, face lifts, Botox. You can't swing a cat in New York without hitting someone who's had work done."

"Stop it, Dad," I said. "You're the last person who should be criticizing someone for making a lot of money."

"You're absolutely right, son. I'm a lucky man. The NHL was very, very good to me and, if you keep your head on straight, it'll be good to you too."

INDI

"What the hell is wrong with you, Dad?" Hudson exclaimed, right at the dinner table. "You need to apologize to Indi right now."

His dad struck an indolent pose, leaning his elbow on the arm of his chair and cocking his head. "For what?"

"*For what?*" Hudson ran his fingers through his hair in exasperation. "Where do I start? The Mother Theresa comment... Saying she was just a pretty face."

"That was a compliment," his dad said.

"For suggesting she was only becoming a doctor for the money."

"And for ruining Thanksgiving," his mom said, which earned her a sidelong glance from her husband. "Honestly, I can't believe you."

Around the table were a variety of expressions from amused, to aghast, to eager. As for me, I was shocked.

Hudson had warned me there would be drama, but I'd thought he meant someone would drink a little too much and dredge up an old family issue or maybe pull a skeleton out of the closet. I'd thought I'd be a witness to the turmoil, not central to it.

With a heavy sigh, his dad shrugged. "All right. I'm sorry. I crossed the line there a little bit. Indi, sweetheart, will you forgive me?"

I mean, what choice did I have? I couldn't exactly say no. But I couldn't seem to voice a "yes" either. So I nodded once.

"There. See?" his dad said. "Everything's fine now."

I didn't know the man well enough to know if he was truly sorry, but Hudson didn't look like he bought it.

"I want dessert!" one of the young cousins demanded, breaking the awkward silence.

"By all means, let's have dessert," Marlene said with forced brightness.

After all the guests had gone and the caterers were cleaning up, Marlene said she had a migraine and sought refuge in her bedroom. I didn't blame her. The barrage of sweets settled things down for the most part, but the tension never completely disappeared.

"I need to talk with my dad," Hudson said. "Alone."

I shook my head. "I don't think so."

"Indi, please. You thought what happened at the table was bad? That was my father being calm and calculated, which is obviously no walk in the park. Believe me, you do not want to be in there when he really gets going."

"So there'll be yelling."

"Yes. And a lot of swearing."

I scoffed. "I'm not a fragile flower, Hudson. I've been yelled at before."

This was a complete lie. My parents were low key. The only time they ever raised their voices was at Slice when they needed to be heard over some racket in the restaurant. My aunts and uncles and cousins were cut from similar cloth. No one had ever shouted at me in anger, but I wasn't about to let Hudson go beard the lion by himself.

"Not like this."

"It won't be as bad if we face him together."

To my surprise, he pulled me into his arms and hugged me tightly. "God, I love you, woman," he said into my hair. "Please say you love me too."

"God, Hudson, I *do* love you. I've been in love with you from the very beginning."

I felt some of the tension leave his body but when he stepped back, his expression was still tense.

"If you love me—"

I balked. "Don't you dare start a sentence like that."

He ignored me.

"If you love me, you'll let me tell you why you need to stay out here when I talk to him."

I crossed my arms. "Okay. I'm listening."

"I'm going to assume that we both hope our relationship will keep getting better and that maybe we can have a future together. Maybe marriage, maybe kids. Who knows? We'll take it one step at a time. Am I doing okay so far?"

"Yes. Yes to all of that."

"That means we're going to have to deal with each other's families and unfortunately, my dad has made one hell of a shitty first impression and if you go with me to talk to him..." Running his hands through his hair, he sighed heavily. "I'm afraid he'll say or do something to make you hate him forever. Yes, he can be an asshole sometimes, but I swear he has a lot of good qualities too and I just...I just want there to be a chance you'll come to appreciate them someday."

All this time I'd thought he was trying to protect me from more of his dad's disapproval and while I appreciated and understood that, I wasn't willing to let him do it. I had a few things I wanted to say to Dom myself, to show him I wasn't a pushover and I wasn't going to take any verbal abuse from him.

But I'd been completely off base. Hudson was worried that the conflict tonight would escalate to the point of no return. That I would be so hurt, any relationship I might have had with his dad would be ruined forever. It was a testament to how much he cared about me and how much he cared about his dad and I had to respect that.

Hudson asked me to wait upstairs in our room while he talked to Dom in the wine cellar. I thought about watching TV to distract myself but found myself Googling his dad instead. What I found wasn't surprising—a lot of evidence that he could be an asshole on and off the ice, but as Hudson had sworn, a lot of evidence he had a heart too. He was quite the philanthropist, supporting a host of charities and foundations. He was outspoken about many issues that I felt strongly about too and, judging from the number of photographs and articles, it seemed as if the Grant A Wish Foundation had his number on speed dial.

I liked to think of myself as a rational person who didn't make rash decisions based on hurt feelings, so I eventually resolved to give Dom a second chance. It meant so much to Hudson that I get along with his dad, and if our situations were reversed and he was butting heads with my dad for some reason, I—

The door to our room burst open.

"Pack your stuff," Hudson said. "We're leaving."

Crap. His face was so red it looked as if he'd just finished playing a tough game of hockey.

"We are?" I asked. It was over six hours back to Burlington. "We won't get home until after two."

"I don't care," he said through gritted teeth. "As expected, Dad doubled down on his dickish behavior, so we're leaving to prove a point. We both need some cooling off time and we'll both be less likely to rehash shit if I'm at school."

Now I really wanted to know what had been said, but I knew Hudson wouldn't tell me and I don't know what was worse—not knowing or letting my imagination conjure up possibilities.

INDI

Two weeks had passed since Thanksgiving and except for the Domholery—a term I'd invented that Hudson found hilariously spot-on—I had an amazing boyfriend who loved me and despite the amount of time we spent in bed, I was still maintaining my GPA. I also felt confident that I'd do pretty well on the MCAT practice test I'd scheduled tomorrow. Like the real MCAT, it was going to be a timed marathon of almost eight hours. The idea was to make the experience as close to the real thing as possible. Afterward, I'd be able to look at the results and see where my weaknesses were.

Hudson and his dad still weren't speaking, but he assured me the situation wasn't permanent and that eventually they'd work things out. But that was the least of his problems.

We'd since cleaned his ears out using the kit from the pharmacy, but he was still suffering from occasional tinnitus. I also noticed more and more often he had trouble hearing me when I whispered or spoke in low tones. These things, along with some troubling balance issues he'd mentioned, prompted me do a little online research. What I found was alarming.

All his symptoms pointed toward otosclerosis, an abnormal growth of one of the bones in the ear, which could lead to varying degrees of hearing loss. There were a lot of careers in which moderate hearing loss wouldn't pose much of a problem. Professional hockey wasn't one of them. Every time I thought about Hudson having to quit hockey because of a medical condition, I felt sick inside. I told myself I was jumping to conclusions and that I should refrain from practicing medicine before I had a license.

Besides, otosclerosis was a rare condition, and the chances Hudson had it were slim.

And yet every time I saw him pull at his ear or had to repeat what I'd said because he hadn't heard me, I wondered if I should say something.

One night after a particularly bad performance on the ice, he was pissed with himself. AJ had gone to the Biscuit in the Basket with the rest of the team, but Hudson wasn't in the mood. Thinking this might be a good time to broach the subject, I accompanied him to his apartment.

"Jesus, did you see me out there? It's like I have two left feet," he swore. "I don't know what to do. Why is this happening? It's like I can't even trust my own body. I wish I knew what the fuck was going on."

I took a deep breath and said in a deliberately quiet voice, "I might know."

"What was that?"

"I said, I might know."

He stared at me. "Really?"

I nodded. "Come sit down."

"I don't like the sound of that."

I didn't reply until he was next to me on the sofa. Deciding a direct approach was best, I said, "I think you have otosclerosis."

"Oto-what?"

"Otosclerosis. It's a rare abnormal growth of bone in the inner ear and you have all the symptoms—difficulty hearing low sounds or whispers, like just now, occasional dizziness and balance problems, tinnitus."

He was scowling at me, but I continued because he hadn't heard the worst part.

"There are two types of hearing loss associated with otosclerosis, conductive and sensorineural. Conductive hearing loss is the better of the two because with sensorineural, there's a possibility of permanent hearing loss."

His face and turned the exact shade of red it had been after his argument with his father. "What the hell are you talking about? Are you saying I'm going deaf?"

"Hudson, weren't you listening?"

"Maybe I didn't hear you," he said with a sarcastic smirk I didn't appreciate.

"Look, don't kill the messenger. I'm just telling you what I know."

"What you know. Let's talk about that," he said. "You're not even in medical school yet. Where do you get off telling me I'm going deaf?"

"I didn't say you were going deaf. See? You *weren't* listening. Permanent hearing loss is only one of the outcomes, but I only told you that because you need to take this seriously. You need to go see an otolaryngologist and get examined."

"Fat chance."

"Hudson, please. I know you're afraid, but you have to get over it. That thing that happened was when you were a kid…"

He started laughing but it was a cruel sort of laughter. "Oh, that's rich coming from you."

"What's that supposed to mean?"

"I mean, I'm not the one who's afraid to even fucking go outside unless I spend an hour in front of the mirror." Then he mockingly mimed me putting my makeup on. "'I'm afraid someone will see my face and call me names.' Talk about living in fear."

This time I was the one staring. Had he really said that, *done* that? I was trying to help him, damn it, and this was how he responded. I'd thought that saying about seeing red was just that, a saying, but right now, my vision did seem to be tinged with red. If I hadn't been so infuriated, I might have looked up the reason behind that phenomenon.

Tears threatened but I swore once to never let a bully see me cry and I wasn't about to start now. With as much dignity as I could manage, I got my purse and left, somehow managing not to slam the door behind me.

HUDSON

When it rains, it pours. Everything in my life was in the shitter and I didn't know how to fix it.

It had all started with that disaster of a Thanksgiving where my dad demonstrated just how big a prick he could be. I'd wanted to look around for the reality show cameras. That's how unreal it had felt. No one in the family had known how to react when he'd started in on Indi.

Not wanting to continue making everyone uncomfortable, I'd waited until all the guests had left and then asked if I could have a moment with him in the cellar. I'd intended to call him out on his dickhead behavior but instead, he started in on *me*, on my erratic game play.

I should have known that was coming. Every time I got on the ice lately it was like taking my chances on a slot machine. Sometimes, I'd hit the jackpot and be on fire. I'd nail my passes, win face-offs, assist, score... But other times, I'd stink. I'd be too late getting into position, misunderstand a teammate, or I'd fucking fall flat on my face.

"It's like some alien kidnapped my son and left a fake Forte in his place," my dad had said. "I can only think of two reasons why this is going on. One, the draft went to your head and you think you've got it made and can kick back. Well, I have news for you, that ain't the case. You cannot afford to slack off until you've signed that NHL contract."

"I'm not slacking off. I bust my ass every night and leave everything on the ice, just like I always have."

"I didn't think so because it's far more likely that you're listening more to your little head than your big head."

"Jesus, Dad."

"How many times have I told you not to let a woman rule your life?"

"She's not ruling my life, Dad. She's adding to it, making it better in every way."

"There's your dick talking again."

"I'm not talking about sex. I'm talking about friendship and support, about being okay with my crazy schedule and how sometimes hockey has to come before she does."

"Exactly! You don't realize it, but she's playing a long game. She wants that golden ring, son." He pointed to the band on his left hand. "She wants to marry you so she can live the life of luxury and never work another day in her life."

The idea was so preposterous, I couldn't even formulate a response. Indi was as laser-focused on her medical career as I was on hockey. *I* was usually the one wanting to blow off workouts and extra training so I could spend time with her instead of the other way around. But my dad was on a roll.

"That's why she's going along with everything you want, accepting that she's a lower priority and fucking your brains out every chance she—"

"STOP!" I yelled, every muscle in my body rigid with rage. "You need to shut your mouth right now or I swear to God I'm going to shut it for you."

My dad looked shocked. I'd never threatened him with physical violence before. Could I go through with it? I had no idea. Those words just exploded out of my mouth like buckshot.

"I have listened to every bit of advice you've ever given me and most of it has been solid, but what you just said is not only over the line, it's flat-out wrong.

"You only met Indi a few hours ago. How could you possibly know what her motives are? Is it so hard to believe that she might just like me as a person? Because I am a person, Dad, not just a hockey player. There's more to me than what I can do on the ice and I have to tell you it's a fucking relief to finally have one person in my life who understands that because you certainly don't."

My dad lifted his chin at me. "I know what her motives are because I know women. I know how their minds work."

"You don't know my woman and unfortunately, you're not going to get a chance to because we're leaving."

My dad crossed his arms over his broad chest and nodded. "Yeah, go on back to school. I've said it before and I'll say it again. College might teach you some things, but it won't teach you jack about shit that matters, like how to avoid gold-diggers."

I knew beyond a shadow of a doubt that Indi wasn't after me for my earning potential. While she had been impressed with the place on State Street, she'd never once asked me about how much I stood to make if I made it to the NHL. With the exception of her expensive makeup, she didn't splurge on fancy things for herself. She never talked about how she wanted of this kind of house or car or lavish lifestyle. Her medical degree represented a dream of helping children, not of making big bucks.

She wasn't without faults, though. Case in point, her tendency to treat me like I was her patient. To have her throw all these multi-syllabic words at me because she thought I had some weird ass condition was ridiculous. It had been like my girlfriend had suddenly transformed into the Nostradamus of the NHL, predicting my imminent doom like it was written in the stars.

Even so, I loved her and felt like the lowest of the low for what I'd said to her. Maybe the apple hadn't fallen too far from the tree. Maybe I'd inherited or learned how to verbally lash out at people from my dad's example. I hated that idea. I hated the defeated look on her face when she'd left the apartment. And yet, in the moment, I had felt a horrible, fierce satisfaction at having hit the mark.

I'd been an asshole of the first water.

I knew I had to apologize, but the relationship reboot wasn't going to hack it this time. I needed to do some major groveling but I was too much of a chickenshit to face her yet. Besides, I knew she was taking that MCAT practice test today, so I told myself she wouldn't want to hear from me until that was over anyway.

As for me, I had something to prove to Coach Keller after Friday night's shit show. I still wasn't completely convinced my problems on the ice were physical and not mental. I had stopped enacting Mac's five step pregame routine four games ago because the nausea and vomiting had gone away, but maybe I needed to start that back up again. Maybe his routine magically corrected more than the anxiety. Maybe it aligned something in my head so I could think during the game more clearly.

I decided to try it tonight in the game against Merrimack. After I had my gear on, I leaned back in my stall and breathed deeply while listening to some relaxing music on my noise-cancelling head-phones. I had a little trouble conjuring up my "happy place," a place where I felt zero stress. I used to think about being in bed with Indi immediately after sex, but that didn't feel right when we weren't on speaking terms. So I imagined I was Deke on his wheel, running for the sheer joy of running. Step four, challenging and rejecting all the negativity in my head, was just as challenging. I'd recently seen an article about me online that said I had great hockey sense but wasn't demonstrating the skating skills I'd shown in the past.

No shit.

The comments below the article were even worse.

I didn't need that crap clouding my brain, so I pictured the article, printed on paper, then mentally lit it on fire and watched it burn. Then I concentrated the rest of the time on visualizing myself owning the ice, executing plays with crisp precision, assisting my teammates in achieving their own highlight moments, and performing so well that Coach Keller took me aside for some words of praise.

Turned out, after the game, the coach pulled me aside all right, but not for praise.

"Forte, what in the ever-loving fuck is going on with you? If I didn't know better, I'd say you were deliberately fucking with me. Just when I'm fed up and ready to mark you down as a healthy scratch, you pull something out of your ass to change my mind. Then the very next day, you're back to your old tricks. Your teammates complain that you don't listen to them, that you see yourself as some kind of wunderkind who can carry the team all by yourself and I didn't want to believe it. But tonight in the third period, I told you to get the puck to Daniels and you flat out ignored me."

I swallowed hard. "Coach, I...I didn't hear you."

"How the hell could you not hear me? I was literally right behind you. Get the fucking cotton out of your ears, will you? And pay attention!"

Getting chewed out by Coach Keller was my come to Jesus moment. I couldn't sit on my ass anymore and pretend things would get better if I tried harder. Maybe my ears really *were* fucked-up, like Indi had suggested, or maybe it was something worse like an inoperable brain tumor. Regardless, if something was medically wrong with me, I had no idea how the Dragons would react. Worst case scenario, they'd neglect to offer me a contract when I graduated.

Thinking Booth MacDonald might be able to help, I called him up. It was late, but the Barracudas had come east for a road trip, so he was in the same time zone at least.

"Young Forte! Good to hear from you. How's that pregame routine working for you?"

"Am I on speaker?" I asked, calling back to his prank from the last time I called.

"Ah ha ha ha ha ha. No, you're not on speaker. I'm in my hotel room."

"The routine is working great, thanks," I said, feeling a little guilty about the white lie. "But now I have another problem and I don't know what to do about it."

"This is why you should always wear a condom."

"Mac, I didn't get anyone pregnant."

"I knew you were too smart for that. Now that we have that out of the way, lay it on me. What's your problem?"

As matter-of-factly as I could, I told him about the tinnitus, the dizzy spells and the fact that I was having trouble hearing, that I'd been having trouble for months. I even told him about Indi's shot-in-the-dark "diagnosis" of otosclerosis.

"Jesus, kid. You need to see a doctor. You guys have a team doc at Burlington? When I was at Dartmouth, there was a team doc for all the school athletes. Can you go to him and tell him what's going on?"

I did a mental double take. In my brain, the team physician was there for game related injuries like pulled muscles or dislocated joints. Consulting him about something that didn't originate from hockey hadn't even occurred to me.

"That's actually a great idea," I said hesitantly. "But…"

"But what?"

I hesitated, reluctant to share my deepest fear, the one that threatened to throw me into panic mode.

"What if he tells me I'm going deaf, Mac? I can't play hockey if I can't hear. The Dragons will drop me like a hot potato and my career will be over before it even started."

Which would make me a pariah in my family. I'd be the one who broke the family's unbroken line of NHL players. I could well imagine my dad disowning me.

Mac said, "First of all, you're not going deaf. You don't know that for sure, not until you see a professional. I looked up otosclerosis while we've been talking and everything I'm seeing says it's a pretty rare condition. So don't get ahead of yourself. Secondly... hold on a sec. Just checking one more thing. There. I knew it. You ever hear of Jim Kyte?"

"No."

"Look him up later. He was the first legally deaf NHL player. Played almost 600 games in the NHL."

"This better not be one of your pranks," I said. My heart was pounding.

"I wouldn't joke about something like this," Mac said. "According to his Wiki page, he was born with perfect hearing but lost it by the time he was three. So there you go. If you do have otosclerosis, and that's a big if, it's not a death knell for your hockey career. And besides, the Dragons aren't going to just drop you. A hearing problem or any other kind of physical problem isn't the deal breaker you think it is. It's all about your performance."

This wasn't exactly reassuring. Even so, I thanked him and he said, "Let me know how it works out, Forte. I'll be crossing my fingers for you."

Immediately after hanging up, I checked out Jim Kyte and got chills. Kyte had been drafted in the first round, number 30 overall, just like me, which was a was a weird fucking coincidence. But that was about the only thing we had in common. Kyte had spent most of his life without hearing, so he had a long time to adapt, to develop tricks to compensate. For instance, because he couldn't hear the players behind him, he sometimes used the Plexiglass as a mirror. He also did a lot of lipreading.

I was glad to see he'd been inducted into the Ottawa Sport Hall of Fame, but he only accumulated sixty-six points in his fifteen-year career. Even for a defenseman, that was not very good. However, I also learned that he wore hearing aids in both ears and had a special helmet to accommodate them. Good to know, considering a hearing aid was apparently one of the first things they tried when it came to otosclerosis.

Unfortunately, the only way to know if I had it or not was to get checked out by a doctor, like Mac said. The idea of going to someone I'd never met before made me break out in a cold sweat. But the team physician, Dr. Neufeld, or Newfie as we all called him, was a great guy with a calm bedside manner. I'd been afraid to talk to him when I was a freshman, but now, three years later, he didn't scare me at all. If after seeing him I needed to see an ear specialist, so be it. I'd have to grow a pair and deal with it because I had momentum now and was done with the torture of uncertainty.

Even though it was after midnight by now, I sent him an email. Right after that I texted Indi.

Hudson: Can we talk?

But I didn't get a reply.

33

INDI

When Hudson pretended to be me at the mirror, putting on my makeup, it was like when you stub your toe hard and the message takes a few seconds to get to your brain.

It was so far out of character for him I literally couldn't believe it was happening at the time. I remember thinking, *he'll realize the crossed the line any second now.* Any...second...now...

But he didn't.

And when I realized he wasn't going to take it back, I couldn't even breathe.

In shock, I'd managed to hold the tears back until I was a couple of blocks away, but once the floodgates opened, I had to pull over because I couldn't see through the tears. I cried, alone in my car, for a good long while. I sobbed until my throat was sore and my eyes felt like I'd gone a couple of rounds with a heavyweight boxer.

When I got home, Ruby knew immediately something catastrophic had happened. Somehow my body managed to produce more tears even though I would have sworn that was impossible. I told Ruby what had happened and when I was finished, she was ready to commit murder. She ranted for a good fifteen minutes about what a horrible person Hudson was and how she didn't think he could have gotten any lower. It really helped. So did the bottle of schnapps she kept in the cupboard for emergencies.

"I want to call him a name but 'bully' just doesn't cut it," I said.

"Ha! We can look some up."

We ended up finding an insult generator and I have to admit, the random creativity of some of the insults, along with the schnapps, made me laugh, despite my broken heart.

Saturday morning, to say I was disappointed to not get a text from Hudson was an understatement. Ruby was outraged.

"You'd think after he had the night to think it over, he'd realize what a...what was it? Insecure cock waffle he'd been."

"Once an insecure cock waffle, always an insecure cock waffle," I said.

I tried to sound like I didn't care one way or the other whether he texted or called or not, but I checked my phone constantly all day. No word that day or the day after. And when he didn't come to class either, I eventually moved from despair to anger, which pleased Ruby. She didn't think he deserved my tears.

"He doesn't deserve to smell your shit. You should block him. Block his number. If he wants to apologize, he should have to do it in person anyway. Don't give him the easy way out. Make him come to you to do his groveling."

In the end, I took her advice and blocked his number, but not for the reason she thought. I blocked him because it was the only way to stop myself from checking my phone to see if he'd tried to contact me. It was a pathetic fact of life that I still loved him and every part of my being wished we could erase what happened and go back to when he was the perfect boyfriend.

I had planned to take that MCAT practice test today, but I'd hardly slept a wink the night before and it was pointless to waste an entire day when I knew my scores would not be a reliable predictor of my real ability.

Instead, I decided to bang out one of the last photography

assignments of the semester, called "Me and Myself." We were to scan an old photo of ourselves and use Photoshop to insert our current selves into the picture. Judging from the examples Larkmont showed us, most people used childhood photos, which made sense. That's where you'd find the greatest contrast between past and present, but all the photos from my childhood probably showed my birthmark.

I was about to troll my mom's Facebook photo album for pictures in which my back was turned or I was in profile with my good side facing the camera when I remembered Denise Snow, that woman from the park, mentioning a Facebook group for people with port-wine stains. She'd said the group had four thousand members. *Four thousand.* Not all of them had port-wine stains themselves, but still, that number had astounded me. Leah had been the first person I'd ever met who had a birthmark like mine.

Curious, I typed "port-wine stain" into the Facebook search box and checked out the top result, "port-wine stain birthmark family," and to my surprise the first post I saw was of Leah. Obviously, I'd found the right group. Their purpose was to provide support for people with PWS or who loved people with PWS. Without really thinking about it, I requested membership.

A notification that I'd been admitted came only a minute later and a welcome post invited me to introduce myself, but I wasn't sure I was going to stick around. For the time being, I'd just lurk.

Most posts were by mothers like Denise who had children with port-wine birthmarks. They talked about treatments, related complications, worries and triumphs. Unfortunately, the posts by adults with birthmarks were few and far between, but then I saw something that caught my eye, a post that I hadn't known I was looking for until I saw it.

Hello, everyone. I'm Michaela and I've been hiding my PWS almost my whole life. Nobody except my close friends and family even knows I have one. And even THEY don't see me often without my makeup.

Because of the many hurtful things that happened to me, I won't leave the house without makeup. I never go swimming. When people told me I was pretty, I'd think to myself, they can't see the real me. They only see the fake me.

But over the past year, I've come to know other people with birth-marks like mine, each one unique. A lot of them try to spread awareness about PWS. Because of them, I now have the courage to accept myself and be proud of my skin, especially that special part of me that is all my own.

So here goes. Here I am, without makeup. Go me.

A picture of the young white woman without makeup followed this heartfelt essay. Her name was Michaela Gibson and she was very pretty. Her birthmark covered a good portion of her chin, jaw and lower lip and her smile was tentative but confident.

The hairs went up on my arms and legs as I read what she'd written a second time. Every single word of it resonated in me. It was as if she'd somehow watched a movie of my entire life and summarized it here.

I spent another hour reading more posts written by adults who had birthmarks and it was as if I'd stepped through the wardrobe into Narnia. I'd never known there were so many other people like me. They were spread across the world, and the fact that they existed at all was a revelation. I'd always felt so alone. Unique, like Michaela had said, but not in a good way. But here were other outcasts who had all lived through their own versions of my life. It was like finding I had long lost brothers and sisters. This was the first time I felt like I belonged to a group.

Then I realized, I didn't *really* belong. Not yet anyway.

Filled with apprehension but determined, I got out my phone

and turned the camera on, put it in selfie mode and snapped a picture, making sure my whole birthmark was showing. Then, heart pounding, I uploaded it to the Facebook group and typed a reply to Michaela's post:

Hi, I'm Indi. Your post really inspired me. This is the first picture of me without makeup that has been taken in eight years. I hope you like it.

Then, before I lost my nerve, I hit return.

34

HUDSON

On Sunday, I was surprised to get a call from Dr. Neufeld.

"I talked with Bart Keller and he's extremely concerned. We both are. This isn't an emergency by any means, but I've already contacted a good friend of mine, Lisa Bourdon. She's a well-respected ENT who's been practicing medicine for ten years. She's agreed to fit you in first thing Monday morning if you can make it."

Even though I was scared shitless, I said, "I'll be there."

Once again demonstrating what a good friend he was, AJ skipped his first class and came with me to the appointment and even though him being there helped, I purposely skipped breakfast so that if I threw up from the anxiety, it would only be dry heaves.

Thankfully, we didn't have to wait long before a knock sounded on the door and Dr. Bourdon entered.

She had long strawberry-blonde hair and kind eyes. She introduced herself to us both and shook our hands.

Surprisingly, we didn't discuss my symptoms at first. She asked me a few questions about my life and somehow got on the subject of pets. I told her about Deke and we spoke a few minutes about hamsters because her youngest child wanted a pet and she wasn't sure she could handle the responsibility.

As I explained what was involved in taking care of Deke, I found myself relaxing. By the time we got around to discussing what was going on with my body, I wasn't even nervous anymore. She examined my ears and gave me a hearing test and while AJ and I waited to hear the results, I prepared myself for the worst.

In a way, AJ took the news that I had otosclerosis harder than I had. The look on his face…it was as if the doctor had said I had six weeks to live, which was pretty ironic, considering he'd come along to be my rock. But he pulled it together as Dr. Bourdon explained exactly what might happen and what my options were for each scenario.

Best case scenario, things didn't get worse, my hearing stayed the way it was and the hearing aids she wanted me to get corrected my problem. However, it was more likely that my hearing would worsen over time and there was no way to know how much or how fast because everyone is different.

"If it comes to it, there is a surgical option called a stapedectomy involving a tiny prosthetic that would allow the sound waves to bypass the abnormal bone and reach your inner ear. I've found it to be the most successful option should the hearing aids prove to be insufficient."

Afterward, we went to breakfast at the Skinny Pancake because, despite the bad news, I was starving.

"I don't understand how you're not freaking out right now," AJ said as we sat down with our food.

"I *am* freaking out. I have no idea what this means for my hockey career. At this point, I may not even have a hockey career."

AJ shook his head. "Don't say that. I'm sure that once you get those hearing aids, you'll start playing like you used to. Hell, I'm thinking about how shitty I'd play if I couldn't hear…" He coughed. "Dom's not going to take it well, you know."

"No, he's not," I agreed. "But after the way he treated Indi at Thanksgiving, I don't really give a shit how he takes it."

"Speaking of Indi...I haven't seen her around the past couple days. Something go down with you two?" He popped a tater tot in this mouth, one eyebrow raised questioningly.

I put a small piece of parsley aside for Deke. "We're actually not speaking."

His fork stopped on the way to his mouth. "Shit. What did you do?"

"What makes you think *I'm* the one who did something?"

"Didn't you?"

"Well, yes, but that's not the point."

"What did you do, genius?"

I told him all about how Indi was the one who suggested I had otosclerosis and that I'd reacted badly, but I couldn't be very specific without telling him about her birthmark and based on how long it took for her to tell *me* about it, I knew she wouldn't appreciate me telling AJ about it.

"Did you try the relationship reboot?"

I shook my head. "Not yet. I've tried calling and texting, but I think she blocked me. My phone keeps saying my messages haven't been delivered.

"You're going to have to go see her," he said.

"Thanks, Mr. Obvious. I know that."

"And if you don't think the relationship reboot is enough, maybe your dad can tell you what will. Maybe he has a backup plan he hasn't told you about yet."

Still in chickenshit mode, I decided maybe AJ was right. Maybe my dad would have some valuable advice for me. After all, he and my mother were, for the most part, happily married. They'd had speed bumps, of course, as all couples do, but they were still going strong. In fact, sometimes my dad went overboard in the romance department and my mom would pretend she was embarrassed but I think she secretly loved it.

Because I had to break the news of my diagnosis to them anyway and the roundtrip airfare home was miraculously under a hundred bucks, I booked the flight that was scheduled for one thirty that afternoon. Then, hopefully when I came back, I'd know what I needed to say to Indi and I could head to Carter Hall straight from the airport.

When I got to the house, my mother greeted me with joy.

"Hudson! What a wonderful surprise." She hugged me tightly and I'm not ashamed to say that I reveled in the comfort of her familiar embrace and held on a few seconds longer than I would have normally. "Your father's at the gym, but he'll be home in a little while. Are you hungry? Do you want something to eat?"

"I could eat," I said.

We went into the kitchen and she made me a turkey and swiss sandwich.

"Are you staying?" she asked. "I didn't see a bag..."

I shook my head. "No, I'm flying back later this afternoon."

She gave me a worried glance and placed the sandwich on the table in front of me. "Hudson, is everything all right?"

"Everything's going to be fine, Mom."

We sat at the table and she sipped a cup of coffee as I dug in.

"Going to be?" she asked. "That's not exactly reassuring."

Luckily, my dad's voice boomed up the stairwell from the street level. "Marlene, honey, I'm home!"

I stood as he came bounding up the stairs. A smile broke out across his face.

"Hudson!"

I returned his hug even though I still hadn't forgiven him.

"Is that one of your famous turkey sandwiches?" my dad asked. "Where can I get myself one of those?"

"I'll make you one."

"You're the greatest, Marlie-bear. Extra mayo on mine. So what's up?" he asked me.

"I'm here because I have something to tell you."

A shadow fell over my dad's face. "Damn it. I knew it! She's pregnant, isn't she? I told you she was just itching to get her claws into you. Isn't it just like a—ow!"

My mother had appeared at his side in an instant and whacked him on the head with her spatula. Mayonnaise splattered everywhere and my dad threw his arms up in a gesture of defense.

"What the fuck, Marlene!" My dad's face was red but my mom was still brandishing her spatula.

"I told you before I wasn't going to listen to any more of that misogynistic bullshit and I meant it. Hudson isn't here to tell us we're going to be grandparents. If he was, Indi—who is a wonderful girl, by the way—would be here with him. Now shut up and listen because I have a feeling the news he has isn't good."

After wiping my mouth with a napkin, I gave my mom a look of gratitude as she took a seat next to my dad, still holding the spatula.

"All right. Here it is. I have a rare condition called otosclerosis. It's not life-threatening, but it is serious."

I laid out all the facts, including the uncertain state of my career. When I finished, I braced myself for ranting and raving. I wasn't disappointed.

"What the fuck?" my dad said. "How long have you known something was wrong?"

Resigned, I said, "Months."

"*Months*?" He jumped to his feet, unable to sit still. "Fucking months? Actually, that makes total sense. I've been wondering why you've been playing like shit. Now I know."

"Dom, don't. This isn't his fault."

"The hell it isn't. I'll bet if he'd gotten looked at right off the bat we wouldn't be where we are today, with his career in the shitter. You nip things like this in the bud so they don't get worse and ruin twenty-one years of blood, sweat and tears."

"You're wrong, Dad," I said, and it felt damn good. "The only thing that would have changed if I'd seen a doctor right at the beginning is that I would have gotten the hearing aids sooner. That's all. It's not my fault. It's not anyone's fault. It was inevitable."

Before Dad could say a word, my mom said, "Dom, your grandmother, Margaret, went deaf when she was in her twenties. I remember hearing the stories about how your father and uncles got away with murder because she couldn't hear them sneaking around behind her back."

"What does that have to do with anything?" my dad asked.

"If Hudson's condition is in any way hereditary, maybe it's *your* fault. Maybe it's the Forte genes."

Because some of the hot air seemed to go out of my dad, I didn't point out that if Grandmother Margaret was the one with the gene responsible, I didn't inherit it from a Forte, I inherited it from a Laramie.

"Regardless of fault, this isn't the worst news in the world." My mom held a hand up when my dad opened his mouth. "There are a hundred worse things I can think of than this. It sounds like he will still be able to play for the Dragons."

"As long as the hearing aids can key into the stuff my ears aren't picking up," I said. "We won't know until I try them out."

"When will that be?" my mom asked.

"I have an appointment with the audiologist tomorrow, but it could be a couple weeks before I actually get them. They said it will take a while to adjust. I can't just put them on and play. I'm supposed to start using them in quiet surroundings first and work up to noisier settings."

"And hockey arenas aren't known for their low noise level," my mom said.

"Right."

"What if they don't work?" my dad asked.

I sighed. "Then we'll have to look at surgery."

But I really didn't want to even think about surgery. The idea of someone messing around in my ear with a laser... What if the surgeon got jostled and fucked up my brain? What if I got out of surgery in worse shape than when I went in?

35

HUDSON

As I was waiting for the Uber driver to pick me up and bring me to the airport, my dad came out of the house and jogged down the steps to where I stood on the sidewalk. A light snow was starting to fall. Wearing a track suit and no shoes, he had to be freezing.

"Hudson, before you go, I wanted to say I'm sorry about what I said. About Indi."

Without lifting my gaze from my phone, I said, "Which time?"

He stuck his hands in his pockets and nodded. "Okay, I deserved that. Both times. I just...you have so much on the line right now and it's not the time to be—"

"Stop." I held up my hand. "I've already heard this lecture a thousand times, Dad. I know what's at stake. I'm not stupid. But Indi is special. I'm in love with her."

He sighed. "I was afraid of that."

"You know, Dad, I really don't understand why. You said at your retirement celebration that you never would have achieved what you had without Mom by your side. Was that a lie?"

"Of course it wasn't a lie." His upper lip curled in indignation. "That was the God's honest truth."

"Then, how about a little faith that Indi could be for me what

Mom was for you? How about you don't jump to conclusions that honestly sound paranoid?"

"I'm not paranoid."

"Then why are you so convinced that Indi's a gold-digger?"

He blew out a breath that steamed in the frigid air. "Because…" He cast a wary glance behind us. "I almost married one."

I stared at him in surprise.

"What the…? When?"

"It's a long story. How about I drive you to the airport and I'll tell you on the way?"

Burning with curiosity, I agreed. I thought I had heard every story my dad had to tell, but I'd never heard anything about a gold-digger.

Five minutes later, we were on Atlantic, headed for I-278E with an estimated drive time of one hour. I was again reminded how powerful the Camaro was and how you could feel it in your tailbone when he revved the motor.

"I was twenty-three, only a couple of years older than you when I fell for Sabina. She was a knockout. Blonde, great rack, big pouty lips. I thought she adored me. I certainly adored her. She was insatiable in bed. I mean, she could—"

"Dad, don't! Let's not go there, okay?"

"Right, right. Sorry," he said. "Anyway, I was like the frog in the pot of water that heats so slowly he doesn't realize he's being cooked. She took her time, conditioning me to do whatever she said, buy her whatever she wanted until eventually, she got me to propose."

"Did she start dragging you into jewelry stores?"

"That would have been too obvious for Sabina. No. After we'd been exclusive for about a year, we were at this rock-climbing place where this guy proposed to his girlfriend at the top of the wall and everybody there made this big deal about it. Including Sabina. I said, 'Hell, that was nothing special. I could do better than that.'"

"I can hear you saying that in my head."

"Right?" my dad said. He was always boasting that he could do this better or that better and the annoying thing was, he usually could.

"So when Sabina heard this, she laughed, patted me on the cheek like I was a little kid, and kept climbing. That's all it took, son. She didn't even *say* anything. That's how slick she was. Two months later after we were knocked out of the playoffs, I took her to Venice and popped the question on a gondola, which, you gotta admit, was out of this world special."

It was hard to picture my dad, in his twenties, proposing to a woman in Italy, especially since the woman wasn't my mother.

"Sabina said yes and we set a date for the following summer. Deposits were made, invitations went out. Everything was all set. Then the morning of the wedding, your Aunt Marty pulls me aside. Says she needs to talk to me, that it's urgent.

"She was at the bachelorette party the night before and at the time she was three months pregnant with your cousin Garrett, so she wasn't drinking. Anyway, the rest of the girls at the party got rip-roaring drunk and at one point, Sabina starts bragging about the multi-million-dollar contract I'd just signed and how she was set for life now because I was too stupid to make her sign a prenup."

I sucked in a breath. "Jesus."

"I confronted Sabina and she denied it, of course, but you know your Aunt Marty. She would never lie about something like that."

Aunt Marty was one of the most stalwart, kind women I knew. She wasn't prone to exaggeration or gossip, so if she said something happened, you knew it actually happened.

"It took me a long time to get over Sabina. I really thought she loved me, but she only loved my money and the life I was going to give her. So, I'm not paranoid, son. I just don't want you to get caught by a woman like her."

"Indi's not like that. She doesn't care that much about money.

If you'd spent more time with her, you would have seen that. She likes economizing. She prefers comfort over luxury. We actually talked about what trip we'd take if money was no object, and she said she'd like to go camping in Yosemite."

My dad didn't look convinced. "She could just be pretending to be like that."

"She could, but she's not. You just need to get to know her better."

He tapped his thumb on the steering wheel thoughtfully.

"Until then, give us both the benefit of the doubt. Innocent until proven guilty."

More tapping.

While he mulled it over, I tried not to think about the fact that this entire Pro-Indi campaign might be moot if she was never going to speak to me again. I had to believe that I could make things right between us and I planned to give some serious thought on the flight back about what I could do to convince her that she should give me a second chance. She was a rational person and, I hoped, a forgiving person, but I was going to have to do something incredible in order for that to happen because in the heat of the moment, when she was telling me things I didn't want to hear, I'd purposely given her an emotional sucker punch that I knew would shut her up.

Fuck. I could still see the desolate expression on her face. Every time I tried to go to sleep, I saw all her feelings for me dim and go out like a candle starved of oxygen.

You know those stupid memes on social media where they ask, "If you could go back in time and tell your twelve-year-old self something, what would you tell them?" Hell, I'd settle for going back two fucking weeks so I could tell myself to not ruin the best thing that ever happened to me.

My dad cleared his throat, bringing me out of my reverie.

"Okay, so I want you to invite her to Christmas," he said. "Tell her I'm sorry but that an apology from me will be coming her way the minute she walks in the door. We'll start over fresh. You can tell her the Sabina story if you think it'll help. Think she'll be okay with that?"

"I hope so. First, I have an apology of my own to give her."

"Eh? What's that? What'd you do, son?"

I told him what I'd told AJ, that instead of thanking her for her concern over my hearing problem, I'd acted like it was all her fault.

"I can't go into detail about what I said to her, but it was mean, Dad. Really mean."

My dad reached out and mussed my hair.

"What the...?"

He was laughing. "That's my boy. A chip off the old block."

"Dad, seriously? You're proud that I was a dick to my girlfriend?"

"Of course, I'm not proud. It sounds like you were a real horse's ass to her. I'm more...amused than anything. Surprised too, if you want to know the truth. It's not like you to be cruel."

"Thanks," I said. "So, what do you do when you've really messed up with Mom? When you've done something that's so bad, the relationship reboot won't cut it?"

He cleared his throat. "If you really want to know..."

"I do. I'm desperate. I don't want to lose her, Dad."

"Son, I'm afraid I don't have any other strategy. The reboot is all I got."

I sighed heavily.

"I mean sometimes I end up buying her something, but that's always a last resort."

"Yeah, I don't think a present's going to work with Indi."

"Does she know you love her?"

"I told her I did."

My dad laughed softly. "There's your problem, son. You *told* her."

"What, was I supposed to keep it a secret?" I snapped.

"No. If you want to keep her, you should tell her every day, but even more important than the words are your actions. You told her you loved her. Fine. Now, I think, you need to *show* her."

INDI

The response to the selfie I'd posted in that PWS Facebook group floored me. I'd been afraid to return to the group for fear of rejection. I shouldn't have been. When I ventured back onto Facebook on Sunday, I saw the people there had welcomed me with open arms and hundreds of messages of encouragement, admiration, support and congratulations. Michaela sent me a private message.

Michaela: You were so brave to post your picture. I'm glad what I wrote helped you.

Indi: It helped me a lot and I'm so grateful. I recently had a bad experience with my boyfriend making fun of my birthmark and I really needed that boost of confidence.

Michaela: Oh no. If you don't mind me asking, what happened?

I poured out my whole story and Michaela reacted much like Ruby had—with anger and shock but where Ruby had a hard time reconciling the cruelty, Michaela and I knew from personal experience, people were capable of that and worse.

Indi: I'm trying to get over him by referring to him as the ICW—the insecure cock waffle.

Michaela posted about twenty laughing emojis.

Michaela: Forget about him. Concentrate on your own journey. Have you thought about taking the next step? Going outside without your makeup?

Indi: Yes, I have. I've dreamed about it but it's…scary. I remember what it was like when I was younger…the pointing, the staring, the name-calling and everything.

Michaela: I'm not gonna lie. You'll still get stared at and people will whisper, but here's what I try to do now. I try to assume it's because they've never seen a PWS before, because a lot of the time, that's what it is, ignorance. It's natural to be curious or confused about something you have no experience with. Like if I saw a person with only one ear, I would wonder what happened. Right?

Indi: I never thought about it that way, but you're right.

Michaela: Okay, so if you're ready—and it's okay if you're not—go out and get some fast food through the drive thru, something like that. Then the next time, go into a store or go for a walk. Tiny steps to build up your strength. Courage is a muscle that has to be used or it atrophies.

After we said goodbye, I knew exactly how and where I was going to reenter the world as Indi, the Original. I just needed to set it up.

Around four o'clock that same afternoon, I was sitting in my car for a moment to gather my nerve. In the rearview mirror, I saw my birthmark was looking pretty eggplanty. We'd gotten a couple inches of snow the night before and cold weather always brought out the purple in it. I resisted the urge to wrap my scarf so that the PWS was mostly covered up.

Not today, I thought. Today was about being fearless, being proud and making a new friend. I'd already walked through the dorm and down to my car without anything bad happening. I could do this last few yards.

The moment I got out of the car, I heard a high-pitched shriek.

"INDI, INDI, INDI, INDI!"

As Denise shouted, "Be careful!" Leah sped down the shoveled walk toward me at high speed. I knelt and laughed as she threw herself in my arms.

"Hey, pipsqueak! How are you?" I asked.

"I'm so happy you're here. And I can see your birthmark!" She clapped her hands in excitement. "Mommy! See? See Indi's birthmark?"

"I see it, sweetie. Come inside where it's warm."

After hanging up my coat and scarf, I followed them to the family room which adjoined the kitchen. A Hallmark Christmas movie was playing at a low volume on a TV. Festive garland adorned the windows and the table had a plaid runner on it, along with lightly golden sugar cookies of various shapes, awaiting decoration.

"What's that amazing smell?" I asked, putting the grocery bag I had brought on the table.

"Hot apple cider," Leah exclaimed. "We put whipped cream and caramel sauce on it so it's extra sweet."

"That sounds delicious. It's clear I'm going to need to see the dentist after today. Now, I hope I brought the right sprinkles. They looked at me funny when I asked for purple but I got a little container of every purple sprinkle they had."

Denise brought us pastry bags of icing and bowls of frosting and after she showed me how to use it, Leah said, "Show her how to do a Leah cookie."

"What's a Leah cookie?" I asked.

"Leah cookies are cookies that have purple icing in the shape of her birthmark," Denise explained. "We made them on a lark last year for her preschool class and I posted a picture of them on social media. They got a lot of attention. Everyone loved the story behind them."

"It's a wonderful idea," I agreed.

"Someone in the Facebook group suggested I sell them to raise money for the VBF—that's the Vascular Birthmark Foundation, but I don't really know how I'd do that." She glanced at me. "I was actually hoping your boyfriend might be able to help me out. That day at the park, he told me about his major—community business or something like that."

"Community entrepreneurship," I said.

"Oh, that's right." Denise smiled. "I didn't know what that was and he explained how it's for people who want to go into businesses that benefit the community in some way. Do you think he'd be able to give me some pointers?"

Not wanting to talk or even think about Hudson right now, I "accidentally" knocked over a jar of sprinkles. "Oh no!" Leah exclaimed.

"No harm done," Denise said. "I'll get the Shop-Vac."

Luckily, no more mention was made about consulting Hudson, but I did end up overdosing on sugar. They gave me an early Christmas present which I adored—a plum colored T-shirt that said, "Port wine is my favorite color."

After I left their house, I stopped by the drug store to pick up some highlighters and shampoo and it wasn't until I was back at the dorm that I realized I'd forgotten I wasn't wearing makeup. I'd forgotten that from the moment I left the Snows until now, people could see my PWS. I'd gone about my business like I didn't have a big splotch of color on my face and nothing happened. I felt like I'd just aced a final. Pride and joy and an exhilarating feeling of freedom suffused me and I wanted to laugh and cry at the same time.

But almost immediately afterward, my balloon of happiness deflated as I came to the bleak realization that the person I wanted to share this accomplishment with most was Hudson.

37

HUDSON

On the plane ride back, I got what I thought was a great idea—a symbolic gesture that might go a long way toward softening Indi's heart and convincing her that I really loved her. It was a long shot and it was going to be a week of sheer hell, but that was kind of the point.

Unfortunately, after we landed, it took me a while to find what I needed, then I had to go home to apply it—no easy feat—and make a phone call.

By the time I drove up to Carter Hall at around nine thirty, doubt began to hammer me. I glanced in the rearview mirror and grimaced at what I saw. This was either going to work out beautifully or she was going to laugh in my face.

I was so nervous, I performed my entire pregame routine in the Jeep—the breathing, relaxation, visualization of happiness, banishment of negativity and the pep talk. When I was done, feeling calmer and more focused, it was gratifying to know the system worked for non-hockey situations too.

"Who is it?" Ruby said, when I knocked on the door.

"It's Hudson. I need to talk to Indi."

"I don't know if she's home. Hold on."

This was total bullshit because their place was too small for her not to know if Indi was there or not, but I respected Ruby's desire to protect her friend.

After hushed conversation, Indi opened the door. Her jaw dropped open at the sight of me and she gasped.

My heart did a hard thump-thump in my chest at the sight of her in a Burlington U hockey T-shirt and sweats. If she was wearing that shirt, she hadn't completely written me off. That gave me hope.

38

INDI

"Oh my God, Hudson, what did you do?" I asked.

A bright purple blotch in a rough approximation of my birthmark covered the upper left quadrant of his face. It looked completely ridiculous. He looked as if he'd just been to a carnival and asked the face painter if, in addition to rainbows and unicorns, they could do an amoeba.

But aside from his face, he was a sight for sore eyes. I'd missed him so much. So many times I'd wanted to reach out to him, but I couldn't. He'd been the one in the wrong, so he was the one who had to make the first move. I loved him and I wanted more than anything for things to be right with us again, but not if it cost me my self-respect.

"It's more about what I'm *going* to do," he said, closing the door behind him. He turned to Ruby, who stared at him with obvious disdain. "I'd like to talk to Indi. Alone."

Ruby looked to me for guidance and I nodded my agreement.

"Okay, fine," she said. "But if you need me to kick his ass out of here, just say the word."

She gave Hudson a threatening "I've got my eye on you" stare then went into her room and shut the door. I liked knowing she had my back.

I felt calm as we each took a seat at the tiny dinette.

"So what's with your face?" I asked, crossing my arms.

"I'll get to that in a sec. First, I want to tell you how sorry I am for what I said to you. I did the worst thing someone could have done to you and the only excuse I have is that I was temporarily insane."

"That is such a bullshit excuse it's not even funny, cock waffle!" Ruby yelled through her door.

Even though I would probably end up telling Ruby what happened later, that didn't mean I wanted her listening real time.

"Come on," I said, "we'd better go into my room."

Once we settled again, him on my bed and me on the chair by my desk, I said, "All right, let's hear it. Tell me how you were temporarily insane, because I have to agree with Ruby. That's a pretty bullshit excuse."

"I know it sounds like bullshit, but I don't know how else to explain it. I just lost my shit. I was scared out of my mind that I was never going to play in the NHL and it would have been all my fault for ignoring everything my body was trying to tell me. Everything *you* were trying to tell me." He sighed. "The truth is, I knew something was seriously wrong with my ears and was too afraid to do anything about it, except lash out at you when you tried to help me. That was wrong and I hate myself for how much I must have hurt you."

"You did hurt me," I said softly, but he frowned.

"Sorry. I didn't catch that."

Of course he hadn't.

"I said, you *did* hurt me. You stabbed me right in the heart, Hudson. After everything I shared with you about my birthmark, you knew how sensitive I was about it and you went ahead and made fun of me anyway."

His face contorted into a mask of anguish. "I know. It was the meanest thing I've ever done and not a second goes by that I don't wish I could go back and do it all differently. But I was freaking terrified my hockey career was over. I just wanted you to stop talking so I could stay in denial instead of face it like a mature human being."

His voice caught and I looked up to see his head bent, his shoulders shaking. He was crying. It hurt to see him suffering like this and I wanted to hug him, but at the same time, part of me was glad. I'd certainly shed my share of tears over this the past couple of days, so I stayed where I was and let him twist in the wind a while.

Eventually, I took pity on him and handed him a tissue.

"Did you at least go to the doctor?" I asked as he blew his nose.

He nodded. "Yes. I did and you were right." He looked up at me, his eyes still bright with tears. "I have otosclerosis."

My hand flew to my mouth and I gasped. Everything shifted. Before he'd said that, my hurt feelings were front and center. I'd been the victim of a bully once again, and despite the pain, that was familiar and even comfortable territory. But now, everything that had happened between us that night faded into the background. Yes, he'd said some heinous things, but no one went through life without saying things they didn't mean. The hurt hadn't completely gone away, but it would eventually. Time would heal this particular wound, but it wouldn't help Hudson.

"Oh my God. How bad is it? What are you going to do?"

He wiped his nose, smearing some of the face paint, then tossed the tissue in the trash. "I'm getting hearing aids. I have an appointment with the audiologist tomorrow. We're trying to be optimistic. It's possible that the hearing aids will work well enough for me to get my game back where it used to be. But the doctor said there's no stopping what's happening in my ears. Whether it'll progress slowly or quickly, there's no way to know. We just have to wait and see."

I went to sit next to him on the bed, close enough so that our thighs were touching. "Have you told your family?"

He nodded. "My dad took it surprisingly well. I mean, first he ripped me a new one for not addressing the problem sooner, but yeah. I'm still standing." He gave me a half smile.

"And the Dragons? Do they know?"

"Not yet. I kind of want to wait until I test out the hearing aids."

I shook my head. "I don't think that's a good idea. They deserve to know what's going on."

"But what if they decide to drop me?"

"Then we'll deal with it. Other teams might want to pick you up. You were chosen in the first round, after all, and that counts for a lot. I asked around."

He looked at me as if I'd sprouted another head. "Who did you—? Wait a second. You said 'we.' You said, '*we'll* deal with it.'"

"Yes, I did."

"Does that mean you forgive me?"

Biting my lip, I nodded and a split second later we were in each other's arms. Relief such as I'd never experienced before swept over me in a giant wave. He was holding me so tightly, I could barely breathe. I kissed him hard and suddenly all I wanted was to feel him inside me.

He seemed to be of the same mind. We got naked as quickly as we could and while he rolled on a condom, I made sure the door was locked. Moments later, he was on top of me, his hips wedged between my legs, his cock at my entrance.

He groaned as he pushed himself inside me and I struggled not to cry out. It felt indescribably good. He went at me with an urgency that demanded a response which I couldn't have held back if I tried. I lifted my hips to meet his hard thrusts and the sensations coalesced into a climax sooner than I'd have thought possible. There had been almost no build-up. It just came out of nowhere.

I muffled my scream in his neck as the waves of pleasure swamped me. Hudson gave one last thrust, grinding himself against me as, shuddering, he came too. I wrapped my legs around him, not wanting the moment to end, not wanting to let him go. He was murmuring over and over, "I love you. I love you," and I'm not even sure he was aware he was doing it.

A few minutes later we were snuggled together in my bed. I could hear music playing somewhere and we'd turned the lights off except for the string of fairy lights that decorated my window.

"So," I said, reaching out to touch the purple blotch on his face, "I think I know what this is, but why don't you tell me anyway?"

He blinked, touched his face then examined his fingers for residue. "I forgot I had this on."

"You did a pretty good job replicating it," I said.

"I had to do it from memory. I don't have any pictures."

"I'll send you one." I reached across him and got my phone from the desk and airdropped him the photo I'd posted on Facebook.

"What's this?" he asked.

I told him about Michaela's "coming out" post and how I'd followed her lead.

"I don't know how to describe what happened after that. The next day there were hundreds of responses. Hundreds. All from people I'd never met before but who acted like I was a long-lost member of the family. I've never felt so much love and support before from total strangers. And they all had stories just like mine. They've all lived through so many of the same experiences I had."

"Indi, that's incredible," he said. "It's also a weird coincidence, because that's kind of why I decided to paint my face." He turned to face me. "Remember when we had that fight at your parents' house and you told me I would never understand what you went through because I have a perfect face?"

"I never said you had a *perfect* face," I said with a smile, "but yes, I remember."

"Well, it occurred to me that the only way to really understand is to try walking around with a birthmark of my own. It's the only way to get a taste of what you went through."

A warmth suffused my heart as he explained that he wanted to wear this painted birthmark, 24/7, for an entire week.

"Obviously, it won't be nearly as intense because I'll be able to wash my birthmark off afterward, but I don't know. It's better than nothing."

I framed his "perfect" face in my hands and kissed him soundly. "It's so much better than nothing," I said, my heart in my throat. "It means everything to me that you want to do this. Everything."

39

HUDSON

Indi couldn't have been more thrilled with the idea of me sporting a fake birthmark, but honestly, I would have worn it for a year if it meant she'd take me back. When she forgave me, the vise that seemed to have been gripping my heart finally eased off and I felt like I could finally take a real breath. And the sex had been unreal.

Even though it had been hurried and frantic, it had surpassed any physical pleasure I'd ever experienced, mainly because it wasn't just physical. We loved each other and when I slid inside her last night, it had been fucking transcendent. In that moment, every one-night stand I'd ever had seemed like a farce, like I'd been going through the motions. I realized why they called it making love. Love made all the difference.

The next morning, we hammered out some details about the birthmark project I hadn't thought about, like what I was going to say to people if they asked me what was on my face. She got a tube of red paint so I could mix a hue that was closer to the actual color of a port-wine stain. The purple that I had gotten was like Barney the Dinosaur purple. She also gave me official permission to include AJ in on everything.

The next day, I stood in front of the mirror and painted the birthmark on, using a photo of Indi as reference. It took me a while, but the end result was startling and pretty realistic. Even AJ was impressed.

Deke was not.

I ventured out to get coffee at the Green Bean before class and was aware of a lot of darting glances and downcast eyes. I just acted like I usually did, like I didn't have a big wine-colored blotch on almost half my face. It was no big deal and I felt like, except for the inevitable shit I'd get from my teammates, this week wouldn't be that bad. But by the end of the day, I was so irritated that I felt like taking things out on a punching bag.

In every single class, as I took my customary seat in the back, my classmates gave me double takes. Granted, they were used to seeing me without the "birthmark," so it was understandable that they were confused and curious. My professors' eyes kept coming back to me as they lectured, but no one actually asked me about it. They just whispered and gave me weird looks. It got to be really annoying.

Later that day, because Indi had given her permission, I told the team exactly what was going on. I thought it would be easy, but I ended up sounding a little ridiculous. Some of the guys even snickered.

"Pipe down, dickheads," Brammy said.

"So let me get this straight," Lex said, "your girlfriend has a birthmark on her face."

"Correct," I confirmed.

"And people give her shit about it."

"Yes."

"So you're painting your face like this for a week in a gesture of solidarity?"

"Exactly." Thank God, *someone* understood.

"It's like when someone gets cancer and you shave your head too," AJ said.

"Sounds kind of sickening, if you ask me," Birdy said, but Birdy was probably the most immature guy on the team and I sometimes wondered if he even liked girls yet.

After the week was over, as I told Indi everything that had happened to me, she started to cry. Because I never know what to do for someone who's crying except hand them a Kleenex, I just kept going.

"I mean, as the days wore on, it seemed like people were going out of their way to avoid me so they wouldn't have to deal with the discomfort of trying *not* to look at my birthmark. Once in the grocery store, someone turned the corner, got one look at my face, and backed away as if they'd made a mistake and didn't want any cereal after all. Jesus, I felt like a pariah."

She was nodding as the tears continued to slide down her cheeks.

"All I kept thinking was, 'just make it 'til Tuesday, dude,' because I wanted it to be over, but the shitty thing is, it's never over for you. You don't have a choice."

"But you did have a choice," she said fiercely. "You *chose* to do this and I'll never forget this as long as I live."

Then she hugged me for a really long time—like longer than the Briscoe Thanksgiving group hug—but it wasn't awkward at all because that hug cemented a bond between us that felt good and strong and true.

INDI

I woke up to find Hudson under the covers kissing me softly and coaxingly between my legs.

"Mmmm," I murmured, caressing his head as he teased my clit with his tongue.

Even though it felt heavenly, I opened one eye to check the time.

"Hudson, we don't have time for this. I have class in fifteen minutes."

We were at his place, which meant a commute of five minutes. That left ten to shower, brush my teeth and get dressed.

He made his way up my body and popped out from beneath the covers. He was on top of me which meant there was no way I was leaving unless he got off.

"We do have time. That's why they call them quickies."

I rolled my eyes, but didn't object and before I knew it, he was sheathed in a condom and entering me with a low groan. His cock felt so good as he buried it to the hilt inside me and then pulled back out only to push himself back in, over and over.

"Indi, you feel so good."

The roughness of his voice excited me and I rocked against

him as he moved with increasingly hard thrusts. I couldn't help myself; I looked at the clock again.

Unfortunately, Hudson noticed and pulled out.

"What the…!" I exclaimed.

Without a word, he dove back under the covers and went at me with his mouth again. I gasped as he wrapped an arm around to hold me immobile while he drove me to a quick, shuddering climax. Before I'd even come back down to earth, he'd shoved his cock back inside me. His guttural grunts as he slammed his body against mine propelled me toward another orgasm that broke over me just as he stiffened and came in a hot rush.

I allowed myself a few moments of dwindling bliss before shoving at his shoulder. It was like trying to move a boulder.

"Hudson, come on. Get up."

He lifted his head and grinned at me. "I told you we had time."

"That remains to be seen," I said as he finally moved off and let me scramble out of bed.

"You can take a girl out of the classroom…" he said then yelped as, laughing, I swatted his bare ass.

We showered, dressed and left his apartment in record time. As he drove us to school, I mused on how he seemed to have regained his confidence. I'd never seen him this eager and relaxed before a game. He was almost cocky.

"Don't take your eyes off me tonight," he said as we pulled into the parking lot closest to my first class, "because I'm going to kick ass."

Hudson was going to wear his hearing aids during the game tonight for the first time. Following orders, he'd been using them in increasingly loud environments, most recently during practice. He'd complained about the adjustments he was having to make to his game and how, in a way, he'd had to learn how to listen again. But finally, it was time to put the tiny devices to the real test, the only test that mattered.

"I finally feel like my old self, Indi, like I'm in control."

"I'm so excited. I can't wait."

"Me either." He flashed me that prescription strength smile. "Because tonight, you're finally going to see what I can do on the ice."

As far as most of the people in the arena were concerned, this was an ordinary hockey game—the Burlington Bulls against the Northeastern Huskies. Nothing particularly important was at stake. We were still three months away from the regionals. But for those of us who knew and loved Hudson—including his parents —tonight's game was critical.

I hoped I wouldn't run into them. It was a big arena. There would be four thousand people here tonight. But of course, as Ruby and I were walking toward our seats, I saw them walking toward us.

"Shit," I said under my breath.

"What's going on?" Ruby asked.

"Hudson's parents, straight ahead."

"You mean Daddy Cock Waffle?" she asked.

"In the flesh," I said as I put on a smile.

"Indi, darling," Marlene said, hugging me. "I was hoping we'd see you." She looked very put together in her black jeans, hound-stooth poncho and white scarf.

After introducing Ruby, I slid a cool glance toward his dad, who actually looked uncomfortable. "And how are you, Mr. Forte?"

"I'll be better after I get something off my chest. And call me Dom. I owe you an apology, a big one," he said, looking me straight in the eye. "I did you a disservice the last time I saw you. I was way out of line and I said some things I regret."

"Thank you, Dom. I appreciate that."

As opposed to the last time he'd apologized to me, at the dinner table on Thanksgiving, this time he seemed sincere.

"I want you to let me know if there's anything I can do to make it up to you. Anything. I mean it."

"How about dinner after the game?" I asked, deciding if Hudson and I were going to have a future together, I needed to try to get along with his dad.

He grinned and I suddenly saw a startling resemblance between him and his son.

"Done!" he exclaimed.

"Oh my God, it'd D-Day Forte!"

Heads turned and several starry-eyed hockey fans began to walk toward us.

"We'll play a game of 'You're Full of Shit: Hockey Edition.' You'll love it," he said, winking at me as the fans descended.

Ruby and I had center-ice seats with a one-eighty view of the playing surface. As usual, the excitement was palpable, and the air was filled with the aromas of hot dogs, popcorn and the excited chatter of Burlington hockey fans.

Hudson needn't have told me to keep my eyes on him. I couldn't help myself. Even when he was on the bench, I loved seeing him in his element. Most of the time he was all business, focused on the job he had to do on the ice. But every once in a while, he'd smile at something a teammate said and I would end up smiling too.

On the ice, he was precision, focus and skill in motion. Every move he made seemed calculated. His passes were connecting. His shots on goal were decisive and it was thrilling to watch him win board battles, steal pucks, and, of course, score goals.

I cheered when he scored the first goal of the game, twelve minutes into the period. It was a beautiful wrist shot that went right above the goalie's left shoulder.

When he scored again in the second period, the puck had

come from AJ and Hudson did this little deflection thing with his stick blade and it caromed into the net.

Then, best of all, he scored one more time at the end of the game. As the clock counted down, the Huskies pulled their goalie so they could have an extra man on the ice. Whenever a team did that, the action was especially fierce. Tonight, Northeastern needed to get one more goal to tie the game which would throw the game into overtime. But our boys weren't going to let that happen.

I was on the edge of my seat, like everyone else in the arena. The other team was furiously trying to score and ours were just as furiously trying to stop them. Hudson was out there when the puck squirted out from a scrum in the corner. Quick as lightning, he scooped it up, took two strides and slapped it toward the other side of the rink.

Where the net stood empty.

I held my breath as the puck sailed down the ice. The crowd roared when it became clear it was going to make it in. I leapt to my feet, screaming. So did Ruby. We jump-hugged as the horn sounded. Hats sailed through the air and even though the beret I was wearing belonged to Ruby, I threw it as hard as I could toward the ice.

"Hey!" she yelled in surprise

"I'll buy you a new one," I yelled back, laughing and giddy as Hudson turned toward us and saluted me with his stick.

THE
END

ACKNOWLEDGMENTS

As always, I have a lot of people to thank. This book wouldn't have happened if not for Lisa B. Kamps and Lynda Aicher who provided much needed encouragement when I was writing my proposal. I owe a debt of gratitude to Melanie Ting, a friend, confidant and beta reader who isn't afraid to tell me she doesn't like my characters (LOL!) A big thank you to Kristine and Kelsey Koelzer for answering my numerous questions about college hockey captains. Thank you Andi Burns for beta reading the manuscript specifically for the hearing loss aspect. As always, I depended on the expertise of Kim Cannon, my copy editor, and Melissa Johnston, my developmental editor. Without them...I don't even want to think about it. The gals in Chatzy, Jaymee Jacobs, Jami Davenport, Kat Mizera, Kelly Jamieson, and Tess Thompson round out my circle of support and friendship.

Finally, I'm grateful to Sarina Bowen, Jane Haertel and Jenn Gaffney. It's been a privilege and honor to be a part of the World of True North.